SEED

The Titanomachy – Book One

S.E. WELSH

LUMINOSITY PUBLISHING LLP

SEER
The Titanomachy – Book One
Copyright © May 2020 S.E. WELSH

Paperback ISBN: 978-1-9993066-9-4

Cover Art by Poppy Designs

DEDICATION

To Katrina—my number one supporter, publicist, beta reader and spectacular sister. Wouldn't want to go through life without you by my side.

PROLOGUE

Chloe

THE **ACRID STENCH OF** smoking plastic burns through my nostrils, startling me into awareness with a jarring cough. I try to cover my mouth, but my hands are bound above me, shoulders already numb from carrying my weight. Attempting to unclench my fists brings a scream of agony, as ropes dig further into my wrists. Even my thrashing is halted by more bindings around my chest and legs, holding me upright. My eyelids feel glued together, weighed down by stones, yet slowly, I manage to part them. I wish I'd kept them closed.

The fire blazes through the warehouse, devouring everything in its path. Shadows flicker across the walls, a macabre dance of black, grey and orange that increases my panic. I struggle more, only to feel the ropes dig further into my already raw skin. Blood soaks through the ropes, snaking its way down my arms to dry in crusty trails in the intense heat.

It doesn't matter.

Doesn't matter how much blood I lose if I can't get out of these ropes. Smoke crawls through the air, clogging the back of my throat and stealing my breath. A series of explosions begin towards the opposite end of the building and I wrack my brain to try to figure out what could be causing it. Frantically, I scan the shelves to either side of me. I'd paid little attention to the contents of the warehouse when I woke, but on seeing the tins of paint and turpentine lining the wall, my panic grows to devastating effect.

Where's Inspiration when you need her? I'm supposed to be from the line of one of the most famous Muses of history, yet here I am, unable to inspire myself into forming a valid escape plan.

Pathetic.

Instead, I continue to wrestle futilely with the ropes as the flames lick closer. Explosions follow the flames, spreading it in swift bursts, propelling it towards me.

"Please, Calliope! If you love me at all, aid me now!" Instead of a response from my immortal foremother, a bottle of turpentine, shaken from the top shelf by my struggles, teeters on the edge of the shelf, then falls in slow motion. It hits a protruding paint can on the way down, lid popping at the impact, turpentine raining from above straight onto my upturned face. I shriek as the liquid reaches my eyes desperately trying to rub them on my shoulder, but that only succeeds in making the pain worse.

Fire jumps from the shelf to the nearest flammable object. Me. I scream my agony into the roaring inferno as the blaze begins to devour me. Starting with my turpentine soaked eyes and hair.

When the smoke and screams steal the air from my lungs, I resign myself to death. Even Asclepius, God of Healing, wouldn't be able to save me now.

Then the Seer gene kicks in.

CHAPTER ONE

Chloe

MY **FEET POUND THE** pavement, a methodical rhythm that takes me away from the memories that threaten to drown me. Bailey, my Hellhound eyes and personal bodyguard, lopes out in front of me, setting the pace, panting happily as he pushes me to my limits. It's exhilarating, the freedom of the early morning, the solitude of the run.

Exercise is the one thing I have left of my former life, of the old Chloe, and frankly, despite the many things that could go wrong, there's no way I'd give it up. Regardless of what the Immortal Council may say about the dangers. It's not like they've been able to figure out who was behind it, for all their power.

The reality is, aside from literal death, everything bad that could happen to me, has already, so I'll continue to do the things in life I actually enjoy.

You'd have to be an idiot to attack me with a hellhound the size of a pony at my side.

It's difficult to maintain the link with the over-eager hellhound, and it only works well when neither of us are stressed or excited, but it's definitely worth it to 'see' again. Somehow this muscular, black-furred monster has become my best friend.

The scent of a mouse has Bailey straying from the path, but I catch him just in time. We don't want a repeat of last week. His last rat hunt left me sightless, freezing in my running gear long after I should've been home in my nicely heated apartment. And he thought I'd be happy that he brought me the rat as a present.

The struggle is real, maintaining awareness of my body while using Bailey's eyes and controlling his natural impulses. Give too much of my attention to the dog, and I lose control of my own body and crumple to the ground. Too little attention and Bailey wanders too far in front and I continually trip over things.

Or worse.

Run into people.

That's something to be avoided. Feeling other's emotions as they catch their first glimpse of my face . . . it kind of ruins the serenity.

Though it could be worse. They could get a look at my eyes behind the sunnies. Horror and embarrassment are not complimentary to relaxation.

There's a shift in my perception and Bailey slows, dropping to the ground and panting a little as he rolls enthusiastically in the dead leaves. His eyes are closed as he wriggles and squirms, so I can't see, but the rustle and crunch are nearly deafening in the silence of the morning. Smiling, I bask in his pleasure.

This is the only positive that has come from the fire—I appreciate simplicity. I used to dwell on every little thing, panic when I missed a deadline, agonise over a client's displeasure. Beat myself up over my failure to inspire.

I come from Calliope's line. I'm supposed to be a descendent of the most powerful muse but my gift for inspiration has always been weak. My family owns a publishing house, has inspired some of the world's top authors. I was supposed to follow in their footsteps.

Fat chance of that happening now.

Our power defines our worth, and until recently I was worthless. Dad was a direct descendent of Euterpe, Calliope's fellow Muse, and was very successful in the music industry for a long time. Mum's a talented descendent of Calliope and me . . . well, let's just say I have more luck inspiring people to walk back out the door than to trust me with their futures.

Mum's always been unkind about it (who wants a Null, someone who's ungifted, in the family, right?), and Dad passed when I was four so he didn't get a chance to have an opinion, but I'm pretty sure he wouldn't have been impressed with his only offspring. As for my foremother, Calliope . . .

I remember her coming to the publishing house once. She was dressed in simple jeans, a white shirt covered by a short, buttery caramel jacket. Even in casual clothes, she turned heads and when the door to my mother's office closed behind her, every person in the room turned to their computers and typed as if their lives depended on it. We had a series of bestsellers that year that hasn't been equalled since.

The troubling thing was, she looked right at me before she closed that door, smiled and I was the only one in the room who didn't start writing. It was devastating.

Bailey attempts to scratch behind his collar and I only just stop myself from mirroring him. Yesterday, I was so lost in thought that when Bailey started chasing his tail, I found myself spinning in circles with him. It wasn't a good day. I give him my version of a mental wake-up call (singing Hanson's "MMMBop" in his head—he hates it) and we are off and running again.

It's then I sense them. My heart sinks as I realise the Council have sent their errand boys to collect me. Damn it, why didn't I feel them sooner?

Now I'm going to be stuck in a meeting with the Immortal Council. There isn't one Immortal in our world who doesn't understand the selfishness of the Council or loathe their duplicity. Somehow it makes it worse to know that though they're thousands of years old, they all look to be in the prime of their lives. Unfortunately for most of them, their archaic attitudes didn't change over time.

I slow to a walk as two figures step onto the path to block my way. Bailey freezes in front of me. There isn't a person with the Immortal gene who doesn't know who these two are. On the left's Deimos—hulking, blond and tattooed. The other's slightly smaller and built like a bodybuilder, also blond with a tousled mane. I find myself struggling with a sudden itch to run my fingers through it. He is just as physically intimidating as his brother, but that doesn't stop me using Bailey's eyes to check him out further. Not a tattoo in sight. Phobos.

I'm glued to the curves and contours of his body, heat pooling in my belly, only to be shaken from my stupor by Bailey's whimper. My skin pebbles as I respond to Bailey's fear with my own. No-one knows, when Ares' sons come for you, whether it's a death sentence or an invitation. Even though Calliope told me to expect a summons, the implications of their presence are ambiguous. Anger stirs and my fists clench as I fight the urge to lash out.

Did they have to send the *scare-tastic* brothers to come fetch me? And did one of them have to be so freaking magnetic?

Bailey senses my anger and nerves, settling into a deep, rattling growl that would have lesser Immortals cowering in their boots. Not so Deimos and Phobos. As the embodiments of fear and terror, the two sons of Ares simply glare at my hell-hound and send him scurrying behind me. Great. Now I'm minus a crucial sense—sight.

My hand settles on the handle of the switchblade tucked into the waistband of my shorts. The man on the left stifles a snort. Immediately, my head swings in his direction as I try to get a bead on his thoughts. They're clouded, and I only just scratch the surface before he notices my intrusion.

Are you always so rude?

His voice is like rich caramel. Even as I wince at the rebuke, I want him to speak again. But I don't withdraw the threads from his mind. Instead, I disguise them.

At least the effort's gained me the valuable information that they're not here to harm, yet it makes me nervous I was detected so easily. The Council won't be happy with the depth of my power and I can't trust these two to keep it from them. Both Deimos and Phobos have been the enforcers of the Immortal Council for millennia and are *very* good at their jobs.

I shift my weight, preparing for an attack.

The douchebag laughs again.

"What do you want?" I snap, both embarrassed and infuriated at being so easily dismissed as a threat. Emotions roll off them almost too quickly, sliding rapidly from amusement to curiosity and a varied array in between.

This is the part about being sightless that really gives me the shits. People can have whole conversations behind your back while you're left in the dark—literally! Apparently, they haven't been around a blind person in a while, or they just don't give a rat's arse whether they offend me or not, because their silent conversation goes on for long enough that my anger starts to spiral out of control.

"I don't have all day, gentleman. Some of us still have a life." It's a low blow. Deimos and Phobos are 'employed' by the Council under an indefinite contract. They were deemed too dangerous to run free in the mortal world so their skills are used to 'protect' inter-racial relations. In other words, they hunt the Immortals who prey on humans.

Ironic, that they do it for the Council, the biggest manipulators in the world.

Disgust and—dare I imagine it—hurt, are the only things I feel from Phobos. Deimos is full of rage, but it's not frightening. I've stirred it, but I don't think it's directed at me.

"You won't have one either, for much longer. The Council wants to see you, Chloe Santos," Deimos says with his quiet bass rumble. At least I think it's him. Phobos' voice seems to be smoother.

I gasp, taking an involuntary step backward that sends me tumbling over my Shetland-sized dog, who has all the ferocity of a bunny rabbit confronted by a snake. I reach out for something, anything to break my fall, but my right arm is almost wrenched from its socket as one of the twins attempts to stop the inevitable. Muscles screaming, I hiss out a breath.

My sunglasses slip from my face with the force of my momentum. I'm hauled awkwardly upright, but from the pain in my shoulder, I think I'd rather have met the ground than feel like someone tried to rip my arm off.

Crunch. Shit. Someone has stepped on my glasses.

"Sorry." It's Phobos, his voice the same warm rumble that came across when he criticised my nosiness. At least I have the voices figured out, since I'll never be able to get a bead on their responses if my cowardly dog continues to keep his eyes closed. "Apparently, I am stronger than I thought—or you are more fragile." I hear scratching in the dirt. "And these most surely are."

My glasses.

I glare in the direction of his voice, the immediate hissed intake of breath serving to piss me off further. Especially since it doesn't only come from one source. Deimos must've moved to join his brother at some stage.

The anger drains as abruptly as it came.

I sigh and hold my hand out for the glasses, trying to stifle the feelings of rejection that follow every person's negative reaction to my appearance. It doesn't work. In fact, it's worse when it's a mortal and the sharp intake of breath is accompanied by a hasty retreat and murmured apology.

Maybe I can say I'm learning to be content with my new appearance, but unfortunately, the fear still follows me everywhere. Probably because for all their powers, no-one on the Council knows who sent me into that fire.

Another reason why they're worse than useless.

A cold sweat breaks out on my forehead as it does at any mention of the fire. I turn away, not quick enough to avoid notice, but the *scare-tastic* twins pretend not to have seen.

They know it's not exertion.

And I sure as shit resent the fact they've seen me like this.

Why couldn't I have met them when I was whole? When I wasn't this fragile shell who can't even go for a run without succumbing to a panic attack?

These days I could give Freddy Kruger a run for his money in scaring kids. My face looks . . . melted. Or at least parts do, particularly around the eyes. When all was said and done, the damage was so deep that not even Asclepius could repair it.

My glasses are placed gently in my hand and I wince, running my fingers over them. The arms are at 180 degrees and I can't see them staying on my head like that. Don't think the massive cracks in the lenses will cover much either. Lucky I have unlimited access to Mum's funds at the moment, 'cos Aviators with a midnight tint cost a mint.

"Again, sorry."

I nod acceptance of Phobos' apology. The man was only trying to help, after all, then whistle sharply at Bailey and attempt to link with him. He's figured out the men aren't a threat, at least at present, so though he's still trembling at least he's receptive enough to loan me his eyes again.

I sigh in relief as I join him. Everything's much easier with sight.

"I need to change—or did they insist you pick me up in my sweaty trackies?" No answer, but I didn't expect any. I continue my run in an effort to show some independence, even defiance. Taking advantage of their distraction, I weave further threads through their minds. I won't be caught unawares by them again.

Deimos and Phobos are amused at my antics, loping silently behind as Bailey stretches out in front. We head around the quay and make our way into the city.

My apartment has a great view of Sydney Harbour and the Opera House, courtesy of Mum and Calliope, but unless the dog is awake and I have the energy to focus, the view is wasted. They may as well have saved some money and bought a ground level unit for all the good it does me. I suspect there's a little guilt money thrown in there.

Calli didn't come to my aid when requested.

It was only when the Seer gene kicked in and I started broadcasting my pain to every person with the Immortal gene that she realised something was wrong. I don't know if I'll ever forgive her for that. She should've known—I've never asked her for anything before or since.

Bailey pads into the apartment first, scanning the living room and kitchen. After snatching a quick drink from the half-keg that serves as his doggy bowl—it's the only thing he can fit his quadruple-sized Staffie-esque head in—he moves off into the bedrooms. Phobos follows, a silent shadow sliding around my apartment.

Despite the fact the males of both species feel the need to check on my safety first, I move deliberately into the kitchen, breaking the connection with Bailey to give myself a rest. It isn't necessary in my apartment—everything has its place and is committed to memory. I've already scanned the apartment for signs of another's presence and found none.

Since the Seer gene kicked in all my mental abilities have been heightened, I suspect, way beyond the abilities of even the strongest of the Council. Precognition is just one thing to be feared from a Seer. Visions, empathy and telepathy are a heady mix, and I'm just learning to use them.

Give me another six months and I'll guarantee that even the strongest on the Council won't keep me out.

And that's another reason Apollo and the rest of his Seer descendants were hunted to extinction.

I really don't want to be interviewed by mass murderers. I'm sure there are still some on the Council who took part in the Delphic Massacre. It may have been over 3,000 years ago but many of our kind have long memories to match long lives. None of them will admit to the murder of Apollo, but no-one else in our world would have had the power or influence to murder generations of a precognitive family in one afternoon. And I'm sure it wasn't just one of them.

"Do you want something to drink or eat while I shower?" I ask Deimos who has triggered the ingrained hostess reflex Mum drilled into me.

There's an awkward silence from the mountainous man in the living room. He must've sensed that it was a reflexive rather than a genuine invitation.

"Sounds wonderful," Phobos replies instead as he re-joins us after his sweep of the apartment, startling me. His presence is pulling me towards him like iron to a magnet, further inflaming my temper. I wonder if it has anything to do with his powers from his mother's side? But if it's an unconscious thing, like many of Aphrodite's skills, then why aren't I drawn to Deimos as well?

I pull Vegemite and cheese from my meticulously ordered fridge, slide my hand to the left until it touches my bread box and take out all that's left. They can eat what I want to eat, or they won't eat at all.

I slap the sandwiches together and pile them on a plate, taking care to balance it well on the edge of the breakfast bar. Two glasses of water later and I'm smiling to myself in pride. Just a few short months earlier the simple act of making a sandwich wouldn't have been possible.

I haven't walked gracefully into blindness, but more of a bumbling fool for the most part. My memory's terrible and even though I've always been good at sport, I found that I'd relied on sight a lot when it came to keeping my balance. Regaining my equilibrium and training my memory has been a long process, with many stupid mistakes in between.

The kitchen was a rite of passage, and now I've mastered it, I feel a little more confident in my own skin. I've also become very good at memorising simple recipes so I don't end up calling for pizza every night.

"Thank you," they murmur hesitantly.

I smile wickedly and bite into my Vegemite and cheese sandwich. It's always amusing to watch the old ones tackle Vegemite for the first time. Not that I'm watching at the moment, but I've managed to weave a sensory thread into both of their minds and that's even better. This way I'll get to experience their discomfort, no matter what polite words spring from their lips.

Phobos' mind seems to shrink in disgust at first taste and I sense him spit the bite out, laying the plate covertly on the floor to be devoured by the bottomless pit, Bailey. It makes me like him a little more, the fact he tries to avoid offending me. I stifle a chuckle, focussing instead on his brother.

Deimos is interesting. The first salty bite hits him like a blow, sending him into a particularly vivid memory of another strong, salty taste. The pickled olives of his homeland. It's a warm feeling, nostalgic but not bitter. How rare are those type of experiences to someone of his background? After all, he's a son of Ares.

I leave the threads in both of their minds and begin to subtly build upon them, making sure they remain undetected. If it means staying safe, I'll invade anyone's privacy. But I'll only steal their thoughts in an emergency.

"This . . . Vegemite . . . is wonderful," Deimos blurts in surprise. I feel Phobos' horror and this time I don't stifle the laugh. It echoes around the room.

Phobos says to his brother, "I think I'll take you to visit Asclepius'. Hopefully, he can heal your mind. You clearly did not eat the same sandwich as I."

I nearly point out the fact he didn't even manage to swallow one bite, but instead rein in my chuckles and retreat down the corridor.

"I'm going to shower and change," I fling back over my shoulder as they continue to argue about Vegemite.

I'm not going to turn up to an interview with the Council smelling like wet runners and mouldy arse. They wouldn't be happy with that luscious aroma wafting around the Council Chambers.

My fingertips trail along the wall beside me until I feel a door frame. The first room on the left, my bedroom. I go to turn inside and crash with a massive *thunk* into the closed door.

"Mother Fu . . ." I hiss as I pick myself off the floor. My embarrassment and anxiety sends me into a rage. Mum always tells me to keep away from people when I lose my temper. Unfortunately, it hasn't stopped me yet.

"Sorry. Between the two of us, we can't seem to do anything right." Phobos is right behind me. My rage now has a target.

"Don't you *ever* close a door in my house again! Do you have any idea what a stupid fucking move that is?" My nose throbs, so I pat it gently to check for breaks and blood.

All good, though it still aches something fierce.

Phobos becomes wary, no trace of humour running through his mind. That's gratifying. They've pushed me far beyond my limit today.

"You have no idea, do you?" I say bitterly. "You and your perfect brother, two paragons of the immortal race. You've never had a day in your life where you felt inadequate, where your physical imperfections made your life a misery. For the God's sake, you're the sons of Ares! How could you ever comprehend what it means to be flawed?"

A tidal wave of rage rolls up the corridor and this time I'm scared, because all that bubbling anger is for me.

"You'll apologise to my brother. He doesn't deserve your scorn and it's you who's misled. Being blind doesn't excuse your ignorance, or have you forgotten all of our history? I assure you we haven't, even if we wish every day that we could."

My mouth gapes like a fish. All my rage slips away, leaving the stinging shame of my hasty words.

Of course, I know their story. Despite being immortal and sons of Ares, the fact that they were also sons of Aphrodite, drove people away. People believed that they both inspired a terrible, destructive love that could only end in death. This hadn't been helped by the fact that Phobos' one and only wife became so unstable she killed herself.

Rumour has it that she was a child of Zeus and a harpy—not a positive combination when you pair the biggest man-whore of the Pantheon with a demi-god whose sole purpose is to help women seek revenge upon unfaithful husbands. Phobos was away constantly, like all the men of Ares line, fighting in wars designed to increase our power. This didn't sit well with his wife. What was her name?

"He wants to forget Alara?" I ask impulsively.

Phobos' footsteps disappear down the corridor.

Shit. I always manage to make things worse.

"Alala," Deimos corrects. "And she was his everything, at one time. Until she started picking at those little imperfections you are convinced we don't possess in a misguided attempt to keep him at home with her." A regretful sigh escapes his lips. "She never understood that we didn't have a choice. At first, we followed the orders of Olympus, now it's the Council. Same shit heads, different name. Our world has grown larger yet our role within is still the same. Slaves. Slaves for four millennia."

I'm a *bitch*.

"Sorry," I mumble, as I grasp the door handle and trudge into my room to shower and change.

I hear Deimos lean against the door as he settles in to wait. One at my bedroom door, one in the lounge room, watching the front entrance.

This is starting to feel like a security detail rather than a simple collection job.

It makes me uneasy, yet oddly enough I feel safe with them. There's more to this meeting with the Council than I anticipated.

In the shower, as the water slides down my back, I try to let go of my foreboding, for at least long enough to enjoy the moment. Nothing good ever lasts long.

With my towel wrapped around me, I step into my bedroom and immediately shivers run up my spine. I'm surrounded by distrust and hatred so strong it leaks through my defences and just about drowns me in the metallic tang of malice. Someone's here, and they aren't friendly. With no sight, I turn in panicked circles trying to find the threat.

I succeed in tripping over the dresser.

My hands have a death grip on the towel, my one shield. As I right myself on newborn calf legs, the door flies open. Deimos barges in, only to stop abruptly, confusion and—dare I think it—fear, lacing his emotions.

The negative energy is so strong, yet I still can't pinpoint a location when, just as suddenly as it appeared, the presence goes.

I plaster myself against the wall, sending out probes left, right and centre. The only beings I touch are those I expect. None with the insane malice of the intruder.

Phobos has moved into the room and joined his brother, yet all three of us reek of fear. What do they have to be scared of? When Terror and Fear are projecting the emotions they are known for inspiring, you know that something big and bad has visited.

"What the fuck is going on?"

They share another of those silent moments of communication that I'm pleased I tapped into.

Do we have the right to tell her?

No. We will be punished like before.

But if we don't she'll probably do something stupid.

Deimos has that right.

How much trouble can one blind woman get into in our company?

"A lot, if you don't tell me what is going on this instant." I'm too frustrated to try and convince them in a way that doesn't reveal the extent of my abilities, so now they know. Surprise!

Of course, their shock and anger are directed at me, and I give them a smug smile. Who knew that after a scare, I could be this confident in a towel? At least I'm not naked.

"I thought I told you it is not nice to eavesdrop," Phobos growls, but I can sense amusement rising to the surface.

"Sorry," I say with insincere contrition, smiling more genuinely this time. There's something about his emotions that appeals.

He sighs, not giving in even though the anger has gone. "We would if we could, but that's what the Council wishes to speak to you about, and things would not go well for us if we were to overstep our bounds. We were charged with bringing you safely to them, and that's what we plan to do."

"So be a good girl and put some clothes on—or not." I can just about feel the smirk on Deimos face and I itch to slap it off.

The innuendo doesn't affect me—there's no interest in his mind bar curiosity. I can understand why, I mean, who meets me and doesn't want to know how far under the clothes the scars stretch? That doesn't mean I like being treated like a freak show.

"Get out and I'll get dressed."

"One of us will stay," Phobos says.

"No, you won't."

"Yes. We will. It has been amply proven that someone can easily infiltrate your quarters. One of us will stay." Phobos' voice is implacable.

Okay. So that's non-negotiable.

"Fine. You stay, but you'll face the wall until I tell you I'm done." I turn in the general direction in which I assume they are standing, hands wrapped securely around my towel, eyes staring sightlessly toward them.

"Done. The hound will be here too," says Phobos.

I'm slightly mollified by this. I'd be much happier if he hadn't proven to be useless around the *scare-tastic* brothers, but at least I'll be able to use his eyes.

I whistle for Bailey and bury my face in his neck, taking comfort in his warmth.

Deimos takes Phobos' place in the lounge room and I attempt to find something to wear in my enormous walk-in robe. Thank-you again Calliope and your guilt money. Bailey pads to my side and I take advantage of his eyes to choose my outfit.

In the days following the fire when I hadn't learned to share with Bailey and Mum was still living with me, my new fashion sense was a constant source of amusement and horror for her. Think floral tops with striped pants. It became so bad that we had to spend a whole day organising and culling my wardrobe—left to right, top coat rack light-coloured tops to dark-coloured tops, the bottom row the reverse.

We even added safety pins to the tags of all my clothes, one safety pin for lights, two for darks. Underwear in nothing but beige, which doesn't help a girl feel sexy, but I guess there isn't much chance of anything like that happening anyway.

A guy would have to be pretty special to get past this face.

I settle on a pair of faded blue skinny jeans and a navy-blue woollen turtleneck jumper. A tidy look, but one that throws the bird in the face of the Council who generally appreciate designer chic.

The silence in the bedroom is extremely awkward. I chose Phobos because he seemed to be the more likely to keep his back turned, but now that he's here I continue to rehash the awful things I said. The tension's unbearable.

"I'm not usually like this, you know. I generally think before I speak, but when I'm scared or nervous, things just seem to burst out and . . . well, I guess I'm trying to say I was thoughtless. And I over-reacted." Okay. That's good. An apology without blurting out the words 'I'm sorry' yet again.

He takes a deep breath before answering. "It is easy to over-react when unfamiliar people are invading your safe space."

I didn't expect him to understand, and yet both brothers seem to constantly surprise me.

"Thank-you." The silence is more companionable. Still, my awareness of him has my over-sensitive skin pebbling, heat pooling in unwanted places when I think about the possibility of him watching me.

I finish pulling on my clothes and send Bailey to look for an old pair of sunnies to cover my eyes. He can't find anything, so I move to the bedside table to see if there's one of those aeroplane eye masks to dim the glow. My frustration's peaking.

Phobos asks, "What are you looking for?"

I let out a sigh of frustration. "No sunnies, no eye mask—you wouldn't happen to have a tie handy, would you?"

"To cover your eyes?"

"Yes of course to cover my eyes," I snap, then take a deep breath and try to control my temper. This whole situation has me so riled up, I've shouted for the second time at someone who doesn't deserve it, and that just makes me feel worse because now I have to deal with guilt.

"Don't apologise or I might have to consider switching places with my brother. Up until now, I was considering this a much more appealing assignment than the front door," says Phobos.

What does he mean?

Nothing about me being appealing. I'm just an assignment and he probably prefers the company instead of door watching. Right? Surely on most missions he—

"Stop thinking. It's hurting me just looking at you doing that. You're dressed, so let's go."

"But I don't have anything to cover my eyes and my hair only covers so much of my face." My jet black hair's cut in a sleek bob that manages to fall over most of my scarring if I keep my head down, but the sunglasses help to not only cover the eyes but any extra scarring as well.

Phobos fills the brief awkward silence. "Leave your eyes uncovered, and put your hair back. Aside from shock value, it will show the Council that you are strong and unwilling to be manipulated."

I sit gaping. Why is he helping me?

"It is also intimidating when you look directly at people with those eyes. So, even if you can't see them, get a lock on their location like you've been doing with my brother and me, and attempt to make eye contact. Remember—you are not their slave." *Like us.* The thought's unvoiced but I catch it anyway.

"Why are you doing this for me?"

"You've been through enough already. The last thing you need is to end up like us. Of course, you still may, but at least you are in with a fighting chance." He pauses and I sense amusement and respect. "Plus, you have attitude. I like that."

He stares at me a moment too long, and there's a heat to his thoughts I can't decipher. To cover the awkwardness I grab some bobby pins and start to pin my hair back as he suggested.

"Let's go," he orders and the moment is broken as all three of us gird ourselves for what lies ahead.

Gods help us.

Or perhaps I should say, forget us.

CHAPTER TWO

Chloe

WE EXIT MY APARTMENT together and I begin to steel myself for the inevitable stares on the plane ride. The current offices of the Council are in Bangkok, and while I don't want to see them, the sooner it's over with, the sooner I can go back to my life . . . or not.

We march along the corridor to the elevator and Deimos rushes to intercept us as Phobos continues a conversation on the phone, voice too low for me to hear. He puts his hand out to stop me and Bailey growls, a little more courageous after their first encounter. Deimos growls back, then laughs as the foolish mutt tries to hide behind me, breaking our contact again.

"Bailey's terrifying, isn't he, Demon?" I say to Deimos. Bailey tries to crawl even further under my legs, almost knocking me over as Deimos' roar of laughter rolls along the corridor. Suddenly Bailey is wrenched away then deposited by my side.

"Sit, hound, you protect your mistress, not her you!" Phobos commands.

Bailey leans into my side but doesn't scurry for cover. Instead, he lets out a whine that almost sounds guilty. I bend to stroke him and am given a reassuring lick.

"And that is not my brother's name," says Phobos.

"Demon?" Brazen, I stir the pot further. "Of course it is! A beautifully accurate English translation. In fact, it'll be my new pet name for him. Congratulations, Demon, on gaining your first Aussie nickname!"

Deimos laughs while Phobos smoulders in confusion, unsure of how to deal with a sense of humour. I find it oddly endearing. Phobos grabs my arm and attempts to guide me away. His brother continues to chortle.

"What about Phobos? Does he get a nickname too or does this mean you like me better?" calls Deimos from behind us.

I turn to retort but suddenly there's no floor under my feet and I'm falling. Pain shoots up my shoulder and neck as my arm's wrenched once again nearly out of its socket.

Again? Seriously?

"What the fu . . .?" I say, trying to regain my feet.

Phobos' hand tightens on my arm in an attempt to pull me up. The pain that radiates from my shoulder now is a sharp reminder of the need to pay attention.

Never trust another with your safety.

The man's wary, probably preparing for another of my outbursts, so I take a few deep breaths. It's not going to help if I lose my temper with Phobos. History should've taught me better. His reaction . . . perhaps I should be a little more forgiving. But damn, that hurt like a bitch.

"Look I'm—" starts Phobos.

"It's okay, I—" Nervous chuckles sneak out my throat as we speak simultaneously. Phobos shifts uncomfortably. All of my senses are attuned to his movement.

"You first," I say, gingerly sitting on the top step while surreptitiously rubbing my shoulder as I wait. I'm tempted to link with Bailey so I can see his expressions, but don't want to split my focus that much. Instead, I weave a stronger tendril between our two minds so I can sense more of what he's feeling as he speaks. I find myself moving closer to his comforting warmth.

His natural scent's earthy, but it's woven with a slightly sharp scent. The closest comparison I can think of is ammonia. Fear has a stronger scent, but with a similar ammonic base.

Anxiety. Interesting.

There's another, more subtle scent there I can't quite identify, but it's fresh, clean and very appealing when mixed with his natural scent. I clutch his wrist, ostensibly for support but in reality gauging his heart rate. His pulse hammers against my fingers, increasing with each second he's silent. He takes a deep breath, steeling himself.

"I'm sorry again." Phobos sounds disgusted with himself. "You are so capable you make me forget you cannot see, and I lack the foresight to plan how to adjust for your difficulties quickly. That and . . ." The strength of that fresh smell increases. "Well, no-one speaks to us as you did in the bedroom. Nor when you were teasing my brother. It is both amusing and . . . disturbing. I am not dealing well with it."

A wave of self-loathing rolls off him and tugs on my heartstrings. He didn't deserve my outburst earlier and he doesn't deserve to feel this way now.

"You shouldn't have been so dismissive of my difficulties. But I'm sorry too," I say quietly. His pulse slows under my fingers and I draw my hands back to my body to maintain some distance. "I lashed out for no real reason earlier and you didn't deserve it." I laugh derisively at myself. "You may have heard that I haven't had many visitors since . . . the fire." I swallow past the lump in my throat, willing myself to continue. The air swirls with the movement of a hand near my hair and I sense his desire to comfort, but it never makes contact.

Disappointment fills me, and I don't want to analyse why.

I rush on, desperate to end the emotionally charged exchange. "I'm defensive and a pain in the arse. So, I'm sorry you guys have been saddled with me but I'll try to be a little more understanding. If you try to be a bit more sensitive to my needs." And that's as much as I'm willing to give. His agreement is pushed back along one of the threads I've left in his mind. He must be more aware of me than I thought.

"Now that you've had your heart to heart, can we please get moving?" Deimos amusement shines through his impatience as I weave stronger threads between us as well. He gives me a mental wink, letting me know he's aware of me and doesn't care.

Should I be worried? I'd care if someone was dipping freely into my mind.

I shake my head. We're heading towards a Council meeting and they're the executioners of the Council's will. I'll take any help I can get and untangle the strings later.

Using the handrail to pull myself to my feet, I link with Bailey for vision and make my way slowly down the steps behind Deimos. Phobos follows at the rear.

"Why'd we take the stairs anyway?" I say as we reach the third-floor landing, trying not to gulp in air. The shock of the fall and my earlier run must have exhausted me. It's almost embarrassing.

"The elevator leaves us open for ambush at the bottom when the door opens," Phobos says hastily.

I frown. I've been here months on my own, perfectly safe. And his logic's totally flawed.

"But if one of you took the stairs, checking before the others came down, we could've still used it," I say. Deimos snorts, his amusement making me smile. "What's so funny, Demon?"

This only makes him laugh harder. I grip the rail tightly and try to concentrate on putting one foot in front of the other, not up his frustrating arse. Wouldn't manage it anyway. Bailey's already at the bottom so my depth perception's non-existent.

Deimos' laughter eventually dies and he answers me, but Phobos is rigid, with embarrassment flooding our link.

"My brother, the mighty warrior, is scared."

I'm confused. Seems to happen a lot with these two but Deimos doesn't explain, dissolving into laughter again.

Phobos shudders and says, "I do not like modern technology. Who knows what could go wrong in there."

"What modern technology? Not, the elevator?"

"Yes." He squirms.

"But you used the phone a minute ago. What's the difference?"

His embarrassment surges like waves over our link, as does a thick, sweet smell, like honey, which I assume corresponds with his emotions. It's not one I've experienced yet but I take a moment to memorise it as we reach the ground floor.

"The phone is a necessity, a useful tool," Phobos continues. "Even then, I still prefer mind speech if I can with someone I have a connection with. Most young ones do not seem to have this ability, so it becomes necessary to use a phone to coordinate strategically. An elevator is not a necessity. It is a death trap."

Chained roughly to the shelving, the flames flick ever closer, metal on wrists and back searing—Blinking blind eyes, I try to shake the flashback. "Not for you. But it certainly makes it easier for me."

Phobos's quiet, contrite. I'm more inclined to forgive now.

I clutch Bailey's harness tightly as we step out of the building. Using Bailey's eyes, I scan for a taxi, but there's none waiting in any direction.

"I thought you would've had transport ready to take us to the airport. Can't really row to Thailand from here."

Both Deimos and Phobos are scowling in agreement, and Bailey scents a mouse, moving eagerly towards the wall so I only catch a glimpse of their faces.

"What?" I ask.

"We did have transport organised, that was what the call was about," Phobos says. His foot taps with impatience. "And we are not going to the airport."

I groan. There's only one other option available if they've disregarded travel by plane, and I don't like it. "You want to use a Hermes!"

Both men share a confused silence.

Most with the Immortal gene would kill to have access to an Immortal from Hermes' line, but I only know one. And I haven't seen him since the fire. "Please tell me it isn't Caleb!"

Bailey's lost interest in the rodent and joins me in time for us to see the confusion on Deimos' face.

"Caleb has a contract with Ares and his descendants," Deimos explains. "He also lives in Sydney. It's convenient."

"Maybe for you, but the person I was with before I was kidnapped was Caleb, and he hasn't attempted to make contact since I woke." I pause, blinking back tears before they fall. I hate crying. Unfortunately, they seem to hover all the bloody time.

And Caleb's absence is a sore point. No phone calls, texts or emails. It's been like he never existed. That hurt's still raw. So's the anger.

I whistle Bailey over and firm our connection as I wrench the emotions back into the vault.

Should we call and cancel the transport, Deimos?

No brother. It'd only prolong the inevitable and besides, she doesn't know the whole story. Maybe we shoul—

I CAN HEAR YOU, YOU IDIOTS!

"Sorry, Chloe," says Phobos. "We don't want to hurt you unnecessarily but—"

His sentence is accompanied by an increase of pressure in the air and punctuated by a loud pop. Caleb appears in front of Phobos with a shit-eating grin. "Sorry I'm late, Boss, but you have no idea the trouble I had getting these god-damned Aviator sunnies! D'you have any idea how much these things cost? It's lucky the Council foots your bills, otherwise, you'd be broke in—"

He's seen me. And his stunning smile disappears.

Caleb's a beautiful specimen of manhood. At just over six foot, his lean frame is defined, but not overly muscular. He has an innate style that I've always envied. Even in jeans and a T-shirt, he managed to pull off the GQ look. With his obsidian mane just a little too long but adding a sense of the untameable that inevitably attracted every single female in a club when we used to hit them.

What his physique didn't do for him in the pick-up department, his smile usually did. Devilishly white, it serves to highlight the deeply tanned skin that's a product of his Indigenous Australian heritage.

He's not smiling now, and neither am I.

Tentatively, I send out feelers into his mind, and what I find shocks me. Caleb's no longer the light-hearted man he once was. His head is filled with pain and shadows that rival those found in mine. And the darkness is recent.

As is the massive block he slams up to try to keep me out!

My hurt still burns with an intensity that's overwhelming. Nearly as overwhelming as my anger. And shame. I both want to know why he hasn't contacted me, and am terrified of the answer. Now's not the time to try have that conversation, however.

I shake my hair down to hide my scars. Despite putting on a brave face for the twins, this is the first time I've been confronted with someone I used to know, and my insecurities about my appearance aren't as deeply buried as I'd like.

"Chloe." Caleb's tone is bland, but the guilt and regret swamp his mind.

"Caleb," I spit out, but can't find the words to express my hurt. Silence stretches into infinity. Bailey barks, breaking the awkward tableau and Caleb turns away from me as he faces the twins.

Good manners has me withdraw a little from the brothers' minds but I can still hear their surface thoughts. Particularly Phobos', for some reason. There're hints of curiosity but by far the strongest is jealousy that hits a crescendo then fades abruptly as he muffles the link.

Muffles, but doesn't cut.

Instead, he wraps it tighter around himself. I think it's an unconscious action, but it fills my chest with an unfamiliar warmth all the same.

"I take it the glasses are for Chloe, Boss?" Caleb asks.

"Boss! Seriously? Boss?" I grin, as Phobos squirms uncomfortably. "I should've known someone would have the good sense to nickname you as well. Also should've known it would be another Aussie." I explode into undignified giggles that stretch the skin around my scarred eyes, a reminder of both the ease of my past life and the pain I'm left with.

It sobers me, and I snatch the glasses case from his hands, hastily pulling out my new Aviators and fumbling them on. Tight muscles loosen, an unconscious reaction to the replacement of my mask.

While the twins had started to ignore the eye thing, Caleb's gaze is disconcerting. There was a time I'd thought him my best friend, that he knew everything about me. Could be trusted with anything.

Until I was broken.

"Done then! Demon and Boss, names for the twenty-first century!" I aim for flippant but it comes out a little strained. Funnily enough, both men radiate pleasure. Caleb's amusement barely touches his black emotions.

Caleb clears his throat. "Are we ready to go? The Council won't wait forever and if we don't leave now, we're going to get stuck in Bangkok traffic."

Knowing the drill, I reach down to grab Bailey's harness when a sharp, burning pain erupts in my shoulder, sending me staggering backwards.

"Chloe!" someone shouts, seemingly from a distance. The scent of copper immediately fills my nose while spots dance before my eyes. I drop to the ground and roll into the foetal position, my hellhound taking his stance protectively over my body.

He's on red alert, senses incredibly sharp as he does what he was bred to. Bailey looms over me, my sense of him expanding with his girth. I don't need my eyes to know that the increase in size has broken his harness, I'm just thankful for the now 200-kilo slab of muscle blocking me from further harm.

The pain in my arm radiates sharp pulses, almost as intense as the smell of my blood.

I've been shot!

★ ★ ★

Phobos

DEIMOS RACES TOWARDS THE apartment across the street to the place where, judging from the trajectory, the shooter is hiding. I raise my sidearm, providing cover for my brother as Deimos searches for the assassin. Rage fills me, the burning overwhelming, but when Deimos reaches the building I drop to Chloe's side, clamping a hand over her wound. I don't let myself think that all that anger may be because a wisp of a girl is curled up in terror at my feet, even as my heart lurches at the pitiable image.

Caleb is crouched on the other side of Chloe and her hound, a hand on Bailey's head and one on hers, ready to whisk them out of danger at my word. I shift his hand so it replaces mine on her wound, then rip a strip of fabric from the bottom of my shirt. It's not pretty, but once I've tied it around the wound it makes a pretty effective bandage, leaving both my hands free. The hellhound glows with fluorescent green flames which seem to have a mind of their own, shying away from Caleb's touch. I am surprised that Bailey will tolerate Caleb at the moment, but the man needs to have direct contact to use his gift.

Screams echo through the building across the street and Deimos bursts through the front doors, sniper rifle over one shoulder, an unconscious man over the other. Nonchalantly, he crosses the road towards us as faces press against glass panes to get a better view. He dumps the body in front of me, and I barely suppress a flinch.

"Do your thing brother, and you," he says, turning to Caleb, "call in a crew to wipe their memories. Quickly."

Caleb immediately takes out his phone and dials. Deimos takes my place scanning the windows and hovering menacingly before Chloe. Hopefully, there isn't a second assassin, but if there is, he will think twice about attacking now that we are alert. I look at the man. He is just stirring dazedly, a bruise already forming on his temple. My stomach roils. I know what Deimos wants me to do, but still, I try to think through other options. Unfortunately, time waits for no man, particularly one of Aphrodite and Ares' cursed union.

"Hurry the fuck up! We don't have time for your squeamishness. I wanted her out of here ten minutes ago," says Deimos.

I steel myself, then fist my hands in the assassin's shirt, slapping him so he opens his eyes.

I breathe my poison directly into the man's mouth, holding his gaze. At least I have control over it now, though it took hundreds of years to master.

The assassin's eyes go vacant and he stares in adoration up at me. One minute the man was shaking off the effects of a punch from one of Ares' sons, the next he was under the thrall of the other. My stomach turns at how easy it is to use this 'gift' my mother bequeathed me, a reaction that she never had, but I swallow the bile and continue with my task.

Self-loathing wars with memories of Alala and I struggle to concentrate on my task, despite knowing its importance. It is then I feel her. Chloe. The warm little thread in my mind she has been stealthily weaving since we met her. The thoughts are weak but she is pushing her emotions towards me and when it registers, I'm stunned. Respect. The tiny slip of a princess respects me, despite what I am doing. It is enough to firm my resolve, absolve me of the guilt I feel.

"Who is your employer, assassin?" My voice is jarring after the intimacy of our exchange, but I wait patiently for the answer.

The man sways slightly towards me, lips parted in ecstasy at the sound of my voice. I want to wipe the look away, whether by my fist or some other means, but experience has taught me what is done cannot be undone. It is only after I repeat myself a second, and finally a third time that he answers. By then I have passed revulsion and moved on to rage.

"Forgive me, my lord, I was not expecting you here. She did not tell me! Please forgive—"

"You will answer the questions as they are given," I snap and the assassin is instantly alert, waiting. "Now, tell me. What was your briefing for this mission?"

"I was to watch the building and wait for an opportunity to take the Seer out. The woman told me she would be here." The man takes a deep breath. "She was supposed to be alone, Son of Ares. I am sorry I have offended you, I was not aiming at you! Did I hit you? She moved so suddenly—"

"Who is this woman?" I cut him off quickly.

"I don't know, Master. She hid in the shadows and took care to disguise her voice even though it was obviously feminine."

I do not like this answer.

What female would attempt to have Chloe assassinated?

I begin the unenviable task of searching the man, clinically stripping him—a task made easier with the man eagerly helping. The assassin starts flinging his own clothes off in eager abandon, throwing himself naked to the ground at my feet. Despite the roiling in my gut, I thoroughly search his clothing, looking for a clue as to the identity of his employer. Burner phone with numbers wiped. Mars Bar wrapper. No trace for us to follow.

It is when the assassin starts to stroke my legs that I decide I have had enough.

"Can you turn it off?" Chloe's voice is weak but filled with disgust, though from the sense I have of her emotions through our link, it appears not to be with me. Perhaps with the situation. Caleb is helping her sit upright. Though swaying, she leans on him as he attempts to get her to stand. She holds firm, waiting for my response.

There is a reason the rest of the Immortal world fears us. We can own a person, in more ways than one, and it is not limited to mortals like the pathetic specimen in front of me. The combination of Aphrodite and Ares' gifts inside us. . . Obsession and terror do not help one form solid friendships.

"Can you turn it off?" she asks again when I am silent for too long.

"Of course he can't," snorts Deimos. "Why do you think he uses it so rarely?"

"There must be something he can—"

"Do you think we haven't tried?" Deimos yells bitterly, startling both Chloe and Caleb who, judging from the expression on his face, has not seen this particular skill in action either. "Being who we are and who we are descended from, there is only one cure, and most can't access it."

"True love," I say bitterly. "Deimos learned that one the hard way, didn't you brother?" Both of us are filled with self-loathing. There is not one day that goes by I don't feel the sting of Alala's death, nor Deimos, the terror of his youth. It is a story he will never voice to another, and one we try our best to avoid. It's no wonder he has reacted with anger to her innocent question, but for me it just makes my heart hurt. The same heart the Immortal world is convinced I don't have.

Deimos drags the man away by the hair and throws an effortless punch towards his temple. He instantly crumples and Chloe's hound slinks over to investigate. I suspect the pony-sized beast is supposed to be both protector and eyes, so I have no doubt she is a little vulnerable right now. There is no way she would want to stare at the assassin's . . . junk? Is that the correct modern term?

"Caleb, stash him in Chloe's apartment. When you've dropped us off, you can return and take him to Hades to be locked up in Purgatory for the time being. Tell my uncle we'll stop by and question him more later."

Deimos' words intrude on my thoughts. It is a smart move. Hades has always been someone to be trusted. He does not take betrayal lightly.

Chloe is on the verge of passing out but turns towards her hound who is still in his fighting form. Green flames lick up and down his back and I catch the moment she registers the heat.

A small shriek leaves her mouth and she tries to backpedal across the sidewalk, away from the monstrous beast whose only interest is in protecting his mistress. Bailey lets out a confused whine, crawling on his belly toward her but I can feel her terror and pain as if it is my own. The blood loss must be affecting her.

Either that or she's stuck in a memory sparked by the heat of her hound's flames.

My heart goes out to her as I push the no-longer-flaming hound away, though surprisingly he snarls in my direction. I did not think he had a spine, but he must have acquired one when his mistress was hurt. A glare in the mutt's direction soon sees him settle, so I turn my attention to his mistress.

Chloe's terror clouds her mind to the point where her impressive mental shields are all but crumbled. That will be the first thing I remedy when I have a moment alone with her. It's a vulnerability she can't afford. For now, though, it is an easy opening to send soothing thoughts her way while I attempt to calm her with my hands. Though it has been millennia since I had the opportunity to do this, there are some things one does not forget.

My hands move in soothing circles on her back.

"It is over now, Chloe," I say comfortingly. "Deep breaths. Find your focus." I try to send warmth through the bond as well, but I don't know if I have managed it.

Eventually, the terror clears and in its place I have become uncomfortably aware of her. The pixie frame plays host to all sorts of interesting curves and in that instant, all I can think about is taking her lips with mine. I know it's not right, the girl has been shot for god's sake, but her emotions seem to be feeding my own and she is pressing closer to me.

An insistent whine breaks the moment and I pull back in embarrassment. This cannot happen. For a variety of different reasons. But the blush that heats her cheeks has me on the verge of doing something to truly earn it.

"Had you forgotten that Hellhounds spark hellfire when they are angry?" My question surprises her, but it shouldn't.

"No," she chokes out. Her cheeks turn an even deeper shade of red and it's all I can do not to reach out and stroke them. "Just memories catching me in a weak moment." She pauses and her head tilts back as she swallows her pain. "Do you think there's any way to train him so I can get used to it?"

It's left unspoken that she probably doesn't want to run terrified from her own guide dog.

"I'll have a think about it." It's then I notice the blood seeping down her shoulder, staining the fabric bandage unforgivably. A red wash of fury almost overwhelms me again, but I tamp it down. "For now, we need to get to Olympus and have someone see to your injury."

She nods, shaky hands still stroking Bailey, as I remove the bandage to get a closer look. Her brows are pinched with pain but she doesn't make a sound. Brave girl.

The bullet has just grazed her skin, but the scar tissue around it is deep. I'm surprised she can feel anything through it. Asclepius did a good job, considering what I've heard about the state they found her in. I gently pinch the sides together, giving the blood time to clot in an awkward sort of healing, before I use her own sleeve this time to rewrap it.

"It's a very poor effort at doctoring, but we have little time and it will be simpler to have you attended by one of Asclepius' line than to get you to a doctor here." She nods her acceptance then reaches up to me for help standing.

I ignore her hand and scoop her up.

The instant our skin touches electricity shoots through my body straight to my groin. I almost groan, the need to draw her closer imperative, but Caleb chooses that instant to touch our shoulders and whisk us both away.

There is a lurch, my stomach churns and I feel like my insides are about to be squeezed onto my outside then suddenly, with a loud pop, we are there.

CHAPTER THREE

Chloe

MY STOMACH ROILS AS we lurch out of Caleb's grasp. Burying my face into Phobos' chest, I fight the nausea that wants to overwhelm me. I take a deep breath of his comforting scent and raise my head. "I'd forgotten how much I hate that."

Bailey's behaving himself but I thread my consciousness more tightly through his and plant the suggestion to stick closely to us. He presses close to Phobos, nudging me with his enormous head before trotting out in front. Taking a deep breath, I look through Bailey's eyes.

The twins are waiting patiently for me to collect myself, Phobos with me in his arms, and I drink in the sight. Despite the fear factor, both are beautiful men. Deimos has his hair cut military short, only the hint of golden blond stubble dusting his crown. Phobos' hair is the opposite, starting to grow out in messy golden locks I still itch to touch. While his body is muscular perfection, I'm irresistibly drawn to his eyes, a gunmetal grey, which by all rights, should be terrifying but instead hold a molten warmth that's mesmerising.

It takes Caleb's pointed cough to bring me back to myself. I studiously look elsewhere as I can't hide behind my hair anymore. Phobos's pretends to look straight ahead though his eyes keep darting to my bare skin and I feign clinical disinterest as I stare at Boss's chest. Who am I kidding? I'm just as fascinated by that as Bailey is by the pole he's currently investigating.

Perhaps this attraction isn't a one-way street.

"I need to get back to pick up the assassin," Caleb says. "I'll organise a clean-up crew to scrub the memories of the witnesses. Gorgons or Sirens?"

"Gorgons," Deimos responds immediately. "They're less likely to enslave the ones whose memories need doctoring. Besides, there are very few Sirens left with any significant power, and the ones under contract to the Council wouldn't have the strength to work on a large scale like this. The others are in hiding."

"Done." Caleb looks at me like he wants to say something, but I turn pointedly away from him. With a sigh and a pop, Caleb disappears.

I'm left to get my bearings.

The smell hits first, a cacophony of incense, bodies and spices. Added to this are the incessant traffic sounds that combine into their own unique melody. It's odd, but not unpleasant. When I finally make use of Bailey's eyes again, I'm lost in the kaleidoscope created by a city with too many cars and people, and not nearly enough space.

Everything's in motion, from the electronic billboards to the motorbikes zipping between and around cars on the roads. People are constantly brushing past, so completely absorbed in their own worlds we stand unnoticed despite our unusual appearance.

I remember that a Hermes descendent has momentary control over the thoughts of those around their arrival when they 'travel'. However, they have to be able to touch those they bring with them. Working in teams they can build a 'gateway' which could theoretically transport an army. Having an army descend on a mortal town could blow our cover though, so I guess they don't use that skill often.

"Time to hire transportation," says Phobos.

We all squeeze into a small yellow taxi, Bailey riding up front with the nervous taxi driver. Like any dog, the great beast sticks his head out of the window, letting his lips flap in the slipstream. His hind legs are squished into the footwell, forelegs on the seat, tail almost an internal set of windscreen wipers, he's that happy.

Much as I love his enthusiasm, I need a rest. Bailey's sense of hearing and smell are intense but I can maintain some distance from them.

It's easy to forget I can't with my own.

The minute I detach from Bailey, everything hits me with full force. The sharp rancid scent of fear from the driver is overwhelming, as are the traffic noises. I'm aware of the cracked leather cutting fine lines into the unmarked flesh of my thigh, even through my jeans.

It's a whirlwind of sensation, made worse by the fact we're in motion and I can't find my way out of this nightmare. I start to panic as I struggle to re-establish the connection with Bailey but fail, over and over again.

My lungs heave, but there doesn't seem to be enough air.

Just as my hands inch towards my ears to block the noise, someone grasps my arm, squeezing hard. The fingers pinch deep into my muscle and I latch onto that sensation, using it as a focus to force my mind to calm. I take a deep breath, filtering out the relatively distant smells outside the car and concentrating on the ones inside.

I'm learning to distinguish between the twins' natural scents. Right now, with his fingers providing a lifeline and his compassion and determination swirling through my head, I recognise the calming, earthy scent as Phobos. His grip eases as I relax, and suddenly all I can think of is the heat radiating from those five points of contact. His touch lingers longer than expected and Deimos lets out an incredulous snort, breaking the spell.

"Maybe we should switch seats, brother. You appear to be losing your composure," Deimos says.

Phobos doesn't say a word but switches automatically with his brother.

It isn't lost on me. The man is desperate to maintain his distance, but is this reaction due to my discomfort or his own? Either way, distance allows us to rebuild some walls while his presence gives me the strength I need to stay grounded.

Heat remains though, like a ghostly touch of his fingers, leaving me wanting.

I re-establish contact with Bailey as the taxi snakes easily through traffic. Pre-nightmare, I would never have driven here; there are too many cars and no obvious road rules. Families ride together on one motorcycle, as do tradesmen and farmers. Bailey barks at a man with live chickens on the back of his scooter.

My wound throbs with increasing intensity but eventually, I catch sight of the blinding white behemoth of a skyscraper the Council calls home.

While it's the Council's general idea to situate Olympus in an area that needs developing for the good of their economy, it's always rubbed me the wrong way. The idea smacks more of a desire for worship and cheap labour than being motivated out of any real desire to better the people or country. The key features of each country they established themselves in are political and economic turmoil that could be used to their advantage. They're worse than Bailey at an all-you-can-eat buffet.

"I hate it that they're here," I say. I have a strong grasp on Bailey's senses, so manage to see Deimos look startled.

Phobos nods in understanding, adding, "It is a tourist mecca, yet so many live in poverty."

The contrast between rich and poor couldn't be greater. Gold leafed temples tiled with shimmering glass, tower over ramshackle lean-tos built against their walls, homes of the poorest. The scent of rich incense threads through unwashed bodies and excrement.

"The sad thing," Phobos continues, eyes glazed with inner pain as he takes it all in, "is that they will funnel money into the country, but these people, the ones who count, will never see any benefit." His words echo my thoughts.

"At least they learned not to meddle since the last disaster," Deimos says. "Attempting to use that narcissistic fool Hitler to improve Germany was a disaster."

I snort. "Disaster's an understatement."

"You are mistaken, Deimos," Phobos states emphatically. "They did not learn that lesson then, nor did they learn it the twenty-odd times prior to it. Caesar. Napoleon. Hitler. Never forget that the one thing they want above all else is power. Even those who think they are seizing it for the greater good." *Both men and Immortals.* I don't say it aloud, but the same thought flits through the minds of the twins, accompanied by a wariness that saddens me.

The taxi pulls in to a hotel of Grecian architecture, ironically named Olympus, which serves as the home of the Council as well as being a very lucrative business. A bellhop in an immaculately pressed uniform opens the door for us to exit, his surprise evident when two brick walls step out first to canvas the area. It must be odd to see a security team step out of a taxi and not a private car, but after the brief flicker, there's no further reaction. Very well trained. He's probably one of ours, one of the most recent generations with the Immortal gene. His power too diluted to do anything with it. Probably a Null. Somewhat like me—before.

Bailey leaps out of the car, snuffling at the sidewalk, and I disengage while he familiarises himself with the environment. I spread my senses out, touching as many minds as I can within a radius of 100 metres. I need to build my mental strength more than anything else at the moment. Interestingly enough, I find I can weed out mortals from those with the Immortal gene by how much I can see.

With mortals, not only can I sense their thoughts, but brief flashes of individual futures and pasts flash through my mind when I make contact. It's a heady rush of information that leaves me feeling powerful when so much in my life is chaotic. The Immortals still register, but I need to actively work at invading their thoughts, and I'm too nervous to try looking at their pasts. However, it's a skill I should perfect. I can't rely on anyone else to protect me from the Council, no matter how hard the twins are trying.

"Come, Chloe, the Council waits." Phobos has slipped into his more formal mannerism, reminding me why I refuse to delve too deeply into an Immortal's mind. With the old ones, their pasts are an eternity behind them, and I wouldn't like to see what lies behind the veneer of civilisation the twins have. No matter how attractive I find one of them.

Their futures, too, are an endless road with many forks along the way that leave me feeling disconnected from reality. When the Seer gene kicked in, the information overload was overwhelming. It took me months before I could screen out others' thoughts, months during which I healed excruciatingly slowly. The pain from both my injuries and the new influx of information from a sense I'd never used, nearly drove me insane.

The bellhop leads us through reception to a small medical bay where one of Asclepius' sons quickly doctors my left arm. Bailey growls threateningly at him when I yelp at his initial touch, then subsides when the cool breeze of the healing runs through me. I heave a sigh of relief. Not even another scar to add to my impressive collection.

The healer's eyes gleam with compassion, but I shrug it off, pulling on fresh clothes someone has found for me. I don't need his pity, but I'm sure he means well. Running my hands along my body to check everything's sitting right, I take a moment to centre myself.

There's no rest for the wicked.

Instead, I'm rushed through the door, even as I send a sightless white nod towards the healer. I'd stay and thank him properly but the Council waits for no man. Or woman.

We enter a vast gold-leafed and marble foyer, making our way to a gold plated elevator that Bailey finds so interesting. I have to suppress his natural instinct to mark his territory. My own nose screws up in disgust at the gaudy display and I sense a thread of amusement from Deimos. Phobos is trying to smother his fear of the 'modern' technology. He stares ahead, not even blinking at the gilding. No doubt they're used to the ostentation but do they truly appreciate it, like their elders? It seems like the type of décor their mother would love—

polished white marble and gilded cherubs. Maybe I *should* let Bailey have at it . . .

Our guide swipes a card over a box next to the door and instantly we're moving inexorably upwards. At the final floor, the doors glide soundlessly open and Bailey drags me through, the twins flanking me. The doors have opened onto a long corridor, plush garish red carpet leading to a set of double doors. I balk, hesitant to move forward and without ceremony, an all-encompassing Prophecy hits me. I drop to the ground as my eyes burn with overwhelming intensity.

I'm watching myself in a forest. I don't know where, when or even how I've arrived, but I feel them stalking me. Bailey's not with me, so the me in my vision moves hesitantly from tree to tree, sending out feelers to find where the hostile minds are. Unfortunately, they're close . . . close enough to hear their voices rather than just in their minds. I attempt to bury myself between bushes and leaf litter, the rich earthy scent a false comfort.

"She is close, Brother. I can smell her fear." It's not a voice I recognise.

"Quiet. I can't hear anything with you chattering in my ears. You know she will try to end us if we fail." They are both silent for a little longer, but the first man can't maintain it.

"Do you think she was telling the truth, that we would be part of a new Council?"

"I think that she would tell us anything to get us to do this job. Fortunately, even without that reward, there is much in it for us." He lets out a short laugh that sends chills down my spine. "Can you imagine it? The opportunity to break a Seer after all this time?"

It's then I realise what they are.

Titans.

I come to with a gasp, fingers digging at the tiled floor the world black around me. Bailey's silken body's pressed protectively against me, offering me comfort from my visions.

I've lost my connection with him so I send out a thin tendril and curl it into the comforting familiarity of his mind.

My heart's racing a hundred miles a minute, jumping like a rabbit trying to escape my chest. The vision is still clear and sharp despite the lapse of time. I know it won't fade. Most do, though this one's too terrifying to disappear. Prophecy. My sweat trickles down the back of my neck, prompting Bailey to attempt to clean me up. Now I'm drowning in dog slobber. The tension's broken.

"Do you want to talk about it?" Boss helps me up, his concern for me still lingering in his voice and mind.

I find that I'm constantly attached now to both brothers, a tendril of my mind snuggling quietly inside theirs. It's as natural as breathing, I'm expending no effort to maintain it. Maybe I'm gaining strength—or they're losing the will to keep me out. I'll talk to them about it later . . . if I get the chance.

"I don't know why this happened now. Usually, there's a trigger for a Prophecy and they're never this clear, but this one . . . It's not your average premonition." My voice drops as I explain the general gist of the vision. "If what I saw is true, then something is truly wrong in our world, and the Council needs to know about it. Though which Gods can we trust? Who would unleash the Titans?" I try to stand only to find myself gently swept to my feet, a hand lingering a moment too long on the small of my back.

Goosebumps pebble my skin, hardening my nipples. Only one of the brothers provokes these reactions and it's embarrassing. Not to mention that I still have a piece of my mind floating around in his, so I can feel both his arousal and his pity.

There it is again. Pity.

No woman wants to be attracted to a man who finds her pitiful.

I straighten my spine and pull away, hurt, resolving to avoid dwelling on the thoughts in Phobos' head. Aside from feeling a little like a peeping Tom, I don't like the heat, so I *really* need to get out of the kitchen.

A smooth wall forms in my mind between my thoughts and his, radically decreasing the amount of information flowing to me. For good measure, I do the same with Deimos. At least this will give us all a measure of privacy.

"I don't know if this is something you want to bring up in your first meeting with the Council." Worry is threaded through Deimos' voice. "From what I can gather from your vision, it appears that someone is at work dismantling the institution, possibly from the inside. There are very few who'd have the power to fill that kind of vacuum and they are all either on the Council already, or have been imprisoned for a reason."

"There are too many agendas amongst the Council to be sure that one of them is not making a move for power themselves. I think there would be only two you could trust with this information—Calliope, and possibly Ares."

I blink, surprised. "Ares?" I ask.

"He loves conflict, but prefers to work from the sidelines, not be the sole figurehead for a political power." His tone suggests there is no love lost between Phobos and his father. "Besides, aside from having a physical presence in the Middle East, the majority of his power in this Age comes from electronic sources."

I'm totally lost. "What power could the God of War have over electronic sources?"

"MI5, the CIA, basically all intelligence agencies make war through the internet. And let's not forget Facebook. Never underestimate the power of teenage feuds." There's a smile in Deimos' voice.

I answer with a grin, releasing some of the tension that's been lingering. "If you really think he would be a good person to confide in, I suppose I could do that. Calliope on the other hand . . ." My gut rolls. Though *logically* I know she did her best, I still haven't forgiven her for the delay that ended in . . . well, *this.*

I lower my head, midnight hair loose from bobby pins lost in the excitement, falling haphazardly around my face.

Surprisingly, I've lost all self-consciousness around the brothers, but the mention of Calliope has me crawling back into my safe place. Flames fill my mind and I have to work hard to shake myself from the past. A hand on my shoulder brings me back.

"She does care, you know," says Phobos. "She asked the others to leave you in peace, at least for a little while, but she was outvoted."

I know she cares, it's just that every time I even think about her, I'm transported back into that warehouse, burning alive again. It's worse that no-one's found who's responsible or even why I was a target when at the time I was a nobody with no power. Maybe this meeting with the Council's a blessing in disguise. The answers are somewhere and I'm going to find them.

Leaning into Phobos warmth, I take comfort where I can.

"I suppose I can talk to her." My voice sounds surly, even to my own ears.

I square my shoulders, latch on to Bailey and continue down the corridor, a little unsteady on my feet. My gut churns at the thought of speaking with both Calliope and Ares, but I know it has to be done. Particularly now I know the Titans are involved.

The burnished doors at the end of the hall swing soundlessly open onto blackness as we approach, an impenetrable veil that seems somehow ominous.

Another step and my quiet life will end, if it hasn't already, and I'll be in a fight for control of my future. I know how it works—they're both terrified and covetous of the Seers' power.

There's a reason the others of my kind are gone.

Deimos disappears through the veil and Phobos grabs my hand, halting Bailey and me in our tracks.

"We *will* protect you, Chloe." Phobos' voice is earnest. "Even if it means pitting ourselves against one or all of the Council."

A bitter, disbelieving laugh escapes me.

"Drop the wall you have built. See the truth. You will find nothing in my mind that will hurt you," he says.

Surprised that he's both detected my wall and wants to allow me unfettered access, I tentatively do as Phobos asks. His memories wash over me, a heartbreaking chorus of pain and slavery. Images of the brothers committing atrocity after atrocity while experiencing their hearts steadily breaking, all in the name of a Council they've steadily lost faith in. Remnants of their last internal conversation, had while I was lost in my memories, flick past.

Will they break her, do you think?

They will try, we will not allow it.

No brother, we won't. No matter their plans.

I feel Phobos' determination to protect me from their fate. Then warmth washes through me, the glow of admiration and attraction, and I try to wall myself away again, confused.

No. Don't. There is nothing to fear here and everything to be gained. Use my memories when you go in there. Perhaps, if we play this right, we can all be free.

His dream of the future floats to the forefront; a house by the sea, the freedom to make his own choices, children's laughter drifting from the shore. He wants it so badly I ache for him, but I also sense his determination to never bring children into a world where their father is a slave to greed and corruption.

You have the opportunity to make a difference. Let us help you, Chloe.

I swallow my fear and reach for him, wrapping myself firmly in the comfort of his mind. He settles around me, his touch feather soft and wondrous. Suddenly I slip, and instead of sharing Bailey's vision, I'm seeing through Phobos' eyes. It's disorienting, but my heart stops as his gaze settles on my face, lingering on my scars. There's anger swirling in his mind, and yes, pity, but it's only for the pain I felt.

By far the most overwhelming emotions are pride and awe. Tears run down my cheeks and I attempt to disconnect, but an intense light's burning within me.

Burning *through* me.

I try to control it, swallow it down again, but it rushes from me to him and back again, fusing us inextricably. The raging inferno propels me through *all* his memories, not only those he chooses to show, and I sense it does the same in reverse. Phobos is subjected to my childhood of hope, womanhood of inadequacy, and more recently my 'rebirth' through fire.

He experiences it all first hand and doesn't flinch. Instead, his mind revels in the merge with mine. *You are a phoenix, Princess. A goddess risen from the ashes.*

A solid thread snaps into place, glowing golden between and around our minds. I know instinctively it's unbreakable, and it shakes me to my core.

What have we done?

My breath comes in harsh pants, as does his, but the most prominent emotion coming from Boss is a wholly male satisfaction.

"What just happened?" I ask shakily, finally able to relax and slip behind Bailey's eyes instead.

He awkwardly gathers me into his arms, relaxing only as I lean into him. "A true joining. I had thought it a myth."

"Joining?" Unease tickles my spine.

"Two souls mated, meant to be, given the opportunity to reside within each other." His fingers touch my face with tenderness, reverence.

There's no need to voice my understanding. We're now entwined so tightly, he senses it. I don't even know if I'm capable of disentangling myself. I know this isn't what he intended, but I don't think he would've offered if he wasn't aware that things could go wrong.

Soulmates. Fuck.

I'll have to think about it later, but despite (or maybe because of) this I know I can trust him. With anything. It's all there in his mind, an open book.

Though there are shadowed areas that smell of secrets I need to know.

"Don't worry," His voice is startling after the intimate connection we just made and I jump. "I understand. Truthfully, it is nice. Not so lonely in there." The silence stretches but it's not awkward, just comforting, and filled with warmth.

I've seen horrors in his mind that no one should be forced to experience, yet by sharing his emotions, all I can feel for the brothers is compassion. They aren't the monsters they believe they are, and I want to help them see it. Particularly this man, wrapped so securely around me.

A pointed cough interrupts us, and I'm surprisingly unembarrassed. The blackness of the gate swirls around Deimos' torso, making him look like a spectre emerging from the wall. "Are you done, or do you two need a moment?"

Reluctantly I pull out of the safety of Phobos' embrace.

"We're done, Demon," I say with a wry grin. "Though you could regret it in the near future."

He looks back and forth between his brother and me, lingering on the hand that's still resting lightly on my back.

"I may, but it won't be today." He beckons us forward with a disembodied hand. "Come. The Council grows impatient," Deimos says as he disappears into the blackness for the second time.

I take a deep breath and walk through behind him, Bailey by my side and Phobos at my back. It feels . . . safe.

Gods know I need some of that right now.

CHAPTER FOUR

Chloe

THE ROOM ISN'T IN the hotel, or at least not in the hotel we just left. As the portal swirls to a close behind us, I stare in wonder though Bailey's eyes. It still has the opulent luxury of the Thai hotel through the door behind us, but this place has an ancient feel, as if built from the bones of some long-dead giant. Judging by who's on the Council, this may not be far wrong. I reach out to Phobos, confused and a little frightened by what's just occurred.

Phobos explains: *This is the real Olympus. The stones and mortar are made from the blood and bones of the Titans, forged by Cronos, and was their base of operations for ages before our birth. Cronos locked it away out of time before he was imprisoned by Zeus. Only Hermes has the power to open the gateway here, which may be the only reason the Councilman is alive today.*

I nudge Bailey towards Hermes, sending out a tendril of my thoughts towards him. His exhaustion floats at the top of his mind.

The portal takes incredible power to maintain. He will be useless for the next few days after expending this much energy. I don't think any one of Hermes' progeny could do it alone, although they have been known to access Olympus themselves by pooling power. Phobos frowns. *Although Caleb may have surpassed him already. He's very talented.*

I'm not tempted to sink further into Hermes' thoughts. The surface is slick and dark, a cesspool of negativity. He stares at me with one golden eye and I suddenly realise this is Caleb's forefather, be it many times removed. I shudder. I don't want to think about how his line continued this long.

Others mingle around the room, more than the twelve who sit on the Council, so I assume this is a social function before the main event. Each of the Councillors seem to hold court, the sea of bodies flowing in circles around them as 'lesser' Immortals seek to curry favour. I wonder what it takes to get an invite to these events. The people here drip diamonds, an aura of wealth surrounding everyone present. My lip curls in distaste. Mum would be right at home here.

A potent smell reaches me. It could almost be termed sickly sweet but's saved from that by a hint of citrus. Ambrosia. It's so rare that it's only served to honoured guests on the most special of occasions, at a birth, death or on a child's twentieth birthday, when their gifts usually amplify to their highest extent.

I've had it on three occasions, the death of my father, my twentieth birthday celebrations and immediately after my rebirth through fire, I think in an attempt to help me recover.

Drowning in smoke as it fills my lungs with silent death—

I clutch the scruff of Bailey's neck and curl myself tighter into Phobos' thoughts, forcing the memories back into their cage and breathing deeply as I hold both lifelines.

My panic recedes and we stride into the room with none the wiser to my little panic attack.

Each of the people we pass has a glass of Ambrosia in hand, a detail that stands out sharply through Bailey's eyes. And nose. If anyone spills any of their drink, my lumbering hellhound will be all over it like a fashionista at a Myer sale. It'd be almost worth it if they did. They've no idea the amount of damage that beast can do accidentally.

As we pass, silence descends, and I can't quite figure out whether the tension is aggressive or expectant. A little of both, I think. Bailey's eyes dart everywhere, assessing the danger. Phobos is by my side, feeding me his observations in a steady stream.

You are correct about Hermes. Avoid at all costs being left alone in a room with him. Women have a tendency to go missing around him then return, days later, broken beyond repair. His fury rises. *They do nothing, the Council. They need him too much. Some even enjoy his 'antics'. I'm sure there are others who participate.*

What happened to his eye? I send to him. *The damage must have been huge to still look like that.*

Rumour has it that one of his 'conquests' did that to him. He was desperate for a Siren, and a Siren he got.

What happened to her?

She hasn't been seen since, though it took Hermes years to recover and Olympus has only just become accessible again. I think whatever she did to him, may have damaged his ability to access his power as well. He has been . . . struggling . . . since then.

I watch the sweat roll off his face and allow myself a small, internal smile of satisfaction. My curiosity's drawing me inexorably closer to his thoughts. I itch to delve into the recent past, see what she did to him. I've never really been someone to pry into others' business, but seeing a monster get his comeuppance . . .? Temptation at its finest.

I don't know if you want to do that, Boss says.

Why not? Surely it'd be worth it, to know if someone lives who's capable of standing up to the Council? Particularly one like him. I feel his hesitation through our bond.

Maybe Deimos can distract him while you work your magic . . .

Done! While still nervous, the prospect of beating a Councilman at his own game's heady. Intoxicating. I flick a thought at Deimos, urging him to begin a conversation with Hermes. So far, no one has approached us, though I don't expect that to last much longer. It's imperative that we get a move on.

Your turn now, Chloe, says Boss.

I send out a thin tendril of my mind towards Hermes' hoping it's fine enough that someone his age won't detect me. I'm pretty confident, but just because I've had some practice on the twins doesn't make me a master.

That first touch is like sliding a hand through a wall of oil. His mind sucks and clings around my thread and I immediately want to vomit, but instead, I push through until I'm safely inside his mind. There's no spark of awareness. He's either extremely good at masking his thoughts, or I'm undetected. I'm surrounded by his hatred and disdain, particularly for Deimos standing in front of him. Their conversation echoes in his mind, stirring bubbles of memory that boil to the surface.

"So I suppose you are enjoying this . . . holiday . . . from your usual duties, Deimos." Hermes' need to anger Demon, to push him into leaving, is a burning desire swamping his mind.

"Yes, it has been rather interesting. Though I hardly think I am the one in need of a holiday. You look exhausted old man! Surely your duties aren't so taxing?"

A wave of red surrounds Hermes thoughts and a storm of images fly through his mind: *A red-headed woman tied to a bed. Gagged. The flash of a whip, dripping blood. Masked faces watching as the woman writhes in agony, eyes pleading for help that never comes. Her body, suddenly limp. The masked faces leave Hermes alone with her, as he bends to check her pulse, her chest not rising.*

I'm struck by fear followed by the almost overwhelming anger from reading Hermes' memory.

He hasn't finished his 'fun'. He unties her gag, about to use his own breath to bring her back.

The woman's eyes snapped open. "Asshole. Shouldn't have ungagged me." Her scream pierces his brain, bringing him to the point of insanity as he flees. There's compulsion in her voice as she shrieks after him. "You will cripple yourself. You will never be as you are now. You will never do this to another again, though every fibre of your being will want to." Her voice echoes with its magic, her scorn a living thing. "A present from all my sisters." The final thread of her compulsion settles around his neck like a noose as she untangles herself from his bonds. Then everything's black.

I disentangle myself from his thoughts, trying very hard to remain calm while horror fills me at the depth of his depravity.

But I also have hope.

She's alive, though he doesn't know where she is. Boss's distress and joy are shared from his access to my information across our link. He then signals to Deimos that we have what we need.

Bailey presses in close to my side, vibrating with his own excitement, possibly feeding off mine. I feel invincible, spine straightening, pride a warm bubble in my chest. Perhaps it's this that has me turn arrogantly at a tap on my shoulder.

"Nice to see you, Chloe." It doesn't take sight to know it's my foremother. Her scent wraps around me, a curious dichotomy of soothing and stimulating.

Just like that, I'm lost again, insecure and angry. Bubble punctured.

"Hi, Calli." She's beautiful. Lush black locks tumble around her shoulders, her skin is flawless and she has the figure of a 60s pin-up girl. I may have her hair, but I'll never hold a candle to the sex-on-a-stick that's Calli. But that's not what attracts people to her. Her voice ripples with power, urging people to agree with whatever she's saying. Already I feel it trying to suffocate me with her guilt and regret.

It takes a strong will to stand against her wishes. Mine's forged in fire. "You haven't changed a bit since I last saw you." Then my voice softens with sadness. "Pity I have."

Her thoughts are a mess of anguish and remorse I instinctively want to soothe. Only I don't know if I'm capable.

Boss sends a blanket around my thoughts and I almost jump, startled. I didn't realise the link would work both ways. At least he's distracted me from Calli's sorrow.

"You know if I had realised—" She starts to explain but I cut in.

"Enough, Calli. What's done is done." Resignation doesn't sit well with me, but this whole scenario's just made me tired. "What do you want?"

Her mouth turns down and even through the filter of Bailey's eyes, I feel it. Even with this buffer, I want to comfort her.

"I need to talk to you, Chloe. In private."

I weave a thread through her thoughts, a little careless with my foremother, enough so she can feel it and rebuff me if she wants. She doesn't, and instead winds me in tighter, almost to the point of discomfort. Her sorrow and pride in me are there in spades, but above these is her caution. She does something with the tendril I'd carelessly flicked her way and suddenly it's firmer, though not so deeply entwined as my bond with Phobos, nor as disturbing.

It's like a piece of my mind floats on the outside of hers, picking up impressions of emotions, opening a line of communication. *We will talk later. For now, just follow my lead. You are going to leave here free in body and mind or it will be the death of me.*

All the nerves I'd previously set aside surface. If I make it out of this without becoming someone's slave, it'll be a miracle.

We will ensure nothing happens to you. The thought from Phobos is reassuring, though a little disturbing. I should've realised he would be listening in.

Calliope's shock is electric, sizzling around her mind before it settles into a quiet satisfaction, tinged with worry. *Soulmates? With Ares' son?*

Yes. Boss confirms quickly with obvious pride. I'm more hesitant.

That's just a myth. Right? I ask nervously.

Boss's hurt's clear, but he muffles it quickly.

Calli doesn't agree. *This is wonderful, Chloe! You should be happy to have found the one person who will never let you fall. That being said,* her thoughts turn wary, *I don't think you should publicise this at the moment.*

I understand where she's coming from. It's not every day Ares' sons show allegiance to someone other than the Council. It's good for me, but promises to be explosive when the

Council realises the shift. And if it's a Soulmate bond, that would scare the Council more than anything else.

"Fine, Calli. I'll see you after," I say. *If we get out of here.*

A hint of amusement comes from Phobos. *Stop being so pessimistic. There are many things that will help us with that.*

We move, as do the Council members towards another set of double doors as Bailey presses protectively against my leg. Fear threatens to swallow me, but now I have four lifelines against the darkness and I'm not letting them go. I move closer to Boss and surreptitiously breathe in his calming earthy scent. My shoulders relax a smidgen.

The next chamber is even more disturbing than the last. The earthen walls are a red so deep it's almost black. They're unadorned, yet light fills the room with shadows from lamps set into the walls. Light doesn't reach the corners of the room, giving the effect that the shadows are creeping closer, eavesdropping on conversations no-one's meant to hear.

In the centre of the room sits the largest table I've ever seen, shaped from one single piece of black marble. An assortment of cheeses and carafes of, I'm presuming from the rich smell, ambrosia, line the centre of the table. Twelve throne-like chairs surround it, each place set with an entree plate and goblet.

One by one these fill with people in various forms of dress, from denim to designer, until Calli takes the second to last chair. She gestures for me to take the last.

I'm an insect under a microscope, the weight of expectation making it hard to breathe.

She wants me to take a Council seat! My thoughts skip wildly around my head. It's an honour to have a seat on the Council, but what's the cost? How much influence would I have?

How could Calli blind-side me like this?

To hesitate is to show weakness. I sit.

This seat has been vacant for over 3,000 years and the collective gasp as I sit, has me squirming even more as I search for the nearest exit. The last person to sit in this chair was Apollo, and he was murdered by some of the very people at this table.

Stop it! Calli's words are a whip in my mind.

I straighten my shoulders, flick my hair out of my face and take Phobos' advice—I stare. With chin up, I scan the room slowly. A wave of fear comes and goes in an instant. The scent is acidic, attacking my sensitive nose almost as aggressively as the floral perfume wafting from the goddess next to me. Persephone takes the 'Goddess of Spring' thing a little too seriously. Bailey stands at my side, nearly twice his normal height and behind me, on opposite sides, are Deimos and Phobos.

A woman stands at the opposite end of the table, commanding an instant hush. Her power rolls off her in waves, intimidating to even the most aggressive. It's easy to see why Hera is called the Queen of Heaven. I've never felt such power. How did Zeus ever have the courage to defy this woman in any way? Not to mention her looks. The brunette beauty wouldn't look out of place on the cover of *Vanity Fair.* Her mind is surrounded by a shield so thick all I get are impressions of both welcome and disappointment. I can't pinpoint who either are directed at, so I wait to see what she has to say.

"Welcome to the first meeting of the Immortal Council since Hermes' accident."

They haven't met since then?

Later . . . says Calli, and I swallow my questions.

"Though we have many matters to discuss, let us first address the most important." Hera turns my way with a genuine smile, raising her glass. "Welcome, Chloe Santos, sole possessor of the Seer gene."

Everyone raises glasses of ambrosia. I fumble mine, a tingle of awareness prickling my skin as all eyes turn to me.

"*Stin iyia sou/sas,*" echoes around the room.

I sip the ambrosia for courage, but not too much or this 'interview' will go south fast. The flash of electricity from that one sip flies through me. It's all I can do not to drain the glass.

"Years ago, the Seers were wiped from our midst. Supposedly for the protection of other immortals." Hera's weighted glare travels the room, her eyes lingering a little longer on some than others. "But it left us without forethought, without insight. In other words, it left us without power."

This causes an uproar.

"It also lets us control our own destiny!" shouts one voice.

"Let the humans live their lives without influence," adds another.

"Kept our thoughts and emotions to ourselves." This last objection leaves them with righteous indignation at my presence.

Many glare my way.

"Let us scheme behind each other's backs while no one could catch a hint of what was going on." The lazy drawl comes from an imposing figure seated next to Hera. Ares.

As the God of War, Ares is refined elegance in an Armani suit, yet there's a wildness about him that raises the hairs on the back of my neck. His energy has the same dangerous edge as the twins', without any of the vulnerability. The room subsides into murmured grumbles. "I shouldn't complain really, all of your machinations cause so much *conflict*, I've hardly had to lift a finger to stir the pot in years."

"Enough, Ares." Hera does not raise her voice, but all in the room subside. "We made a grave mistake in eradicating Apollo's line. Hopefully, that wrong will now be rectified. I call for submissions on how we should proceed with this new development."

Development? I'm a 'development' now.

A beautiful man with green eyes gleaming with mischief stands, staring intently at me. An unwelcome heat spills through my body, making me surreptitiously rub my legs together, trying to dispel the sudden ache between my thighs. My mind reaches for Phobos, hoping he can explain. Instead, he locks on my heat, increasing it with his own passion.

"You know the laws, Eros, none may use their power on another Council member," Deimos growls, projecting his anger at me, to clear some of the lust from my head.

Clarity comes in a rush and I immediately disengage from Bailey. No-one wants a hellhound humping their leg.

"She is not a Council member, at least not yet." Eros' voice is smug, but he reins in his power. "Now we know our powers will work on her, as they didn't on Apollo." Satisfaction and relief surround us.

Calli, is he right? Could Apollo block others' powers?

It was his only defence, something to do with the strength of his mind. She pauses. *Although I suspect it was a developed skill. Apollo worked actively at both shielding his mind and reading others.*

I'll have to do the same. No way will I leave myself at the mercy of vultures like Eros.

"We have nothing to fear from her and everything to gain, if we can bend her to our will." His thoughts are hungry, lustful, and not just for my body. Either option scares me. Eros is very friendly with Hermes. Too friendly.

"Eros is right." Hermes' voice is as slimy as his oily mind. "She need not take Apollo's place on the Council." His attention burns into me. "After all, we already have two slaves to do our bidding, why not one more?"

Phobos presses in closer to me, his body heat and anger providing security in this nest of vipers.

"Did you just call my sons slaves, errand boy?" Ares stands, as the heat of anger fills the room.

The twins remain still. Hermes and Eros' insults have no barbs anymore.

"And what would you call them, Ares? Bearing in mind they have not been free to act of their own volition for millennia?" Hermes' words fuel the tension in the air.

"I agree. This is something that needs to be addressed." Ares' attention focuses on the walls of muscle behind me. "If one of my sons is deemed capable of controlling himself, surely the other two have just as much right to their freedom?" I'd forgotten Eros was his son as well.

"Agreed, Ares," says Hera, once again taking command. The twins are bottled hope. "All in favour of the only two Immortals not in control of their destiny finally being free to choose on their own?"

I latch on to Bailey, desperate to see the outcome of this vote.

Slowly the room fills with a sea of hands, some immediate, others hesitant. Only two remain down. Hermes and Eros. A sneer mars the latter's otherwise perfect features, directed at both of his brothers then at his father. "Fine. Don't come crawling to me for help when you see what they unleash on the world." Hesitant hands drop, but there's still enough for a majority vote.

"By consensus, the Council has spoken. All contracts and chains that bound Phobos and Deimos of the Warrior line are now broken." Hera looks at the brothers as her voice softens. "You are free to act on your own behalf now." Both bow with respect to Hera then resume their stony-faced stance behind me. Surprise and a hint of wariness cross her face before she masks it. She knows they'll bear watching.

Why are they still behind me? Surely they would go to their father?

I want to believe it's for me, but experience has made me cautious.

"Back to Chloe Santos." Her tone's a little harsher than before, and I'm not sure whether they've made a mistake, making their interest so obvious. "The Council will now take suggestions on how to deal with the first Seer in millennia."

Calliope stands. "I put forward that Chloe be granted Apollo's seat on the Council, as she is the last of his line."

Outraged shouts come from a few while others remain thoughtfully in their seats. "Furthermore," Calliope's voice cuts through the cacophony, "she should be given the freedom to choose her own path, as we have done."

"If she becomes a member of this Council, then she should be made to serve, Calliope. She should not retain the right to refuse requests of Council members acting for the benefit of our kind." Asclepius the Healer I remember as gentle, yet his words are tinged with steel. He also can't refuse a Council member who asks for healing, though he can delegate to one of his line. "I agree with giving her the status—Gods know we all need some forethought right now—but her skills should be used for the benefit of all."

More than a few look towards me with avarice shining in their eyes.

"Chloe is one woman, Asclepius. You are one among many. To leash her with the mandate that allows all to ask for her services, with no right of refusal, will burn her out. She will have no true freedom at all." Deimos' voice is bitterly harsh with remembered pain.

"A pity you do not have the seat to vote, Deimos," Eros interrupts cuttingly. "Leave the discussion for those who can."

"Nevertheless, Deimos is right. However" —Ares' eyes pierce through me and I'm rooted to the chair— "it would not be poor form to ensure she owes each seat on the Council one favour a year."

There are grumbles at this, but most of the Council seem to like the idea.

"Do you have any objection to this, Chloe?" Ares asks.

I hesitate. Is this the best offer I'm likely to receive?

"But I don't have control of my powers yet. I've only had a few months to come to terms with this." My hands flick towards my face and eyes. "I don't even know how to use them voluntarily." Hermes guffaws and I turn my sightless gaze towards him, staring. He squirms uncomfortably.

"Then I think a period of training is in order. All in favour of granting Chloe Santos one year to come to terms with her power, before she is beholden to one boon for each line, per year?" Hera's words echo around a silent room as all at the Council table raise their hands.

Twelve favours. I think I can do that.

"Done. Chloe Santos, you are granted a Council seat as head of the Seer line, on the proviso that you voluntarily offer your service according to the terms mentioned." Hera concludes the matter.

I nod warily.

"Good. We will have one of Athena's line draw up the contract," she continues.

A contract implies terms. Maybe I can negotiate further.

"Hephaistos?" Hera nods to the most enormous man I've ever seen.

When he stands I see Hephaistos is taller than Ares, and twice as wide though none of it's fat. He is so dark and heavily muscled if I came across him in a deserted alley I'd run screaming in the opposite direction. The God of Fire hasn't come far from his blacksmithing days.

"I will get started on her badge of office, as soon as we conclude this session." He smiles in my direction and I'm struck by the way it transforms his frankly intimidating features.

Crippled, Hephaistos is actually beautiful. The only emotions coming from him are those of welcome and warmth.

Phobos throbs with angry intensity once in my mind, before a wave of mortification follows it. I don't know what his problem is, but I'm sure going to make the effort to find out.

"Next order of business," continues Hera. "The disturbing increase in attacks against our kind. It carries whispers of the Titans."

The room's awash with fear and hatred. It's so thick I start spiralling under its weight. Suddenly a hand grips my shoulder, fingers digging deep enough to pierce the fog of terror in the room. It's Phobos. Again.

Thanks, Boss. I inhale, licking dry lips.

You're welcome. Now pay attention. This might be related to your vision.

"Ares has information to share," says Hera as she cedes the floor to Ares.

"This morning there was an assassination attempt on Chloe." Speculative glances are turned my way. "If we hadn't sent my sons to collect her, we would again be without a Seer."

Am I mail you *collect*? Luggage at a bus station?

"How many others have been attacked?" Hephaistos' voice is like gravel, but his concern's genuine. You can't fake the worry floating in his mind.

Ares' answer is quick. "The majority have been Sirens or from Calliope's line. Anyone with any chance of influencing others it seems."

I gasp at this news. Is this why I was targeted? Kidnapped? Was I practice?

A pit opens in my belly, the iron of the chair cold and smooth between tightening fingers.

"Though there have been others—a harpy, some dryads. All over the space of the last year." A shocked murmur makes its way around the room at Ares' words.

"How many survivors?" Asclepius' voice is barely a whisper.

Ares hesitates, and I know his answer before it leaves his mouth. "Just Chloe."

Asclepius' anguish is a living thing, writhing through the room.

"The others have all been found dead, or are still missing." Again Ares pauses. "All trace of a connection to their forbearers has been severed."

This. Is. Horrendous. The connection with our forbearer is there for times of need, danger or sorrow. It's what enabled me to contact Calli when I was dying. Though this information makes me rethink that whole situation.

What if Calli wasn't ignoring me?

What if I had been cut off too, only when the Seer gene kicked in I gained the strength to bypass it?

Conversations strike up in hushed bubbles. No-one wants to miss the discussion, but everyone has questions.

Hera remains calm at the head of the Council. She says, "The part of most concern is that the connection with the forbearer is severed *before* there is any chance of them calling for help."

I don't need Bailey's eyes to know she's staring directly at me. I swallow cold, dry air through my thickening throat.

"They have not made the same mistakes with the others as they did with Chloe," Hera concludes ominously.

I was the first.

The test run.

And now the Seer gene has made me a bigger target.

Hephaistos asks, "What are we doing to protect our people?"

"We have called this Council meeting to gain your approval on our plan," Hera replies. "Hades, I believe this is where you come in?"

An unassuming man in plaid shirt and jeans who I had previously overlooked stands to address those assembled. He's not unattractive but his features are plain. The only thing unusual about him are his eyes. They're black as night and galaxies seem to swim in them.

This is Hades? So not your stereotypical image of Death, Guardian of the Underworld. Though he doesn't reap souls for a living, just makes different realities for them to wait in before their next cycle. Bailey's ecstatic at the sight of his former master, tail thumping against the back of my chair. I swear I hear a grunt from Deimos. That tail packs a punch.

"Targeted groups will be coming to dwell in the Underworld," Hades says. There's uproar as the smell of fear thickens in the room. "Stop this superstitious nonsense! Am I dead? Is Persephone?"

A tinkle of laughter comes from the petite blonde seated next to him. Persephone is the epitome of Spring, right down to the flowing green cocktail dress she wears. It's nauseating. Or maybe that's the perfume I caught a whiff of earlier. In comparison to my borrowed jeans and T-shirt, with their familiarity that settled my nerves when I changed from my blood-splattered gear earlier, she *is* a goddess. Maybe 'comfortable' wasn't the best choice of outfit.

"How do you think we dwell in the Underworld? It is not just a place for souls to wait, but a haven for those in need of sanctuary." Her words embarrass some, release the fear in others. "You forget I am Demeter's daughter. Where I walk, so does sunshine and life." There's a kind of arrogance in her voice that rubs me the wrong way, but I can't deny the truth of her words.

"So how will this work?" Hephaistos rumbles.

"The remaining descendants of Calliope and the other Muses will come to us directly. Calli can get in touch with them all and we will have a few of Hermes' team on hand to ferry them to us." Hades is matter-of-fact. "The real issue is locating the surviving Sirens."

"I think that Chloe may be able to help with that," Calli says.

My scars tighten as I raise what's left of my eyebrows at that. "I can?"

"Yes, you can." She laughs and others join her.

I scowl.

"I'll explain more later. It's a bit complicated," says Calli.

"Can we trust you with this one, Calliope?" Hera asks bluntly.

More importantly, can *I* trust Calli with my life again?

"Once Chloe has mastered this skill, she will find it relatively easy to track down the Sirens." Calli's defensive retort makes me wonder whether she's telling the truth. For the life of me, I can't think of a skill that would allow me to find missing women.

"Fine." Hera stands and I sense the meeting's over. "For now we usher as many as we can to safety with Hades, Chloe will track down the Sirens, and Ares' twins are now free to act of their own accord and not at the demands of the Council. Though" —her glare pierces through Ares who, to my amazement, suppresses a shudder— "their father will still retain responsibility for their actions, as he does for all of his line."

Calli grabs my hand and holds me in my seat as the Council leave. None of them linger, except Ares, signalling something to the twins who then quickly exit with him.

We will be just outside, Boss says through our link and I imperceptibly relax.

"What is it, Calli?" I ask, turning to her.

Silently, please. You are in very real danger. I believe others on the Council are involved in this mess. I need you to come to my rooms with me.

Her words send terror straight to my gut. When I realise I'm all but cowering in my seat, I straighten my spine. *Okay. I'm not going to roll over and take anyone's shit.*

A wave of relief wafts through our link.

Even yours, Calli.

Surprisingly, this fills her with pride.

We make our way into the antechamber where Deimos and Phobos wait.

Ares is no-where to be seen.

The chill of premonition that runs up my spine tells me that's a good thing.

CHAPTER FIVE

Phobos

I NEVER THOUGHT THE day would come where the Council decided on freeing Deimos and me. That it comes now is probably because they were too concerned about Chloe to think more closely about unleashing us. I am not going to complain, but it speaks a lot of their fear of Apollo's line that they will free the scourge of the Immortal world rather than sacrifice time debating Chloe's fate.

As we exit the Council chambers behind our father, Deimos and I allow our thoughts to mingle.

Well, that was a development, brother! And to think dear old Dad actually suggested it!

I send a silent, wry grin through our link. It wouldn't do to have Ares cotton on to the fact we were talking behind his back. *If he had known everything that has happened in the last few hours, there is no way he would have supported that, and you know it.*

Yes, particularly with the plans he has for your Chloe.

My gut churns, a red haze of anger and jealousy builds that I find difficult to dispel. Deimos' laughter echoes through our connection. I clench my teeth and will down my errant thoughts. There is no telling what Ares will do if he thinks I have betrayed him.

Do you have any idea why he wants us? I ask my brother, mainly to divert him from his current line of thought.

No, but we are about to find out I think.

Ares has come to a halt outside the Council chambers. Though he has walked the Earth for millennia, the man still appears only slightly older than Caleb, and he is from the most current generation with the Immortal gene. His strength is legendary, as is his ability to charm women, though there have been fewer of our line born in the last couple of hundred years. He has been nearly as immoral with that sort of thing as Zeus, so it is surprising we don't have any more little brothers or sisters floating around.

This will be quick, boys. His thoughts bludgeon into ours with no subtlety. I don't think we will ever be anything but 'boys' to our father, despite being grown men for thousands of years. *I will come to see you in Chloe's rooms later, but for the moment you will need to stay by her side. The woman must be protected at all costs if Apollo's last prophecy for our line is to come to fruition.*

Deimos and I exchange glances, a fact our father does not miss. Deimos jumps in before he can start picking us apart. *You didn't believe in the prophecy before, Dad. What's made you change your mind?*

He pauses long enough that I'm not sure he is going to answer. *Before, there was none of Apollo's line left. Now, here she is, and all I can think about is the power floating in her veins.* He hesitates. *There has been none to rival Hera and Zeus in power for generations. Doesn't the thought of it excite you?*

Neither of us want to mention the obvious but Deimos, ever the bold, makes the attempt. *You've had problems with this for generations, Dad. How do you think—*

It is my right! He snarls initially, then realises who he is talking to and calms. *And if that fails, then one of you may try. But until then, the woman belongs to me.* He pauses. *Make sure she is at the feast. This begins tonight.*

He turns abruptly, striding towards the elevators as Deimos and I try to conceal our shock.

This is the first I have heard about him being willing to share, Boss. My brother sends slyly. *Maybe you will have your chance with Chloe after dear old Dad—*

I whip around to face him, eyes going heavy with the weight of my anger. The one thing I can guarantee as a descendent of Ares, is that it's obvious to all when the bloodlust overtakes us. Deimos holds his ground but eyes me warily when my red-tinged sending reaches him.

Neither of you will touch her. For once my brother has stopped joking, instead nodding in confirmation of his own thoughts.

Then we must work out a way to discourage Ares, or you will be facing a lot worse than enslavement to the Council, Phobos. His worry for me is clear and it's that which lets the bloodlust recede, seconds before the door opens once more and Calliope and Chloe step out.

I nod to my brother in silent acceptance then we both fall into step behind the women. The connection between Chloe and me is so bright and true it is almost visible to the naked eye. Sensing my turmoil, she sends a wave of comfort my way and I smile, for what seems the first time in millennia. I send her some of my warmth, basking in the unity.

Careful how you handle this, brother. Deimos' warning is timely. All I can think about is sweeping her off her feet and taking her somewhere private. *There are other things to consider than your emotions, though,* he pauses and I feel his own smile. *It is good to see you living again.*

It is good to *be* living. I will take his warning to heart. What is between us is too precious to lose through misjudgement and error. I will not have a repeat of my first marriage, not if I have anything to say about it.

Secrets have a way of sneaking out when they are least wanted, Deimos sends soberly. *Be careful how you time your truths.*

I will. Believe me, I will.

CHAPTER SIX

Chloe

CALLIOPE'S ROOMS ARE SPARTAN, but the walls are filled with the most incredible artwork from across time. Through Bailey's eyes, I spy an early Da Vinci sketch (I suspect the model's a nude Calli), a Picasso and a Titian, again with a voluptuous Calli-esque model. It's not tasteless, but it's easy to see the influence of this Muse across time. The walls are also lined with many first edition novels, bound carefully in hardback or locked under glass. I know from experience these are signed. It's become common practice in our publishing house to collect signed first editions from our authors.

There's so much space here that even the twins, a hellhound, Calliope and myself in the room can't seem to fill it.

"Is it safe to talk here?" asks Deimos immediately, as Boss moves to close the curtains and survey the other rooms.

"You won't find anything in here, Phobos," says Calli. "The rooms have been secured by Hephaistos himself." She looks towards Deimos. "Does that answer your question?"

Both brothers seem to relax and I take a seat. Hephaistos' security's impenetrable.

"Okay, Calli, what's this about?" I throw my question at her as I disconnect from Bailey. A headache's blooming and maintaining the connection will make it worse. The loss of sight makes everything else stand out in stark relief. Worry saturates the darkness, permeating the air.

Boss has attempted to block himself off from me, but his fear and residual shame from earlier, leak through. Deimos makes no attempt to block me out, but all that comes from him at the moment is anger and worry.

"We need the Sirens, Chloe. I think this is much bigger than Hera is letting on and I think you will be at the heart of it," Calli says gently.

Her fear still has that metallic bite, but underneath her concern for me is a thread that shocks.

Love!

Calli does love me! It's a sugary sweet taste that sends warmth through me, etching itself on my heart. My own mother may think I'm useless, but this one sensation tells me I'm at least loved by *someone*.

My hand's swallowed by a warm grip and I don't need sight to know it's Phobos. *Others care too, Chloe.* I take a firmer grip on his hand and with that motion, the others' attention drifts towards curiosity and humour. Perhaps some wariness.

"Also . . ." she hesitates.

I don't know if I want to know what comes next.

She takes a deep breath and continues, "I think you have a right to know about your background."

This confuses me. We're all aware of our background. Most of our forebears are still alive today, so you'd have to be pretty dense to not know your own lineage. Or wilfully ignorant.

"Yes, Calliope, I think you have some explaining to do." Deimos' voice is firm but not aggressive.

I guess there's some story here that I'm not privy to. Curiosity has me in her grasp, whispering sweet nothings in my ear. I lean eagerly towards Calli.

"Did you not wonder where you inherited the Seer gene from, Chloe?" I jolt. Phobos' words make me feel foolish. It's something I should've questioned.

"I guess I just thought some ancestor way back had a slight touch of the sight. Maybe a human ancestor?" I don't really believe anything I'm saying now, and it seems stupid that I did before. Calli laughs.

"No, hon, we have assured your line remains unpolluted for the last 2,000 years." My jaw hits the ground, but just as quickly anger rises.

"Unpolluted? You're starting to sound like Hermes and his posse, Calli. I didn't know you hated humans so much."

She snorts, that one sound containing the wealth of her disgust. "So quick to jump to conclusions, Chloe. Perhaps you should wait for the explanation first?"

I nod my head, gesturing for her to go on.

"I'm sure you aren't aware that Apollo knew he and the others of his line, were going to die."

The men give none of their surprise away, but it's there regardless. My shock's palpable, but then I realise it makes sense. Why wouldn't any of the most powerful precognitives have foreseen a massacre of that scale?

"As I'm sure you are aware, none can foresee their own death, so the Council took advantage of that in their planning—time and day undisclosed, all to be hit at exactly the same time."

I shudder at her words.

Visions flit through Calli's head, ones that sicken me to my stomach. Calli's hands reaching to touch bodies stiffening with congealing blood. Men, women, children. All sacrificed to greed, the desire for power.

And Apollo, butchered in his own seat of power. Drawn and quartered to ensure there was no chance of his body healing the damage done to him. Calli's grief's so raw, I'm left with no doubt about her feelings for Apollo.

She's always said a man's desire for power makes him a monster, but his capacity for love can absolve his guilt. I'd say Apollo didn't even need absolution in her books. The Council, on the other hand . . .

"Though he didn't know the time or the place, Apollo had seen the mass pyres in a vision and made the connection between them and the shady dealings of Olympus at that time. He came to me . . ." Calli's voice is drowned by her tears. The twins and I wait in silence as she composes herself. "You see we were best friends. And while there was never any sexual relationship there, Apollo asked—"

"Asked you to continue his line." Deimos has understood before I have.

If you knew your entire line was about to be wiped from existence, what would you do?

"And you loved him enough to do it," I add.

Calli nodded. "He had a final vision, one in which a sole survivor with his powers would help to defeat the Titans when they returned. Without this child, all would be lost."

No pressure Chloe.

"So, I retired from Olympus in grief and gave our child to my grand-daughter Nerissa to be raised as her own." That's sacrifice. My heart thuds inside my chest.

"You kept Apollo's child hidden within your line?" Deimos asks, but I want the clarification too.

"Correct. Though it wasn't hard, as none of our descendants to date have ever exhibited any Seer abilities." I feel the warmth of her regard. "It has been hard pretending that the children of this union were not . . . special to me."

All my feelings of anger and resentment flow to the surface. Surely she doesn't expect me to believe that her favoured great-many-times-removed grandchild would have been ignored while she roasted to death?

My tone takes on a cutting edge. "So now you have me, and you think you'll train me. How're you going to do that, Calli? And how're we going to find the Sirens? You don't really expect to be able to teach a Seer how to control their powers, do you?"

My scorn is unwarranted, but the way I'm feeling at the moment makes me want to lash out in any way possible.

A soothing warmth washes through my head and I realise my anger's left me wide open to Phobos. I relax into his mental embrace as I run my thumb over his palm, silently thanking him for the support. It's amazing how quickly I've come to rely on him. He's now the one person I trust implicitly in this fiasco.

"I don't have to teach you." Calli's words sow confusion, but when she continues, everyone's awed. "Apollo will."

She reaches out and something soft brushes my fingers, which I quickly grab. Bailey's in the other room, so I desperately feel the package, running it through shaking fingers. As I unwrap the cloth, my fingers brush the spine of a book and I flick through leaf-thin pages.

Let me be your eyes, Boss offers.

I hesitate, not wanting to intrude again, but he gives me a mental nudge, making me smile as he moves closer to me. It seems effortless to pour myself into his head, not like it is with Bailey, or even with Hermes. His eyes become mine and the steady thump of his heart calms me like nothing else.

We look in the parcel.

Nestled within the cloth is a small, palm-sized book. Though its cover is leather, it doesn't appear to be too old, and when I flick through the pages, the ink's a sharp, bright black. I look questioningly towards Calli.

"I have hand-copied it every ten years. It's not due to be redone for another eight."

"And the other copies?" Deimos is confident. He knows they haven't been destroyed.

"Locked in safety deposit boxes across twenty different countries until they are no longer legible."

I marvel at her dedication, but the draw of the book is stronger. I flick the pages, and Boss looks over my shoulder, his breath heating my neck and sending all sorts of crazy thoughts I shouldn't be having flitting through my mind. He chuckles briefly across our connection and then I feel it from him too, only what he shows me is a fierce hunger he has no urge to deny.

My face flames, but perhaps I can get away with people thinking it's excitement over the journal?

The muffled laughter from Calli and Deimos tells me not.

"Quiet, Demon, I'm trying to read here." This just prompts a louder laugh that takes all of my self-control to ignore.

Deciding to be the bigger person, I nudge Boss, holding the book higher. His eyes immediately flick back to the page from the glare he was throwing his brother:

> *My Descendent,*
> *If you are reading this, you have come into your Seer powers as prophesied. I am sorry for what you have had to go through to get to this point. I have only seen snippets of your journey, but it breaks my heart that you have suffered so much, and that you will suffer more before this is done.*

Hold on. How much did Apollo know about my 'suffering', and how much did he tell Calli? It's all I can do to rein in my temper enough to finish the letter.

> *I have left this book with Calliope, as she is the only one I trust. Others appear my friends, but they all have their own agenda, which may not align with mine. Ours.*
> *There is but one thing we need to do as a species, and that is to protect humanity. Although Olympus will claim that is what we do now, every move we make is used to further our own quest for power. Those with the Immortal gene need to use their talents to foster the greater good. Unfortunately, our barbaric forefathers care even less for the fate of mankind than my fellow Olympians do.*
> *That brings me to my visions. The Titans. Despite the devastation of the last war between Olympus and our parents, I have seen that there will be one on the Council who will free some, or all, of our forefathers to further their own agenda. I do not know when this will happen, but it may have been part of the catalyst for your own change. These beasts must not be allowed to go free, they must be*

destroyed or reimprisoned. Sirens and Muses were invaluable in past battles, as were Hephaistos and Athena.

You must ensure that your potential is reached. I have written detailed instructions for your training in particular skills, as we would begin to train any child of my line. Progress through as quickly as you can. You never know what will be needed. And under no circumstances, allow this book to fall into an Olympian's hands. You would not be safe if they understood the breadth of your abilities.

I wish you well, Child of my Heart.

Apollo

Calli is wringing her hands.

"Got something to tell me, Calli?" The snarky comment has weight. That ammonic scent of her anxiety fills the room. "You've copied Apollo's words faithfully every ten years. You can't tell me that you didn't know there'd be trouble, Calli."

"I didn't know it would be you!" Calli's guilt and regret stun me to silence. "I've waited millennia for a Seer to arrive and over time I got . . ."

"Complacent," growls Boss. His anger swirls in a raging tornado through mine.

"You could call it that." She slumps.

Chasing calm, I flick through the pages. If I open my mouth now, I'll say something unforgivable.

"You have to understand, his instructions for identifying the one were vague at best, totally incomprehensible to most. 'Black hair' and 'athletic' doesn't help when it describes more than half of our offspring." I understand what she's saying, but it doesn't soothe my anger. She should've been keeping a closer eye on me. Particularly with this unrest.

Swallowing my anger's hard, so I continue to read through Boss's eyes, both of us calming as technical jargon fills our minds. Calli's become a distant thought. That doesn't mean I won't revisit this conversation later. At the moment though, I won't risk my relationship with the only person who appears to care for me in the heat of rage.

Maybe I'm growing up.

Back to the book.

Some of the skills Apollo lists I have already, others are completely unfathomable. One catches my eye as I skim past.

"Distance mind search?" My question sees Calli's enthusiasm burst from her in waves. Her relief is palpable, so the excitement is a touch grating.

"Yes, this is what I alluded to in the Council meeting. You should be able to pick up anyone's mind signature from a distance and follow it to its source."

"Wouldn't I have to know the person to find their mind?"

"Apollo could do it with just an image of that person, but you are correct. For most Seers, it was a skill they could only use with those close to them."

"What makes you think I'd be capable of this now?"

"Apollo said it would come quickly for you—perhaps too quickly. He said it would be as it was for him—a matter of discovery and exhaustion."

"Exhaustion?"

"Every new skill learned causes our body stress. You will most likely be in a perpetual state of exhaustion while you are training. It is the same for all of us, but worse for you because touching time and minds at the same time is beyond stressful."

I don't like the sound of this. So far, my little excursions into people's minds and pasts has been relatively easy. I really don't want to have to live my life in a vacuum again.

"We can try now if you like? What does Apollo say about it?" Her enthusiasm is contagious, even as I can't seem to let go of my scepticism. Boss looks back to the page.

Fix an image of the person you seek to locate in your third eye.

"What does he mean by third eye?" I ask.

"Your inner eye. Some say it is located on your forehead between the other two."

Extend your senses, particularly those defining place. If you maintain your focus on the individual, you should be able to visualise their location and approximate distance from you. You will feel a draw in your solar plexus towards that individual that becomes stronger the closer they are.

"This doesn't sound too difficult," I say to Calli, though my nerves are playing havoc with my senses. A beep from a phone draws our attention to Deimos. He smiles in relief.

"Why don't we test it then?" I nod nervously. Deimos moves towards the door. "I will take a little walk, and you will find me. Give me two minutes." He disappears.

"Are you ready for this?" Phobos' voice holds concern, but it sparks my anger a little.

"You should know by now that I'll do anything to stay alive." I feel anger from him in turn, and it confuses me until I hear his next words.

"You will not do *anything* to stay alive. That is what my brother and I are here for."

Boss has a protective streak. I shouldn't be surprised after all I've seen in his memories, but I think the rumours about the brothers have clouded my perception of them. His hurt at my thoughts is clear and I realise we're still too tightly entwined as I've been using his eyes.

Bailey comes galloping into the room at my whistle, dropping at my feet. I disconnect from Boss and, though there's a sense of loss from both of us, join again with Bailey. It's too tempting to be so close to a person, particularly when they have warm feelings for you. Almost addictive. I may have to try and maintain my distance.

It can't be healthy to be this attached to someone in such a short space of time, despite the fact I know him now almost better than he knows himself. The moment we had before entering the Council chambers left him—us—bare. Thoughts and emotions long thought buried, experienced in an instant. And with none of the judgement we heap upon ourselves. I wonder what he thinks of me now he's had a chance to think things through, but I'm too shy to ask, quickly attempting to mask my thoughts from him. Maybe not quick enough.

"Okay, let's go find Demon." I follow Apollo's directions, trying to think first and foremost of Deimos' face. Unfortunately, it's the other brother's face that keeps leaping to mind. After an exasperating five minutes of trying, I let out a sigh of frustration. It's then that Boss's amusement hits me, so I glare in his direction, which only makes him more amused, though that granite face of his remains stony.

I'll help you. An image of his brother's face appears in my mind, clear and crisp, so I work on solidifying it in my thoughts. Almost immediately I feel a tug in my gut, like butterflies are struggling to get out, so acting on intuition, I follow where they lead.

We exit Calli's apartment, turning left down the corridor. I feel like we're moving in the right direction, but we're too high. "Is there a lift around here somewhere?"

"At the end of the hall," says Calli.

Bailey snuffles away in front of us, unrestrained, while Calli walks by my side and Boss brings up the rear. When the elevator arrives, I press every button on the way down, much to the others' amusement. They'll soon see. We arrive at the first floor down, the lift stops and the door inches open. I take one step out, holding the door with my hand, and then hop back in. The others look at me, confused. "It's pulling me lower. We'll test each floor."

It's three levels down that I finally feel the tug prompting me to move. I give Bailey a mental nudge to get him moving forward, then start out myself. All of a sudden Bailey's pace increases and he lets out a cheerful yip. Some guard dog. Seems he's adopted the *scare-tastic* brothers as his pack now, busily making a fool of himself as a grinning Deimos rubs his belly outside the door to a room. "Found you!" I mentally pat myself on the back. That was easier than I thought.

"Maybe next time you can do it without help." I swear I see Boss's lip twitch upwards a little so I decide that my new mission will be to see him smile. His brother's quite capable of it, so it isn't genetics that makes him so stony-faced.

"I'm assuming it was the similarities between my face and someone else's that was the problem?" Deimos laughs at his own joke and instantly my hackles rise.

"Nothing of the sort!" Boss is amused but doesn't contradict me. "This isn't as easy as it looks you know, and your face *is* rather forgettable." This comment has Calli smiling too, though Deimos' smile is not quite as wide as before.

"Aren't you in the least bit curious as to where we are?" he asks.

"I was wondering whose room you'd dragged me to, but I supposed you'd get around to it when you finished feeling smug." A growl erupts from Bailey's mouth and I sense a figure behind me.

"Stand down hound, I'm not going to harm your mistress." The tone's gruffly amused, the deep voice one I remember.

"Hello, Hephaistos. Are these your rooms then?" During the Council meeting, I sensed no ill will from this immortal, but it never hurts to be polite, especially to someone as powerful as Hephaistos.

"No, little Seer. I have just finished securing these rooms for our newest Council member. Any idea who that may be?" His good cheer is infectious, and again I'm reminded not to form my opinions based on rumour. Human mythology would have you assume Hephaistos was a bitter, self-centred man, when from what I've seen today, the opposite is true. It wouldn't hurt to be wary however—after all, this is the man who actually invented the internet, giving it to the humans for free to help them advance their own technology. He's also been credited with the design of the first computer, and the first spaceship, leaking the schematics to the appropriate people when technology caught up to his inventions.

"Thank you," I say.

"Would you like to tour your new accommodations?" It takes me a second to realise he means would I like to see my rooms. It's been a long day. And the use of my new skill has drained me more than I expected, though I think it'll get easier with practice.

"Again, thank you."

"We thought you may like to get settled before you meet with our father." Deimos' voice is a confusing mix of affection and wariness when talking about Ares. I try to pick the story from his thoughts, but he locks me out so well, I only get vague hints of an earlier conversation that disturbed him.

Interestingly, this glimpse has Boss leaking angry, jealous fumes before he too shuts down. Or at least begins thinking of hellhound puppies. I toss a glare in what I assume is his direction and grab hold of Bailey, slipping behind his eyes as I ruffle the big mutt's jiggly black fat back. He pants in ecstasy, making me smile in turn. Let Boss keep his secrets for the moment.

"Shall we?" Hephaistos is amused by our behaviour. Bailey looks towards him and I catch a glimpse of a fleeting smile that makes my breath catch. Yep, that smile . . . Beneath the scarring, Hephaistos is beautiful, transformed.

He turns to make his way into the room, gait hitching as he accommodates for his lame foot, and I shake myself out of it, trying to ignore the waves of jealousy radiating from Boss. What the hell's his problem? It's not like he has any claim on me. I'm conveniently ignoring the fact he may be my Soulmate. So what if I find another man attractive?

Bailey's head is perfectly positioned to appreciate the subtle play of tight, arse muscles beneath Hephaistos' jeans, so take advantage I do. It's not like anyone would ever—

"Excuse us for a moment, Chloe and I have need of some privacy." Unceremoniously I'm flung over Boss's shoulder, my connection with Bailey thrust from my mind. My anger rises as I realise how this must look, chuckles chasing us down the hallway, my blood rising to a boil.

"Put me down, you arse!" I thump ineffectually on his back until I'm airborne. I stifle a shriek, not wanting to give the big brute any satisfaction, but fear's creeping steadily past the anger and to my mortification, tears slip over my cheeks. There's nothing worse than the feeling of falling without sight. It doesn't matter that I quickly land in what appears to be a heavenly soft king-sized bed. Unfortunately, this is the icing on the cake of an already over-baked day. I curl up into a ball and wait for his anger to hit me, too tired and heartsick to deal with anyone's shit right now.

Instead, my mind is washed with a comforting warmth.

Boss cuddles me and I curl into him, exhausted and embarrassed. "Don't think because I'm crying on you, I've stopped being angry, because I haven't." I sense his amusement, but behind that's still the anger. Now though, he's aware of my fears and treads carefully.

"I didn't like being privy to your thoughts in there, Chloe." I sit bolt upright incredulously, fury rising again. Anger definitely trumps exhaustion.

"You've got to be kidding me! I take one look at a guy's arse and you pull this caveman routine."

"Chloe—"

"Launching me over your shoulder, embarrassing me in front of Council members—"

"Chloe!"

Frustration building, I plough on.

"What makes you think you even have the right to make a comment like that? You haven't even—" His lips smash into mine, igniting a fire that goes well beyond fury.

Unfortunately, it's over all too soon. A brief bonfire he lights then leaves to burn. The man pulls away, hesitant. Waiting.

With a strangled moan I throw myself at him, moulding my lips to his, stroking the flames hotter with my tongue. *This. This* is what I need.

My fingers fist into his shirt as I draw him in tighter. There's no hesitation as I yank his shirt upwards, desperate to touch the chest I've been fantasising about for what feels like forever. He helps, drawing it over his head, grabbing my hands and pulling me in, chest to chest. His skin's smooth and hairless, yet so hard I have trouble believing he's flesh and blood, not a marble statue of Adonis.

I move my lips to his chest, tongue flicking out to taste his salty flesh. With another moan, I trace my hands back to his head, fisting my hands in his hair and yanking his mouth back to mine. Boss's teeth tug at my lips as his fingers dig into my arse, bringing me closer, trailing his fire up my back. It's those same fingers on my scarred face that throw me back into the present.

And the people in the other room.

I scoot backwards on the bed, in my haste nearly falling off the side. Shaking my head so my hair hangs over my face, I turn my useless eyes downwards. He sighs, edging closer on the bed, all the heat from a moment ago gone. Boss takes my hand in his, tracing circles in my palm, and the rhythm calms me. I relax into him, snuggling into the earthy scent of his shirt. The silence isn't awkward, but he breaks it anyway.

"I don't care that you may find other men attractive, Chloe," he says haltingly. "I do care about the way you seem to see yourself."

I don't interrupt, though I can't say I'm happy with the turn of this conversation.

"You are beautiful, Chloe, despite the scars. They are not hideous as you imagine, but are a delicate web of lines I itch to run my fingers over."

His fingers do just that and I relax into his touch.

"Run my lips over."

His follow suit and I melt.

"They make me wish to trace every inch of you, to see what other surprises await."

I moan as his lips capture mine briefly and then pull away again.

"And those eyes," I stiffen slightly but his lips ease the tension, feathering kisses on each temple.

"When they blaze white I become rock-hard. Nothing could make me tear my eyes from you." *Except possibly a threat to your safety.*

I brush a quick kiss to his full lips. It'll take me a while to see his truth, but that he believes it, I've no doubt. It's enough to make my heart pound a relentless rhythm in my chest, trying to force me to accept the connection between us. I squash it ruthlessly.

"We'd better go out to the others." I slide out of the bed then hesitate, totally lost. *Shit.*

"Come on, Princess, I have you." His calloused fingers lace with mine and Boss leads me gently out of the room, allowing me time to count steps before each turn. I'm tempted to use his eyes, but I know I'll more easily remember if I'm forced to do it with my other senses. He doesn't make the offer either, but I sense our minds are so tightly entwined that they'll never separate.

For a moment, a jolt of fear flies through me. I'm literally waiting for him to see just how disappointing I am, then do a complete one-eighty, and run in the opposite direction. He tries to pull me to a halt beside him but I plough on, tugging him with me while I trace the walls, and Boss doesn't have the heart to start another argument now.

Later.

We make it to an open space and I feel the walls recede, the fresh sea breeze filling the room with its light.

"This is an interesting development. You work fast, warrior." Hephaistos derision is clear, and I can't understand where it's coming from. Bailey comes snuffling to my side, a little shamefacedly, so after a moment I bend to scratch behind his ears. The dumb mutt has no real reason to protect me against Phobos or Deimos and he knows it. Suddenly, his nose bumps against my crotch and he lets out an enthusiastic yip.

"Get off you dumb mutt!" My face flames and everyone's chuckles just make it worse. I elbow Boss in the ribs and he lets out a satisfying grunt as I try to divert everyone's attention back to Hephaistos. "What do you mean by that, Councillor?"

"Only that you should be wary of showing others this *attachment* you have formed." His tone's bitter, a crack in his walls letting me see his heartache. I float briefly through his memories until I find her, a blonde waif who's most definitely not his ex-wife, Aphrodite.

The woman shines in his memories like the sun, his love for her burning brighter than anything I've seen before or since.

The vision fades and a flash of bloody eye sockets and matted golden hair replaces it.

The Seers were a greater loss than many realised. Pairings between Seers and other lines are feared greatly.

The depth of his anguish brings tears to my eyes. "Others on the Council will fear this pairing, just as they fear anything outside of the norm that could impact their power." Hephaistos' focus shifts to Boss. "And from what I can gather, your father has his own plans for Chloe."

Phobos' thoughts turn dark and ugly at the mention of his father.

"Yes, we know," says Deimos, surprising me. I'd no idea Ares had plans concerning me. A chill sinks into my bones and Phobos draws me in tighter.

"We will deal with that when we come to it." Boss's blasé attitude irks me, especially when I'm in the dark. "For now, we need his support in this search, so . . ."

"Yes, you'll have to tread carefully around Ares. Don't antagonise him." Calliope's worry steals through the room, her gift urging us to caution.

If Ares is against us, our task will be doubly hard.

"On that note, Chloe, you should rest. We have a dinner to attend and I still have some questions for you," Calli continues. I groan.

All I want is to close my eyes on that warm, cozy bed and let go of the day. Now, I'm going to be stuck socialising at yet another formal event where I have to watch my tongue with ancients. Anger stirs slightly at her attempt to baby me, but I don't have the energy to follow through.

Instead, I grab the scruff of Bailey's neck and give him a gentle nudge in the direction of the bedroom. I don't even have the energy to use his eyes, so I trot along beside him and hope he gets it right. As Bailey stops, I reach my hand out, feeling the bed right in front of me. I drop on top of the covers, dirty clothes and all. My eyelids close for what seems like a second when I'm woken by a gentle whisper.

"Don't you want a bath, Princess?" I nod, not even bothering to open my eyes, so Boss gathers me in his arms, gliding soundlessly towards the bathroom. Gently he removes each article of clothing, each touch stirring the heat within, before lowering me into an already full bath.

The water's almost too hot, especially on my newly healed skin, but soon the heat and the scent of frangipanis send me into a stupor. Boss's hands knead the tense muscles of my shoulders, sending shocks of electricity running through me. My body wants to sleep, but all I can think of is sampling those lush lips again. I roll over to do just that but suddenly his hands are gone, only to be replaced by the softness of a towel brushing across my face.

"Time to get out," he says, threading his hand under my elbow to help me up. I sigh. Apparently, we wouldn't be continuing from where we left off earlier.

And maybe that's for the best. Things are moving so quickly, I need a night by myself just to let it sink in. He wraps the towel around me and scoops me up, depositing me in the middle of the bed. I snuggle into the Egyptian cotton sheets. Things always look better in the morning.

CHAPTER SEVEN

Phobos

CHLOE IS ASLEEP BEFORE I even have her dry and back in the bed. She sprawls inelegantly across the mattress in a way that makes my mouth quirk upwards. Though the sight of her bare body has me up in flames and stiff as a board, I gently pull the sheet up over her shoulders, sneaking a kiss on her forehead. She is such a curious dichotomy of innocence and tempered steel that I know it will take me lifetimes to figure out every nuance of her character, but that is fine by me.

I'll do whatever it takes to see to a future for us.

This will not end with her death as it did Alala.

That in mind, I force myself to go so I can catch Hephaistos before he leaves. He and Calliope have been plotting while I dealt with Chloe, but Deimos has indicated that is winding up.

"Hephaistos!" My raised voice is not loud enough to wake Chloe—though I'm not sure even an explosion would wake her at this point—but it stops him in his tracks nonetheless. Calliope with him. "I will walk with you to your apartment." I turn to her. "Alone, if you don't mind, Councillor."

Calliope eyes me curiously from under her thick lashes but immediately her face lights in a smile. "I will see you at dinner then, Phobos." Her grin turns wicked. "Try not to let Chloe be *too* late, will you? Though I'm sure Deimos won't let that happen. The man is a stickler for punctuality." I nearly grin, she does have my brother pegged, but her other words have me blushing. It has been so long since any innuendo has been directed my way.

I cough. "We won't be late." With a satisfied smirk, she floats away down the corridor.

"You need my help, Phobos?" Hephaistos asks as she disappears into the elevator.

"Can we be heard out here?" I ask perhaps a little too sharply.

He flicks his wrist, the light shining on an intricately carved metal cuff. "No-one will hear our conversation if I don't allow it." He swipes his finger across it and a slight hum starts then subsides. "Sonic technology. Interferes with any devices that can be used to listen from a distance, with an added little extra of mine that blocks all conversation within a two-metre bubble."

I hesitate, even though I'm sure this is the one man who can keep Chloe safe.

"What do you need, Phobos? I have my own preparations to do before dinner tonight."

"I need a favour, Councillor." I try to keep my tone respectful, but I may be harsher than intended. Worry has a habit of making me curt and short-tempered.

"A favour for you," he asks. "Or one for the little Seer?" He is perceptive, seeing straight to the heart of the matter.

"For both of us." He stares at me a minute, his eyes piercing my soul. I acknowledge the half-truth. "Fine, mostly for me. To ease my fears."

"I am short on time as it is, Son of Ares. Why should I do you a favour?" His words are bitter. I know he suspects one of our line of the murder of his love, but neither I nor my brother has any knowledge of it. "I owe you nothing."

"I don't think you ever heard the full story about Alala, Hephaistos." The words are drawn reluctantly from my mouth.

"And what does your wife have to do with this favour?" He is intrigued. None outside of the family know the truth about her demise. There are many who would give everything they own for information to use against one of Ares' line. I hope my faith in his honour is not misplaced.

"Alala was, while not quite sane towards the end, not as unstable as rumour would have people believe." It is hard to talk through this, but if I am to achieve my goal, I know he will settle for nothing less than the whole truth. "Contrary to what most believe, ours was a marriage of convenience, though there was some affection there. You see Father had arranged it after one of Apollo's last prophecies had surfaced and it had come to light that Alala may carry Seer blood."

"I know the prophecy of which you speak, though most do not." My eyes flick to his in surprise. "Apollo was my friend. Surely you didn't expect that he would have told no-one else?" I suppose I shouldn't have assumed that, but now I have to wonder just who else knows. Just how safe can Chloe be if it has been bandied about freely?

"Well," I continue. "We had been married in haste, before her background had been investigated properly. But by the time we found out the truth, I had come to love her." Nothing like the depth of what I now shared with Chloe, but we were happy. At one point she was my world. "Alala was not of Seer blood but Ares did not see the need to dispel the rumours she was, and I was not there to protect her." This is the hardest part of my retelling. My throat constricts and I try to force the words out but nothing happens.

"Yes," Hephaistos' words are full of compassion, his sudden hand on my shoulder squeezes in comfort. "Your father often dismisses the small things if they are not important in the grand scheme of the battle."

I nod wordlessly. "He doesn't understand emotion. I suspect that is why your mother's absence barely registers, despite the fact they were together so long." I am amazed by the lack of anger in his tone. His history with my father and mother is legendary.

He gives a wry chuckle. "I moved beyond that years ago young one. I'd found a love that eclipsed all others. Now," he continues, "how does this relate to the present?"

I take a deep breath and forge on. "I came home from one of Father's battles to find Alala missing, the house a mess and my wife's blood on the floor." Hephaistos' eyes grow shadowed. He knows what is coming. He experienced it before I did. "We of Ares' line are nothing if not skilled trackers. I found her, not too far from our home." The sight of my wife in pieces, lying in a pool of her own blood, is one I will never escape. Not even if I live another three thousand years.

I look Hephaistos directly in the eye as I come to the end. "She was still warm," I spit out. "If I had found her an hour earlier, minutes even, she might still be around today."

The other man nods slowly, taking in what remains unsaid. He understands what I need now, without me having to ask him. Just in case, I share my last concern. "Chloe had a vision," I tell him, "and in it, she was being hunted in a forest." My anguish leaks out into my words. "Alone, Hephaistos! Can you understand what that means to me? To know she is to be alone and hunted and I am not there with her."

His face is pale.

"Though you may hate me and mine please, help me help her."

He takes a deep breath. "Fine. For the love of two good women long in their grave, I will help you." His eyes flash with fire but I can see respect in them. "God help you if you cannot save her then."

Satisfaction races through me along with my terror. This will have to be enough.

"And, Phobos," he flings behind him as he leaves. "Tell her everything. Secrets have a way of escaping when you least want them to."

The advice is no less true despite the fact it's unsolicited.

Tomorrow will be soon enough for judgement day.

I cannot lose her.

CHAPTER EIGHT

Chloe

"WAKE UP, CHLOE! YOU have half an hour to get your arse ready for dinner." The Demon's voice comes from outside the room, an annoying insect that won't leave me alone. He's turned the volume on the television up as high as it can go, David Attenborough's commentary on the mating habits of the walrus serenading me through the walls. I groan and roll over, throwing my head into the pillow beside me. As I breathe in, I realise Boss's scent is all over this side of the bed, but the man himself is nowhere to be found.

"I don't hear the shower, Chloe!"

"Do I have to go?" Even to me, my voice sounds whiney and I cringe, instantly wishing to take it back.

"No, you don't. But if you decide to stay here, be prepared for some pretentious arseholes to knock on your door and suss you out under the guise of checking on your safety." I leap out of the bed, but then stand hesitant. Which way's the bathroom? I realise I've never been there on my own. I don't know the scope of the room, have no fucking idea which way from my bed the bathroom is . . . Bailey's big furry head nudges my arms and gratefully I latch onto his harness and see through his eyes. The room that greets me is a revelation.

It's a cool white, with pale blue accents worked into the décor. For once, nothing's too pretentious. Aside from the size of the bed, everything else is minimalist. The sheets are white, Egyptian cotton if my guess is right. The room's incredibly bright with the curtains open. I've no idea how I have managed to sleep as long as I have because the setting sun's more than enough to light the room with its warm glow.

"Chloe!"

"All right! Stop getting your knickers in a twist!" Bailey pads towards the bathroom at my urging and immediately I stop. The room's stunning. Marble sinks, a huge sunken bathtub I don't think I even registered in my stupor last night, giant fluffy blue towels, and the mother of all double-headed showers. There are even shampoo, conditioner and bath foam dispensers with their names in braille dotted elegantly on the front. I breathe in a relieved sigh.

"Out mutt!" Bailey whines in disappointment as I push him out the door then disconnect. He scratches at the door moaning pitifully, but a girl's got to have her shower time. One arm extended, I move towards the cubicle, running the fingers of the other hand across the plush towels, just to test them.

"Twenty minutes, Chloe! Move your arse!"

I scowl as I move into the shower, running my fingers across the names to make sure I have the right dispensers. Braille was the first new skill I learned after the accident. I don't know what I would have done if I couldn't read. The scent of frangipani surrounds me, making me smile. I suspect Hephaistos had a hand in this. I don't think that any other with access to this room would have the sensitivity to remember a blind person's issues. Or the tools to see it done.

The water beats down in a soothing hot stream, but conscious of the time, I don't linger. Drying myself is no chore and it seems like only seconds before I'm ready to let Bailey in. I link with the dog and open the door confidently, only to stub my toe on the frame.

"Fucking . . ." I suck air in through my teeth in pain, automatically dropping my towel to clutch at my abused toe. The sharp jolt has knocked me back into my own head, so as I search for the towel I reconnect with Bailey, only to find him staring at a large, muscular presence.

Boss is standing stock still, eyes glued to me, filled with fire and yearning. I rise slowly, turning in his direction, the towel forgotten in my grasp. A deep breath lifts my breasts for his gaze and defiantly I straighten my shoulders, watching his eyes trace my curves, the web of scarring that runs all the way down the left side of my body. He doesn't flinch and those eyes lose none of their fire, even as his hands clench on the dress forgotten in his hand. Moisture pools between my thighs and I tighten them, struggling to strangle my instant desire.

He shakes himself out of his trance, smoothing the crumpled material and loosing an embarrassed cough. "I thought you might need something to wear tonight." His hands caress smooth red silk, making me imagine those hands doing the same thing to me. I break the connection with Bailey in a desperate attempt to escape by body's response to his actions.

Though all is black, the soft footfalls of Boss as he crosses the room stirs further anticipation in me, and I realise maybe I was premature in thinking the darkness would make his presence easier to bear. I suck in my breath in anticipation when he stops before me, and I swear I feel his presence like a furnace on my chest. Gently, he takes my hand, stretches my arm out and lays the dress over it. I'm trembling as his touch lingers then recedes.

"I'll be right outside if you need me."

Can I call him back now? Because gods know I need someone to slake this desire burning inside me. He chuckles as he closes the door, bringing a smile to my lips as well, before I remember we're on a time limit and I need to hurry.

With a little creative help from Bailey with my searching, I eventually find my meagre belongings have been unpacked in a large walk-in wardrobe. I quickly grab some underwear, ignore the bras and attempt to throw the dress on by myself. It's then, as the silk hugs my body all the way down to my legs, that I realise it's sleeveless.

"Boss! This dress is missing something!"

"The only thing it was missing, Chloe, was you in it. Now hurry up!" Great, now both brothers were being bossy about the time.

"Two minutes, Chloe!"

"Just shut up, Demon, I still have to do my make—" I don't have to do my make-up, do I? You can't hide scars like this, so why bother? "Okay, I'm coming."

Throwing on some strappy sandals—no heel, I don't have a death wish—I take a deep breath, grab Bailey's collar and walk out the door. The dog leads me down the corridor and I trace my hands along the wall, counting steps and doors. My memory's getting much better. The swift draw of breath as I enter the room makes me nervous, and I stand fidgeting as I wait for them to speak. "Well?" The silence's become too much.

"You look beautiful, Chloe." Deimos' words hold only truth, which is a relief. I wouldn't trust Boss's opinion. The man's entirely too biased at the moment. Across our connection, his awe warms me—and his arousal. It makes my skin break out in goosebumps and I shoot a shy smile in their direction. And a flash of warmth through our bond to Boss. The red silk and bare flesh are like a flag to a bull.

I have plans for you later, Chloe Santos. I smile in anticipation.

They had better be in line with what I have planned for you. His gaze burns a hole through the dress as I turn away from them toward the door. With Bailey pressed tight to my leg, and the *scare-tastic* brothers moving quickly into position behind and in front of me, I feel safer and more content than I have since the fire.

The event is being held in the ballroom, a fact which makes me nauseous. Too many people will be there with too much opportunity to stare at the Seer. But I square my shoulders anyway, nod for the door to be opened, and find myself striding in to the sound of my name and new title.

"Chloe Santos, Councillor of the Seer Line."

Pretentious arseholes. Anyone would think we were royalty, the way they behave. To be honest, though, there are more than a few in the room who still see themselves as gods, so I guess it isn't surprising. We make our way into the room and are immediately accosted by Persephone.

"Have you made progress on finding the Sirens?" Blunt much?

"She has been resting, Persephone. It was a long day." Boss's tone is placating but firm. "She will make a start on it tomorrow."

"This is urgent! We do not have time for your—"

"Persephone, I do believe you're also at this entirely useless event." My inner bitch has come out, and I'm not doing a very good job of hiding it. Never have been good in social situations. "Shouldn't you be organising accommodation for my family and the sirens we manage to find?"

Persephone's face purples with rage. Anger's not a good look on her. Surprisingly, my darling hellhound steps in front of me, a rumble sounding deep in his throat. Boss also moves in closer, as we all watch this goddess work to control her temper. *Be careful, Chloe. She is one of the old ones, her talents are strong.*

Hades moves into the fray and I swear her expression turns to disgust for a fraction of an instant when he touches her, but I must be imagining things. She turns towards him and it's like he hits an instant off switch on her temper.

She's all smiles.

I suppress a shudder as I watch her press into him. "Why don't you go and get yourself a drink, love, while I talk business with our newest Councillor?" Hades' tone is slightly patronising, and I wait for her to lose it like she was about to with us. Instead, she smiles sweetly, placing a kiss on his cheek and floats off without a backwards glance.

"Please excuse Persephone. She has a terrible temper and is not used to being challenged." That's an understatement. From what I've heard, her mother spoilt her rotten and it looks like her husband isn't much better. And that split second change of face . . . the woman's terrifying.

"I'll be staying out of her way I think, Hades." There! I *am* capable of diplomacy. I didn't tell him I'd run very fast in the opposite direction if I ever had a glimpse of his wife in a dark alley.

Bailey's belly is to the floor, the great lump whining to catch Hades' attention. He laughs, leaning down to scratch the rolls around his neck. My hound dissolves into a slobbering mess.

"Have you started working with Calliope on locating the Sirens yet?" He's hopeful, not accusatory, and I realise he's genuinely concerned. A vibe I didn't get from his wife. It makes me a bit more open with him.

"We have made some inroads, but an undertaking that big will require me to be well-rested and relaxed." I give an ironic laugh. "Unfortunately, I'm anything but at the moment." He takes in my appearance, the rigidity of my spine, the black circles around my eyes my afternoon nap has done little to fix.

"Yes, you should take some time for yourself. Shall I fend off hostiles for a while so you can at least try to enjoy the party?"

I smile. "That's the best offer I've had all night!"

Really? Boss sends across our link. *I may have to make my offer more appealing.* I blush furiously as Hades walks off, hoping no-one notices what an interesting shade of tomato I've become. Deimos coughs behind me, smothering a chuckle, waves of amusement washing over me.

"Got something to say, Demon?"

"Don't need to, do I?" His amusement gets stronger. "Have fun trying to block all that out." I attempt to master my emotions, because making a futile attempt to knock out one of Ares' sons in the middle of a crowded ballroom wouldn't endear me to the rest of the Council. Unfortunately, this thought has both brothers laughing internally. Indignant, I grab hold of Bailey's harness and march us towards the bar, thankful I have the love of my simple mutt. Demon is still amused behind me, but Boss is feeling a little more contrite, so I decide to forgive him.

But in an instant, he cuts himself off from me as much as he can. Puzzled, I try to strengthen the connection but he blocks me again. Then Ares comes to a seat beside me at the bar. "And what will you be having, Chloe Santos?" The man's confident and hasn't touched me, but something about the situation's making my skin crawl. Particularly since Boss's mind's a haze of red I can't access.

"Just water, Ares. Can't afford to have a fuzzy head in this pool of sharks." The moment the words leave my mouth I want to take them back. Instead of the angry outburst I expect from one of the old ones, Ares throws his head back and laughs uproariously.

"Well, aren't you a breath of fresh air?" His eyes turn hungry as he scans me from head to toe but his thoughts, though shrouded to a certain extent, show clearly enough that lust's not the dominant emotion. Though it's still there, more prominent is greed. Both emotions confuse me, making me wary. Why Ares would find me attractive after being the Goddess of Love's consort for millennia is beyond me, as are his feelings of avarice.

"I like honesty in a lady, it makes life easier." Again, this comment confuses me. He elaborates. "Aphrodite was always playing games."

Aha.

"I loved the woman," he continues, "but I never knew where I stood with her, and eventually it got too difficult to keep trying."

My heart almost goes out to him, but something holds me back.

"I find honesty's always the best policy. Lies are too hard to keep track of, particularly when you live as long as we can." Score one for Chloe in Diplomacy 101.

Deimos and Phobos are silent at my back, and when Ares puts his hand on my arm, a red wash of rage comes from behind me. I half expect Phobos to rip his own father's head off, and to be honest, at this point, I might even enjoy it, but he doesn't move, his expression unchanging. His lack of outward reaction has my stomach taking a dive.

"I will need to speak with you about the current predicaments, Chloe. There are many reasons for us to collaborate on this." He smiles at me in what I'm sure is an echo of the charm Eros dishes out, but from Bailey's point of view, too close and looking up, it makes him look demonic. His hand traces my arm as he stands to leave and I suppress a shudder.

"Bring her to my chamber afterwards, boys."

Again Boss's anger surges, washing my skin, turning it to goosebumps. He still doesn't say anything, but Deimos tosses a spanner in the works.

"She'll come in the morning, Father. Tonight, she needs her rest." For a moment Ares looks angry at the challenge, but then he takes a good look at me and nods.

"'Til tomorrow, Chloe." He shoots me one last speculative look and leaves, snaking a glass of ambrosia from a passing waiter's tray as he goes. I breathe a sigh of relief.

"I don't like that man." Belatedly, I remember I'm talking about their father, so I grab my glass of water to hide my grimace. Both are studiously looking in other directions but I can tell they've heard me. "Where's the food?" My attempt at distraction doesn't go so well. Deimos laughs at me while I feel Boss's smile inside my head. Finally, the idiot is letting me in a little. Though he's not as open as earlier.

We know what you're doing, Chloe. Just be aware, we don't particularly like him either. His thoughts get a little darker. *Our mother wasn't the only manipulative one in that relationship, so don't believe any of his sob stories.*

Any idea what he wants? Curiosity's burning a hole inside me. The brothers exchange loaded glances. *I could steal the information from you at any time, boys. I'd prefer to hear it from you.*

Please don't ask us to tell you. If we told you, I believe our father would pull us from this mission. Boss sends a wave of warmth through me that comforts as much as it excites. *And both of us feel we are where we need to be at this time.* A flash of humour shines through. *Though Deimos has vastly different reasons than I.*

And just like that, I want him.

When can we blow this joint?

You can't leave until after dinner. It would be the height of rudeness. Though I can sense his agreement with my sentiments.

We make our way through the crowd, stopping for me to say a couple of words to each of the Council members I haven't met. Most I know by reputation already, and some downright scare me, but it's all part of a role I must play if I want to avoid the fate of my predecessors.

A bell's struck signalling a move to the banquet table in the next room. I barely avoid running as I hear it—my stomach's telling me in no uncertain terms that I'd better feed it now.

It'd better stay a silent voice.

I end up seated between Calli and Hephaistos, the latter being the more desirable dinner partner. Calli's still not on my 'nice' list, but I need her if I'm ever going to learn my heritage.

For a moment I'm confused that Deimos and Phobos are not seated at the table, but then I realise it's only the Council seated here and that the others all have staff of various kinds behind them. Some are muscle, like the twins, but Hera has two nymphs behind her and Hephaistos has turned up with no one to give him aide.

"I was hoping you would be here tonight, Chloe. I have something for you." He passes me a wooden jewellery box that has the familiar smell of eucalypt. It stirs a deep longing for home. The smooth grains slide effortlessly through my fingers as I rotate it, searching for the latch. Hephaistos takes it from me gently and opens it.

Bailey's just as curious as I, snuffling the inside of the box before I prompt him to pull back a bit and *look*. His priorities aren't always mine.

The bracelet's silver, but that's the only ordinary thing about it. Vines, leaves and flowers are laced together in an intricate tapestry. A series of images that call to my soul.

"It's beautiful! Thank you!" I move to put it on but he stops me. Hephaistos' mind strains at mine so I form a tentative connection. *Put it on but do not be alarmed. It will tingle for a second as the binding activates. Another plainer cuff lies underneath the cushioning in the box. It will allow the wearer to find you anywhere. Give it to your man.*

He's not my—

He is. Do not deny either of you that connection. The depth of his sadness sends an ache deep into my bones. I lean over to kiss his cheek as I put the bracelet on, a sound move it turns out, as I start imperceptibly when it seals around my wrist.

"I'd better not regret this, Hephaistos," I whisper to him as we move apart. Surreptitiously, I slide the box to Deimos, knowing he'll see it safely back to my rooms. Despite Hephaistos' words, I'm not sure I want to give Boss that much power over me.

Ares is sending antagonistic waves from across the table towards Hephaistos, and I remember that Aphrodite had often been a source of conflict between the two. The feelings I'm picking up from behind me are also tinged with a hint of anger—and the green-eyed monster.

Speculation's moving like a whirlwind around the table. This innocent gesture of Hephaistos' could be seen as something entirely different.

There's another knocking at my mental barriers and I let Hephaistos back in. *It may be wise to allow others to think I have a romantic interest in you. They are more likely to be indulgent with that than if they knew about Phobos.*

I agree. We both smile at each other, hamming up the attraction in front of the sharks. Their amusement floats around us during dinner, but between Calli and Hephaistos I'm kept so entertained I lose track of time. The storm cloud behind my shoulder continues to grow in intensity with every laugh. As the last traces of dessert are gone from my plate, I turn to my dinner partner.

"Thank you. I wouldn't have made it through this meal without you."

A smile twinkles in his eye. "Rest assured it was no hardship, little Seer. I hope to see more of you in the coming months." His attention shifts to the brothers behind my back. *In fact, if it wasn't for a certain brooding son of Ares already having caught your eye, I may just have laid a courting wreath at your feet myself.*

There's humour in his tone, but I sense his sincerity. It confuses me a little. No-one has flirted with me since the incident, and I'm stunned into silence.

"Come, Chloe," Calliope says, dragging my attention away from the man on my left. "We still have work to do." Curiosity prompts me to follow Calli from the room, my ever-vigilant entourage trailing behind me, one finding the situation absolutely hilarious, the other about to chew nails and hurl thunderbolts.

I don't understand why he's so furious, but then I realise he hasn't re-established the connection well enough after the earlier incident with Ares to have been sharing my thoughts. The idiot has watched me flirt with another man all the way through dinner and quietly stewed in his own negative thoughts.

My own anger's rising. Just as I'm about to turn and let loose with some vitriol, we arrive once again at Calli's door.

Once inside, she wastes no time on preliminaries.

"How did it happen?" she asks, eagerness overflowing.

"How did what happen, Calli?" I return wearily. All I want is to sink into that heavenly bed and meet oblivion. Surely she knows that?

"We didn't get a chance to discuss this development between you and Phobos before, and it may well be the most important thing to have happened in the Immortal world since the loss of the Seers." She's almost vibrating with energy and I don't have the heart to tell her it's none of her business.

Besides, she has information I need.

"We had an . . . incident, in the hallway before we entered Olympus," I say. Boss snorts.

"Incident does not begin to cover it," he adds and proceeds to share the details with her. I'm surprised by how freely he speaks, but he did say he thinks she's trustworthy. "We bonded."

He's quiet, contemplative. But over our link flows a wave of happiness so strong, I don't want to do anything to break it.

"A Soulmate bond!" Calli's voice is filled with awe and a hint of jealousy. "We haven't seen any Soulmates for millennia!"

"Calli, are you sure about this?" I ask. "I mean, has anyone ever met someone with a Soulmate bond?" I'm slightly creeped out. It's one thing to be attracted to someone, quite another to realise you've met the one person in eternity who's the other half of your soul. By modern standards, this shit doesn't happen.

"Once," she says, "long before my granddaughter was born, I met a Soul-mated couple." Her voice weaves a spell of its own. I'm lost in her memory. "They were unremarkable, a man of Asclepius' line and one of the Nereids, Poseidon's attendants. They lived humbly in a hut by the sea, taking in the weary and the sick and sending them away whole. Their love . . . every time that man looked at her, it was as if he was offering a galaxy. There was nothing in the world richer than their love."

"Where are they now, Calli?" I ask. It'd be priceless to be able to ask them about this.

"Gone," she says. "Gone like so many of the truly peaceful over the years." Her sadness drowns us, but she reins it in quickly. "The Council rarely lets a thing of beauty live untouched."

"Envy is definitely the curse of the Council," agrees Deimos. I'd almost forgotten he was here, I was so lost in her story. Calli's sadness becomes mine.

Bailey whines and slurps a big wet tongue across my face.

"Ugh, you great dumb mutt! Gross!" Despite my words, I grab his monster head and snuggle into his neck. "Love you too."

"I'm sorry, Chloe," Calli says quietly. "I lose control sometimes when locked in the past."

The grimace I make tugs at the taught skin of my scarring.

"It's fine. I'm just a little sensitive at the moment." I take a deep breath. "So, what you're saying is, Boss *is* my Soulmate, we have the potential to be blissfully happy, but we're probably going to have to bust a few heads together if it's going to last?"

Rueful laughter breaks the tension.

"Correct," Calli grins. "Have a think about what you want, Chloe. You're going to have to address their concerns sooner or later."

"I vote later," Deimos says. "Time to go to bed, princess. You can deal with all your shit in the morning." I nod wearily, too exhausted to argue with the bossy bastard. Bailey nudges his head under my hand and I grab his collar, saying a quick goodnight to Calli on the way out.

"I'm going to assume you'd prefer my company on the way back to your rooms than my brother's." Deimos' tone is suggestive.

"Well, you know what they say about 'assume', Demon."

"What?"

"It makes an 'ass' out of 'u' and 'me'." Boss guffaws.

Calli gently kisses my forehead, hands on either side of my face.

"Know that you are loved, Chloe, since well before you were born. Loved for the person you are now and the woman you have always been." I touch my forehead to hers shocked to find tears welling. I blink them back. "Even if you now have someone who will love you more."

"On that note, it's time to go. When women get teary it's time to implement an exit strategy." At Deimos' words, I am plucked off the ground and slung over a broad masculine shoulder. The scent of the sea after storm surrounds me. Definitely not as nice as Boss's earthy fragrance.

"Put me down, you oaf! I can walk to my own room."

"No can do, little Seer." Great, it's rubbing off. "We'd never get back to your rooms if I left you in charge." Bouncing around like a sack of potatoes is so humiliating.

"You could at least carry me in a more comfortable position."

"Nope," he chuckles. "Any other position and my brother may think I am trying to hit on his woman."

From the feel of the thundercloud walking behind us, he may have a point.

Just before I think I'm about to faint from all the blood rushing to my head, we arrive back at my rooms. "Hand out, Chloe." I bristle at the order but, curious, follow his directions anyway.

He presses my hand against a touchpad on the door, which then opens with a whisper. Deimos answers my unspoken question while Boss stomps past to scan the room. "Bio-thermal print scanners. Looks like Hephaistos has given you all the best toys." I still don't think it stands up against the thoughtfulness of his gift in the bathroom, but a lady has to have her priorities. Bailey takes the open door as a sign he's no longer needed. On hearing a great *whumph* from the lounge, it's clear Bailey's claimed his space. I wince at the thought of all that immaculate whiteness.

Finally, Boss comes back, swings me unceremoniously into his own arms while grunting at his brother, "You have door duty." It doesn't take him long to get to the bedroom, but by then my temper's had a chance to smoulder.

"Do you want to tell me what your problem is?" He doesn't say anything, just lays me gently on the bed, which has the unwelcome effect of cooling my temper some. "You can't shut me out then let your temper run away with you when you don't understand a situation." With that, he drops his walls completely and the floodgates burst.

Red-tinged images of me and Ares, me laughing with Hephaistos, even me with his brother flood through me, but along with the anger lies a hurt and longing that brings me to my knees. And fear. As much as he desperately wants to claim me in front of all the others, his fear for my safety trumps everything. As open as he is at the moment, there's still one secret I know he's hiding.

"Okay, Boss, I get it. But when are you going to tell me about Ares?" Again that red flash of rage and I get glimpses of a conversation with his father that's quickly shut down tight, under lock and key. Just like that, I'm angry again. I'm on a fricking rage rollercoaster.

"You'll find out tomorrow."

I open my mouth to give him a piece of my mind, but he stops it with his own. Instantly my bones turn to liquid and all thought flies from my head.

I'm not tired anymore.

Where our first kiss was all fire, this is a slow, melting exploration of my mouth that has me yearning for more. His tongue dances gently with mine and all of a sudden it's not enough. I pull back, catching his bottom lip gently with my teeth, eliciting a gasp and a hungry growl.

"Why do you have so many clothes on?" I ask. The sensory thread between the two of us explodes and I've no idea where he ends and I begin. I reach for his shirt, desperately tugging it from his pants, running my nails across his moulded abs to get my fill of skin. His own are busy too. Instead of undoing his buttons, he rips it over his head, allowing me to explore. My hands trace his contours, moving up towards his pecks and, as my fingers reach his pebbled nipples, my mouth joins them.

Boss lets out a moan, his hands fisting in my hair then tracing down my spine. All of a sudden I'm on my back with a very aroused man on top of me. He grinds himself into me, the hard length of him rubbing against my clit, dress hiked up around my waist as I wrap myself around him.

His mouth latches onto mine again in a bruising kiss. I work at his waistband, desperate for the feel of him in my hand, sliding his slacks and underwear downwards as I caress his rock-hard arse. He helps, moving back momentarily to slip them off.

Grasping his length in my hand, I pump him to feel his breadth. A drop of pre-cum is at his slit and I use his own wetness to pleasure him. He grabs my hands, pinning them above my head.

"Any more of that and it will be all over before we start."

I feel his breath on my neck before his free hand traces its way down my neckline, sliding under my breast and popping it out of my dress. Goosebumps pebble my skin in anticipation, his breath enough to have me panting for more.

Without warning, he sucks my nipple deep into his mouth before rolling his tongue around it. Moisture pools in my panties and I writhe helplessly beneath him, eager for more. His hand traces across the other breast, freeing it as well, the two now presented like a feast for him between the vee of my dress.

I feel the hunger in him burn at fever pitch, as he gives my other breast the same attention as the last, this time culminating in a gentle nip before he releases it. My back bows off the bed, thrusting my breasts further into his face. He smothers them in kisses before wrapping his arms around me and lifting me upwards.

"Someone else has too many clothes on." Boss's throaty rumble has me panting for him. His hand snakes behind me, lowering the zipper on my dress. "I confess, I don't know how well I was concentrating on my job during dinner." He kisses my shoulders as he slides my dress downwards.

"Everything about you was tormenting me. This," he says as he drops more kisses on my collarbone. "These." His tongue traces a line in a swirl around each of my nipples and I bite back a moan.

I raise my butt off the bed as he slides the dress the rest of the way down, holding my breath for his reaction. Even knowing he has already seen me like this, it's not the same as having my scars bared during sex. He sucks in a deep gasp of appreciation so I relax.

"And I have been particularly desperate to discover what is under this." His fingers hover above the waistband of my black lace thong.

"You aren't going to discover what is under there if you don't keep moving, warrior," I tease, a poor attempt to hide my desperation from him. I feel his smile through our bond. There's no disguising the anticipation is killing me.

His fingers slip underneath the sides of my panties and he groans.

"Gods you're wet!" It comes out through clenched teeth. A finger slides along my seam, flicking the little bundle of nerves above it. I cry out wordlessly as he applies more pressure, his finger moving in relentless circles. My hips rise with each rotation, breath coming in pants and gasps. The orgasm I'm chasing is hovering when the bastard takes his hand away.

★ ★ ★

Phobos

SHE IS SO FUCKING beautiful spread out beneath me, the dress a rumpled silken mess underneath her, bare but for that tiny scrap of lace that conceals nothing.

"Stop fucking torturing me." That is my cue to move. I flick the lace down her toned runner's legs, kissing up the inside of her thighs on the way back up before I stop. Her folds glisten with her natural wetness. Hungrily, I take my first taste of her, a long slow stroke from her tiny pucker to that bundle of nerves she is so desperate for me to touch. Her back arches off the bed and I grasp her hips, holding her still as I continue my assault on her clit.

She tastes like ambrosia, and I know I will never be able to get enough. Surely, I press a finger into her, hooking it upwards as I rub it along her walls. She lets out a little mewl so I add another.

Gods, she is tight!

Long slow licks turn to tiny circles and when she is writhing on the silk, I suck her little bud into my mouth and gently bite. Chloe explodes around me, into me, and I'm electrified, feeling her orgasm as if it is my own. I look down to check that I haven't lost all dignity but no. As her orgasm recedes, I find I can't hold back any longer.

"I need you now, Chloe."

She opens her legs wider in silent invitation, too exhausted for words. I crawl upwards and kiss her as a lazy smile spreads across her face.

Oh no, she will be as desperate for this as I am in just a second.

I trail my hand down her side, the scars reminding me how tough she is. If anyone is able to handle my love, its Chloe. I flick my shaft against her clit and her eyes spring open, her body rocking in a mini orgasm. Dragging her to the edge of the bed, I grab her hips and flip her onto her stomach, lifting that gorgeous arse in the air.

"Pay attention, Princess." She nods feverishly and I rub myself through her moisture. It will be a tight fit. Anticipation rises as I rest at her entrance, then with one swift stroke, I push myself in. She cries out in ecstasy, clutching at the sheets as I drive into her to the hilt. She is so fucking tight, her walls still pulsing with the remnants of her orgasm.

I know I won't last long, but I want to make this as good for her as it is for me. "Touch yourself."

A red wash flies through my thoughts and I realise she is embarrassed, but it doesn't stop her from following my directions. I take a few experimental thrusts, the slap of my balls on her flesh punctuated by her little moans.

My thumb presses against her pucker and she leans back into me, letting me in to my knuckle. Her tight hole clenches around me, and I dream of the day when I can take her there as well. I begin to gather speed, careful I'm not hurting her. It is easy to lose control of your strength when you hold the Warrior gene.

She runs her hands over me, then reaches between us to stroke my balls, giving them a little squeeze. I almost come in that instant, but the little minx just says, "Stop being a gentleman," and slams back onto me. I lose it. Quickly flipping her on her back, I throw her legs over my shoulders, pounding into her as deeply as I can in a frenzied rhythm.

"Yes, Boss, just like that. Don't fucking stop!" Far from hurting her, she matches me, thrust for thrust. Her nails rake furrows across my back and it's enough to send me over the edge as she comes too, pulsing around me.

CHAPTER NINE

Chloe

"*I KNEW THIS WASN'T a safe place,*" *says a statuesque Siren. Her black wings are unfurled and rigid with her anger. "I can't believe they trusted you." It takes me a moment for it to register but the burnished red hair gives away that it is the same woman who bested Hermes in the vision I stole from him. "Where are my sisters? My nieces?"*

Mad female laughter echoes through the vision. Hellhounds race into the room from all directions, converging on the furious Siren. She opens her mouth to sing but it turns into a shriek as one of the hounds latches onto her calf. With a mighty roar, she attempts to shake him lose but another tears into her wings, scratching and clawing at her. She leaps into the air, grasping both hounds and wrenching them from her back. They fly into the wall with a resounding crash as the Siren laboriously fights her way upwards.

"You can run, Ligeia, but there is nowhere you can hide." Again, the laughter fills my vision and I realise just who is talking. "No-one can hide from me."

As the vision fades the Siren lets out an angry shriek—

Automatically I reach for Boss, thrusting the memory of the vision into his mind before I forget. He's already awake, sitting up in bed patiently rubbing my back as I calm down.

"Is this present or future do you think?" Boss is all business.

I think it through. "It had a sense of immediacy about it, I don't like." I think a bit more. "Most likely either just now or in the very near future."

"We need Calli." I nod, but Boss is already on the phone to my foremother, telling her to get up here now. I didn't know anyone talked to Calli like that, but apparently, urgency gives my warrior certain allowances.

It seems like no time at all before she arrives. I've managed to bundle myself into an over-large T-shirt I usually reserve for sleeping and a pair of loose trackies. Comfort wear. Boss hasn't bothered with a shirt, just his slacks, and I feel a little rude ogling him through Bailey's eyes as he lays his pony-sized head in my lap. His golden mane is a dishevelled mess around his head, and I remember tugging at it last night when his mouth was latched around my nipples.

Definitely shouldn't be having these thoughts while in Bailey's head.

I don't regret it though. Even when Calli catches me eye-fucking him and coughs pointedly.

"Not that I'm not thrilled with this relationship development, Chloe," Calli drawls as I blush. "But I'm assuming there is another reason you have called me up here at five o'clock in the morning?"

Deimos moves from outside the door to inside, chuckling at Calli's teasing. Boss glares at him, saving me the hassle of doing it myself. Gotta love teamwork.

I explain my vision to Calli. She frowns but doesn't ask me the expected question. "Ligeia you said?"

I nod.

"Are you sure?"

I roll my eyes, but then realise that won't register. Hard to see an eye roll when the eyes are white.

"Boss will back me up." He nods, just as intrigued by Calli's response as I am.

"She is correct. Why is this important?"

"Ligeia is one of the original three Sirens, former handmaids of Persephone." With Calli's words, everything clicks into place.

"The ones Demeter supposedly punished for not protecting her from Hades?" Boss asks, still confused.

Calli hesitates before answering. "No-one is sure exactly who punished them. Rumour has it, it may have been Persephone herself."

This is news. And it fits with the rest of the vision. "Calli, I'm convinced Persephone has done something to those women. Can you check in with any of our family you sent to Hades for protection?" My gut's swirling with anxiety.

Calli dials a number.

And another.

I watch her expression move from worry to outright fear as every number she tries rings out. She closes her eyes and I know she's trying to contact them with her mind, the direct line to those of her descent. Finally, her eyes open and she turns to me in despair.

"One last call." Her fingers are a blur as she searches through her contacts list, turning the screen to show me where she stopped. HADES. She hits dial then puts it on speakerphone so we all can hear.

The dial tone seems to echo through the room, an endless wait that culminates in a *beeeeep*.

"Phobos, go and get your father," Calli orders, automatically taking charge. "And take a quick shower on your way. You don't want to anger him." He nods and leaves.

I've no idea what she is talking about, but somehow, I think I won't like it.

"You might want to get yourself organised too, Chloe. I suspect we will be sending you on a little trip in the next few minutes," she continues with her instructions. As Bailey and I turn to go, I hear her order Deimos around too. "We'll be needing Caleb, Demon, can you—"

"Way ahead of you, sister. He's on his way and will meet one of us in the lobby in twenty minutes." I smile as I make my way to my room. At least one person has the drop on Calli.

★ ★ ★

ARES (FUNNY THAT IF YOU rearrange the letters a bit it spells arse) seems to take up much more of the space in the sitting room than is comfortable. He keeps staring at me with a burning intensity that rubs the wrong way. I want the couch to swallow me whole just to escape his gaze.

Deimos has picked up Caleb from the lobby and sat him down next to me. I catch him sneaking looks my way but instead of speaking, he spends the time ruffling Bailey's ears, laughing when the traitor slurps his face. Boss is brooding in the corner, his thoughts a wash of green and red that I don't have the time to decipher.

Through Bailey's eyes, I see Calli trace her fingers over ornate columns in each corner of the room. She answers my quirked eyebrow swiftly. *A gift from Hephaistos. When activated in sequence, none will be able to hear what transpires in this room, through gift or physical means.* Good news for us, considering what my vision implies.

"So, why the five a.m. wake-up call, Chloe?" Ares leers at me and I barely suppress a shudder of revulsion. "Not that I don't appreciate the invite to your chambers, but there are too many people here for us to get further acquainted."

Ignoring the innuendo isn't easy, particularly when Boss feels like he's both about to explode with anger and hide in shame.

"Ares, I've had a vision I think you need to be aware of," I say.

Immediately he sits up straighter, all business and I nearly breathe an audible sigh of relief. As I share the details with him, his expression worries me. It reflects both his worry and his desire. When I weave my way through his thoughts, I'm disturbed to find him aroused at the thought of a battle ahead.

"This will need to be a covert operation. The way I see it, there are two missions." Deimos and Phobos are both nodding along with their father, already having come to the same conclusion themselves.

"Someone needs to collect Ligeia, ensure that she is safe."

The fact that he had no idea she was alive comes through his thoughts loud and clear. "The second will need to be on a rescue mission in Hades. Our people are no longer safe there. Persephone is obviously unhinged."

"Yes, because a man striving for power is ambitious, but a female is unhinged," Calli says wryly. "It would be wrong to assume she is insane. That would imply she is unable to think clearly, or reason."

"Well said." Boss nods in agreement. "We must all be very wary when it comes to someone of Persephone's power."

"We'll send Chloe after Ligeia, along with Caleb and Phobos," Ares interrupts, dismissing Calli's comment.

"Does this mean I get to pull off a rescue mission in Hell?" Deimos is practically rubbing his hands with glee. Ares smiles.

"Pick who you want to go with you. Caleb, I need you to secure a meeting with your forefather for me this afternoon." Caleb leaves immediately, giving my hand a squeeze in parting.

Ares turns back to Deimos. "Be on the lookout for Hades. We don't know whether he is in on this or not, which could be problematic."

"That and he is overly protective of Persephone. He won't like it if we have to eliminate her," Calli adds.

"I don't think you'll have much choice." My voice is barely a whisper, but it stops them in their tracks. "From what I saw she's too far gone to be reasoned with."

"What I don't get," says Calli. "Is why? Persephone has the world at her fingertips. What does she hope to gain by this?"

"That is exactly what I plan on finding out." The steel in Ares' voice sends a shiver down my spine. I don't want to know what he plans.

"Deimos, Phobos," Ares says, curtly. "You will each go plan your separate missions. Be back here in no more than a half-hour. Is that clear?" Both of the twins' eyes lock on me and Ares *harrumphs* his exasperation. "She will be safe here with Calliope and me."

They relax slightly at the mention of Calliope, both moving off to do their jobs. Boss hesitates at the door.

Will you be fine here with them? The ammonic smell of anxiety's flying thick from Boss. I hasten to reassure him, despite the fact Ares makes me nervous. The man feels almost . . . expectant?

Calli will be here so don't worry. I'm sure you'll be back quickly anyway.

Still, he hesitates. Ares glares, motioning him to keep moving.

If you don't hurry, we won't have a chance of finding the Siren in time. I project the confidence I'm not feeling into my voice. It doesn't fool him, but he leaves anyway.

I know he's going to set the record for the quickest expedition plan ever.

When the door closes behind them, satisfaction seems to radiate from Ares.

I almost go to the door to stop Boss before he hits the elevator but Calli, oblivious to the underlying tension, starts talking again.

"Do you think you'll be able to find the Siren, Chloe?" she asks.

"It shouldn't be a problem," I answer truthfully. "Yesterday wasn't hard after I figured out how to focus. I just hope we find Ligeia."

"Yes," says Ares. "The woman is likely to go off half-cocked on a suicide mission if you don't find her before she heals." That wasn't what I was thinking, but it adds a whole new element to the mission. My biggest worry was finding her before Persephone does.

"Good," she says, picking up her phone again and moving towards the corridor. "If you'll excuse me, I have some calls to make. I may be able to secure us some allies in unusual places."

Her exit sends me into panic mode, particularly when Ares slides in closer. Bailey lets out a deep, rumbling growl of warning, increasing his size and moving protectively in front of me.

Surprisingly, the man stops.

"Call your hound off, Chloe. I'm not here to hurt you, just to talk." I hesitate. Even knowing we need Ares, something tells me it'd be a mistake.

Unfortunately, I can't alienate an ally on a hunch.

At my silent command, Bailey backs off, though he's still eyeing Ares as if he's lunch. And he doesn't decrease in size. My hound looms a head taller than the God in front of us, making my vision awfully peculiar.

Ares takes immediate advantage, moving in closer. Too close. The smell of his aftershave wafts around me, sickening in its thickness. I leap from the lounge but in my haste, trip on the coffee table. Ares is there in an instant, his arms stopping my fall, but the panic's so overwhelming I lose my connection with Bailey and my vision burns to blazing life. Images of the future shatter my hold on the present.

Flashes of two children with gleaming silver eyes moving like a blur in a mock battle, happy laughter weaving its way through the scene. My hand entwined with a calloused male one, rings on wedding fingers, such joy rising I'm overwhelmed by it. A naked me moaning in total abandon in a bed as someone feasts between my . . .

It only takes a moment, but unfortunately, I've been projecting snippets of it.

Ares is so still, hands almost bruising my arms, I've no idea what's floating through his mind. I even try to lock-pick his shield, but all I'm feeling is calculation. And greed.

"Interesting," he says finally, setting me down on the lounge. "It seems you are meant for a Warrior, Chloe." His satisfaction seems to flow around the calculation. "Apollo was not wrong."

Bailey's had enough. While I remain silent, trying to gather my thoughts, the hellhound plonks himself on the lounge, settling his enormous head in my lap. He rumbles a warning Ares should heed.

Calli chooses this moment to return.

"I've done it. I'll have to take a short trip to . . ." Her footsteps stop and attention sharpens. There's no way to disguise my nervousness, even if I wanted to.

"Ares," her voice is steel. "Do you want to explain before I assume the worst?"

"I'd say you already have, Calliope," he replies arrogantly. "And you would be wrong."

Half wrong.

I've no idea what he intended before I tripped, but it felt like a seduction. An unwanted one.

"Ares?" The word's a command. I'm surprised he answers.

"You know about Apollo's prediction, Calli."

She nods. I've no idea what they're talking about but I'm beginning to get some idea.

"Well," he continues. "I thought I'd address it with Chloe, but as soon as I got close to her she panicked and it threw her into a vision."

His avarice increases, but so does his confusion. "A vision which confirms what Apollo foretold. Somewhat."

"That a Seer will produce powerful children for the Warrior line?" Calli asks. She's stalling and now the anger's building as I put two and two together.

"I think it's time you both left," I say icily. Ares goes to argue but I cut him off before he can start. "Your twin spies will be back any time now. I think I can take care of myself 'til then."

Calli moves closer, fingers brushing my shoulder, but I step away.

"It's getting very hard to trust you, Calli. This is just another one of those secrets you keep to leave me in the dark."

"It's not like that sweetheart, you have to—"

"I have to!" I laugh, devoid of joy. "I don't *have to* do anything, not for you, foremother, and definitely not for you,

God of War." Bailey rises with me as I stand, my fists clenched tight, but I still don't reach for his eyes. My own are burning and I have the sneaking suspicion they blaze with my anger.

"If it weren't for the fact I actually care about the people missing, or that this mission may help me find out who did this to me and why, I'd let all of you drown in the ocean of your own mistakes." Ares seems almost aroused by my fury. Calli in awe.

I don't give two shits. I just want them gone.

"Get. Out. Now."

Calli leaves first, towing Ares in her wake.

The door closes behind them with a fatalistic *thunk*.

Hours? Minutes? Seconds pass before an insistent hammer starts on my door. I know who's behind it, but my hurt's almost as great as my anger.

How could my Soulmate do this to me?

"Let us in, Chloe! It's not safe for you to be on your own."

Is it any safer with them around? I sigh. Unfortunately, the past few days have shown I need more protection of the physical kind.

When I open the door they tumble inside, instantly wary.

The hurt is eating me from the inside out.

They knew.

They knew what their father was plotting and didn't bother clueing me in. Boss attempts to wrap me in his arms but I ram my elbow into his stomach, catching him by surprise. He lets out a satisfying *oomph*.

"You arseholes knew about Ares and you let me walk straight into it, when a few words would've at least helped me keep my eyes open."

"What did he do?" The man has the audacity to be angry.

I whip around in fury towards Boss's voice. "You gutless piece of shit!"

He steps towards me, but I back away, connecting with Bailey who's stuck to me like glue. "All you had to do was give me a heads-up. Do you have any idea what it was like to be alone in that room with him?"

"You weren't supposed to be alone! Where was Calli?"

"Calli has her own agenda," I spit. "Much as you do. Or . . ." I say slowly, horror dawning, "is this a family thing?"

"No!" Deimos shouts emphatically. Phobos is trying desperately to beat down the shields I've erected around my mind, but I'm having none of it. "Ares was told years ago that a child of his line would be powerful enough to unite the Council," he continues. "And that this child would be born of a Seer."

My anger's still simmering, but so are tears. Not going to happen. "So he thinks I'm his own personal broodmare sent to see him and his line into more power?"

"In essence," says Deimos. "But I doubt he sees it that way. I'm sure he thinks you were made to be his perfect match, a partner where our mother went her own way." He shrugs. "The power is just a bonus."

"He hasn't had a child in centuries—what makes him think it will happen now?" They look at each other but I'm too slow to catch the communication. Then it hits me. "He can't, can he?" My gut starts churning when neither of them answer. "So one of you had to make a sacrifice, for the good of the line."

"It's not like that, Chloe, you know—"

I don't give Boss a chance to finish. "I know what? I should've guessed the fact someone would find me attractive was a stretch. Hell, my own mother can't even look me in the eyes, and facing my mirror each morning does wonders for my self-esteem." I conveniently forget I can feel his emotions in the heat of the moment.

"Chloe—"

Rounding on Phobos, my words turn to frost. "So is that all we are, a ploy to help your father?" He's opened the barrier between us but my anger's overwhelming both our emotions. I can't see anything else clearly.

"I become your father's little whore and you bang me on the side to see which one of you gets me pregnant first?" He grabs my arm to shake me but Bailey lunges towards him, snapping his teeth awfully close to his hand.

Boss withdraws quickly, but not far enough. I can still feel his heat. "Will you tell him your plan, or will you just continue to fuck me until he has another little brood of monsters to unleash on the world?"

My chest's heaving with the force of my anger. Bailey stands guard in front of me, a steady rumble of warning coming from deep within his breast and Deimos has retreated into the suite. A drop of water lands on my chest and it's then I realise I'm crying. Nothing bloody registers when I'm angry. Fuck this.

Boss makes another move towards me, but I throw my hand up. "Enough. We have a job to do, and we'd better do it. Otherwise, we'll have blood on our hands."

"We need to settle this, Chloe. You need to know the truth."

I laugh.

"The truth, Boss?" My laughter's a little manic and a whole lot of hurt. "You people wouldn't know truth if it slapped you in the face. You've all spent so much time manipulating others for your own gain that it comes naturally now." I take a breath. "I don't want to be like that, become that."

"Gods, Chloe, can't you feel the truth of what is between us?"

I stare at him for a moment, eyes burning as I reflect on my vision.

The silence stretches, an infinity in a moment.

"I don't know what to believe anymore."

I brush past him, Bailey a solid wall between me and Phobos. I turn to look back.

"Maybe we're all monsters."

★ ★ ★

I TAKE OUT APOLLO'S journal, familiarising myself with the process one more time as I will myself to calm. Ligeia needs me. Us. I focus on her face from the visions, her spirit, her anger and heartache. It doesn't take long to form a connection, probably because her feelings almost exactly mirror my own. The pull is strong, close but muffled.

"She's south," I tell the others, my only acknowledgement that they're in the room. Caleb's finally made it back while I've been focused on the book. "It feels close, though it's like I'm sensing her through a barrier. The feeling comes in waves . . ."

"Water. She is on or over water." I ignore Boss's comment even though his desperation for me to acknowledge him is leaking along our connection.

"Directly south you say?" Deimos pulls out his phone to check Maps, Phobos looking on in anti-tech disgust. "South are more islands, but we'll check Koh Samui first."

"Koh Samui?" I ask.

"Another of Thailand's islands. There is an entrance to Hades nearby, so it would not surprise me if she was close, waiting for another chance at Persephone." Deimos stares intently at the map, nodding to himself.

"She's injured, you idiot. She's probably still recovering." Exasperation fills my voice.

"She's a Siren, Chloe. The woman would probably stab someone from her deathbed if they annoyed her enough," he shoots back.

"And she is an old one," says Phobos, making it hard for me to forget he exists. Harder to forget he asked if I wanted him to stay. "Older than us. She won't be healing for long."

Caleb looks thoughtful. "I can get us to Koh Samui, I've been there before, but from there I'm going to need a line of sight to travel short distances. We'll need a boat."

"And you'll need to rest," I say. When it looks like he's about to argue, I pull out the big guns. "I've seen what over-exertion does to you. We'll need you on the way back. And the next day." The last time Caleb had been worked too hard he was returning from a stint in the Middle East and landed on my lounge room floor, comatose on arrival. It had taken him three days to recover enough to travel short distances, a scenario we don't need right now.

"Agreed," says Deimos. "We'll use Samui as a base for both the attack on Persephone's forces and your search. The Ang Thong National Park holds an easy entrance to the Underworld, so it is strategically sound."

"We also have a villa on Samui we can use as a base of operations." Trying to ignore Phobos is fruitless. Unfortunately, we need him. Still not willing to admit *I* need him. "I doubt Persephone knows about it, so it should be a safe place where we can relocate any survivors, including Ligeia."

Deimos takes charge. "Pack a light bag to drop at the villa. Anything else we can get there."

I hope the new wardrobe someone bought me has some arse kicking clothes in it. Maybe a pair of funky Doc Martins?

The boys waste no time exiting the room, Boss's attention staying on me right until he leaves. Even then I can still feel the heat of his mind entwined with mine, but I do my best to shut him out, despite his feelings of hurt. He doesn't deserve my consideration at the moment. Finally, I'm left with just Caleb.

"Want me to pack a bag for you, Chloe?" I start at the sound of his voice, lost in my thoughts.

"Oh. You want to help me *now.*" So, he wants to pretend nothing happened? Like everything's rosy? I may want my best friend back but I'm not stupid enough to let him in without a damn good explanation. "Well go ahead, and while you're at it, you can explain why you stayed away so long." His skin turns an interesting shade of green, but he nods his head, taking my hand and leading me up the hall, Bailey a hulking shadow behind us.

It's odd seeing myself from this angle. I'm in better shape than I thought.

He pulls shirts and shorts from my wardrobe and throws them haphazardly in a bag. I wince at his packing style but don't say anything. I'm too interested in what he has to say. At least it'll be a distraction from thinking about he-who-shall-not-be-named.

"I'm waiting, Caleb." Impatience sharpens my anger.

"Guilt's a terrible thing, Chlo—" he starts to say but I snort.

"Guilt?" I butt in. "The only thing you need to feel guilty about is not being there the last few months. Why, Caleb? Why would you leave me like that? When I desperately needed my friend?"

"You don't get it! I couldn't be in the same bloody room as you without being reminded that it was my fault!" He runs shaking hands through dark hair and sits, packing forgotten. Bailey nudges him and whines for a pat, skewing my vision by getting too close.

"What are you talking about?" I clench my teeth, trying to get a grip on the anger. "You weren't there, you'd gone home ages before I did." Well, maybe not ages, but certainly enough to be home before I left the club.

"But I didn't go home," he says, startling me. "I'd picked up some chic, taken her outside and fucked her in a blind haze in an alley outside the club." His self-loathing's evident.

Fuck.

"Not an unusual move for you, though," my sarcasm's thick. I can't seem to stop. "So many nights ended like that when we went out. Must admit, I'm surprised you didn't make it to your apartment. Didn't think alleys were your style."

"They weren't." He shakes his head. "Aren't. I think . . ."

"Yes?" I ask, curious despite the anger.

"I think she was a Gorgon."

His mention of the mesmerising Immortal women has me pause.

When he turns his head to look at me, I almost disconnect from Bailey in shock, his anguish is so clear.

"I saw you leave," he says, and it's then I want to throw up. I remember leaving the club, starting to walk down The Cross but then . . . "I even saw the van pull up beside you."

A van. I remember the van.

A blue van pulls up beside me. I ignore it, thinking it's a delivery for the club, until I'm grabbed from behind. A rough cloth's shoved over my mouth and in moments, everything fades to black.

"I saw that goddamn fucking van and I fucking finished what I'd started before I turned to check on you."

The rage wants to come, but his words hit home.

"I waited 'til I'd finished fucking some chick whose name I can't even remember while my best friend was abducted and left to die." Caleb attempts to hide his emotions by stuffing more things into my bag. It doesn't work. His anguish fills the room with its musky scent.

Bailey looks back and forth between us, whining quizzically. It's enough to make me dizzy, so I disconnect. Ironically, this is the best thing for me, as the comforting dark allows me to collect myself.

"They've recruited a Gorgon." Before the Seer gene hit, this would've terrified me. Now I have my own weapons to fight back. "That bitch and her friends are going to pay."

"I've tried that, Chloe." He sighs, defeated. "It's like she never existed."

"I searched for you all night. On foot at first, but gradually I sobered up and was able to jump short distances, looking for any sign of that fucking van." He shakes his head, exasperated with himself. "It took me too long to connect the dots with the Gorgon. By the time I did, she was long gone. Eventually, your call roused Calli and together we found you in that warehouse."

His tears still flow freely, but I sense he's letting go of the guilt. At least most of it. "It was the most horrific thing I've ever seen in my life. We didn't think you could live through it, but your heart kept beating, even as your skin flamed. I held you for thirty seconds." He takes a breath. "Thirty seconds to get you out of there, and in that time, I ended up with third-degree burns." Barely a whisper comes from his mouth. "I don't know how you're still here."

I nod, squeezing him in understanding. "Let it go, Caleb. It's not worth wallowing in misplaced guilt. Besides" —I attempt a smile— "I'm sure your Gorgon will turn up somewhere and when she does . . ." My smile turns feral.

"I suppose it's fair you get first dibs on revenge," he says as he flicks me a smile with a hint of his former cheekiness. It's almost reassuring. "I've searched for her the last sixteen months, but something tells me all of this is connected."

"True, but right now we have bigger fish to fry, so hurry up and finish my packing!"

He laughs, but I can feel his earnestness when he says, "I'll make it up to you, Chloe. Somehow, I'll make it up to you."

I don't reply. Promises like that have a way of coming back to bite you on the arse.

CHAPTER TEN

Chloe

CALEB OPENS THE GATEWAY in a storeroom at the airport on Koh Samui, standard procedure in less hectic cities. No-one wants to have to deal with a bunch of panicked mortals when a black doorway pops out of no-where.

As we walk to the car rental stand, I can feel the burn of Boss's eyes on my back. My anger's mellowed to a slow simmer, so while I'm still pissed at him, I'm curious why he kept me in the dark. I'm also curious about the devastation I can feel forefront in his mind. Deimos grabs my hand before we get there, slowing me down to a crawl.

Useful skill to practice here, Chloe. Try and bend the mortal's thoughts. We don't want to have to put our names on any piece of paper, or show documentation, so make him think he has seen everything.

Seriously? That's theft, dude, and the people here can't afford that.

We'll send them a hefty pay packet anonymously when we finish this, Chloe. We can't have anyone getting wind of our presence here before we do what we came here for.

I nod tightly, clinging to Bailey as my stomach churns. This feels wrong, but I know it's necessary. It's natural for Gorgons to mesmerise mortals with their eyes, well, mostly mortals, but it was considered one of the deciding factors in the decision to eradicate the Seers that the strongest of them could easily manipulate immortals as well.

Could the Gorgon's powers have been severely underestimated?

I walk by myself up to the desk, already weaving fine threads through the mortal's mind. "Hello, madam. Can I help you today?" His English's very good, but I ignore him, lost in his thoughts. Boss steps up next to me and I can't help but lean closer. When I remain mute, he continues the conversation with the attendant.

"Hi, my fiancée and I are looking for a large SUV, big enough to fit ourselves, the dog and my groomsmen over there." The man's attention flicks over to Caleb and Deimos, who are trying to look innocent in a corner. They aren't very successful. He nearly panics when he sees my monster dog. I soothe his riotous thoughts and he continues to serve us.

"Any particular make or model you were looking for?" Their conversation no longer registers at all, though I try to shake off the happy feelings being described as Boss's fiancée has given me. I'm not ready to forgive him yet. If ever.

The attendant's mind is simple in comparison to an Immortal, and I weave a net around his thoughts, gradually tightening the strings. Suddenly they snap together and a silver glow seems to form around his mind. I nod slightly in Deimos' direction, then pay more attention to the conversation.

Boss has almost concluded the negotiations. Time for me to see if this little trick will work.

"Now, sir, I need a copy of your driver's licence, and that of anyone who is going to be driving the vehicle."

You just saw our licences and made copies.

His mind flashes silver as the suggestion settles, and he immediately launches into the next part of his spiel. Bingo!

"And how will you be wishing to pay for that, sir? We will also need a copy of your credit card for security purposes."
You've seen and made copies of his credit card too.

Again, I tighten the net, and again his mind flashes silver.

"Excuse me for a moment while I call the car around."

I almost do a victory dance but control myself.

Deimos sends a silent congratulations, my moral high ground from earlier vanishes in the face of victory. Fortunately, this skill seems an easy one to perfect on mortals, though I think Immortal sensitivity will make it harder to manage.

We walk out the front where a valet waits with our car, holding the keys out to Boss. Waves of disgust roll from Caleb.

"A Toyota Fortuner!" His groan makes me laugh. Caleb's obsession with off-road vehicles in Australia is a well-known fact. "This piece of shit has no guts! We won't be able to do anything with it!"

In between snickers from everyone else, Deimos pipes up, "It just has to get us up the hill, Caleb. No off-road action required." I'm tempted to stir him further but at the moment, I'm just tired.

"Let's get out of here, shall we?" I open the front passenger side and Bailey lunges in before me, settling himself on the driver's seat. "Off, mutt! Someone else needs that seat or we aren't going anywhere!" I tug on his collar but there's no way the big lug's moving, so I settle in the passenger seat waiting to see what the boys will do.

Bailey's decided to have a sleep, so I lose my eyes once again, but it brings a smile to my face anyway. I don't mind being sightless for this battle. I'm sure there'll be lots of entertaining language from the old ones I haven't heard before.

The driver's side door opens and there's a moment's silence where I giggle internally. A low growl comes from the man at the door and Bailey leaps up, scrambling through the middle and into the back in record time, whining in submission. I burst into laughter as Boss settles into the seat next to me. My mouth tightens instantly.

Silence is king in the front seat, though there's an open discussion in the back between Caleb and Deimos, and I wish I'd chosen to sit there instead of the front. I hang my head and let my hair hide me from Boss's view.

"The villa isn't too far, nothing is in Samui, but it is up the mountain so at least we'll have some privacy." His attempt at starting a conversation falls on deaf ears. "You will love it there, Chloe. It is right in the middle of the jungle, no-one else is in sight, and the villa itself is stunning." I can hear the desperation in his voice, but I don't want to talk to him right now. Whatever I have to say to him will be said where no-one else can hear us.

"Boss." Caleb thankfully breaks the tension, drawing Phobos into their conversation. "I know you've been here plenty of times. We were just discussing our best options for Demon's launch point . . ."

Their conversation continues as we climb further into the mountains, the path getting narrower and unsealed. Greenery writhes around us, wet and lush, and despite myself, I begin to relax, eventually nodding off to sleep.

Chloe. Boss's voice in my head gently wakes me from my sleep. I slam up my shields and ignore his internal sigh. "We're here."

Without hesitation, I join with Bailey who has just been let out of the back by Caleb. So many new smells and colours assault my senses that I immediately drop the connection, wincing. A hesitant hand touches my shoulder.

"You can use mine if you like." The olive branch Boss extends is too tempting.

I've missed being close to him, even if it has only been a few hours. This Soulmates thing sucks when I want to be angry. Hesitantly, I merge with his senses, trying my best to keep walled away from his memories and thoughts. His mind wraps around mine and, despite myself, I feel safe. Home.

His eyes open to a world of green.

An enormous villa's nestled in amongst the jungle, not so much one building, but a collection of slightly smaller ones, of varying shapes and sizes. They're all nestled around a large structure with a domed roof, which is almost open air.

A man is waiting for us in front of this building. He's dressed island-casual in T-shirt, boardies and thongs, but the bulkiness of his build gives away his lineage. A smug smile tilts the corners of my mouth when I see Demon give him a quick man hug.

Yep. One of Ares' brood for sure.

Aeden is our cousin, a few times removed. I don't reply to Boss but he answers my curiosity anyway. *The man runs operations from here. He hates cities and hates his forefather Eros with a passion, so we try to keep him away from it all.*

Curiosity peaked further, I start towards the man who has the good sense to hate Eros.

Apparently, the interest's mutual, 'cause the minute he sees me he strides over to meet me halfway.

"So, you are Chloe Santos." His smile's easy-going as he extends his hand to me. "I must admit I was expecting someone a bit . . ."

"Taller?" I ask cheekily, unashamedly using Boss's eyes to shake the offered hand.

"More intimidating," is his immediate reply. Aeden's honesty's refreshing and I find myself gravitating towards him. Boss growls but I ignore him.

Bailey makes a grand entrance covered in dirt, leaves and smelling like something dead.

"Gods, Bailey! I can't leave you alone for a minute." Everyone's caught between laughter and choking coughs, attempting to move away from the enthusiastic hound whose excitement has him leaping from person to person, searching for love.

Aeden grabs at his collar and surprisingly, Bailey calms and lets him lead him away.

"I'll catch up with you later," Aeden flings over his shoulder. "This mutt is going to get the biggest bath of his life." At that Bailey digs in his haunches, but the warrior just drags the whining hound along behind him.

"He shouldn't have said the word bath until he was safely in the water," I quip. The others laugh again, and a sense of peace settles over the group.

Then I remember why we're here.

It's easy to see as Boss looks around why they use this as a base for operations. The 'villa' looks like it could sleep hundreds. The smaller buildings are connected to the communal hall via a series of covered walkways that seem to blend into the lush vegetation.

A large swimming pool is almost camouflaged behind the central dome, and it's calling me.

I make a move in its direction but Boss's hand on my arm stops me short. "Please, Chloe, we need to talk." His anguish softens me, so I allow him to lead me away while Deimos and Caleb move off, pretending to be oblivious.

Boss takes me towards one of the furthest buildings, slightly smaller than the others. Inside is as lush as the surroundings, all sleek mahogany furniture and white linen. He turns to face me and I disconnect, not wanting to see myself through his eyes.

I can't bring myself to shut him out completely though.

A nervous cough escapes me. "You wanted to talk? So talk." I know I'm being bitchy, but I'm nervous and angry. Never a good combination.

The silence extends into infinity, drowning us in tension. I can't take it. Throwing my senses out to search for Bailey I turn to go but Boss has other ideas.

"I'm sorry." I freeze. Is that it? A fucking half-arsed apology?

"Sorry for what, Boss?" I whip around, my earlier calm gone. "Sorry, you led me on? Sorry, you kept big fucking secrets from me? Or sorry I found out?" Tears stream down my cheeks, showing my weakness, which only serves to make me angrier.

"It is nothing like you are thinking, Chloe! Nothing!"

"Did you or did you not keep me in the dark about your father, because I sure as shit don't know how I could interpret that differently."

"We are under oath! Do you have any idea what that means?"

"Under oath for what? What could have possibly prevented you from at least warning me what could happen?"

His frustration fills the room, increasing my impatience.

"We are under oath to never move against our father. It would spell our deaths and the deaths of everyone we love." This stops me short.

"Who on Earth has the power to enforce something like that?" I'm horrified. I know Ares is power-hungry but to have virtually crippled his sons? Is what the Council did to them any worse?

"Hera is the only one on the Council capable of taking us down without risk to herself. All Father has to do is contact her and in an instant . . ." The words are bitter. "Despite the fact that neither of us would harm our own kin, he is power-hungry and proud he muzzled us."

I can hear him pacing the room, back and forth, his agitation likely to wear a hole in the floor. How could Ares call for their 'freedom' in Council, and still keep them chained himself?

"Never before now have I thought of harming my father. Not when Alala begged me to stop my father's warmongering and come home to her, not when his harsh words to her drove her to the brink of despair, not even when I found her dead in a pool of her own blood and he told me to leave her to rejoin his forces. Not even then!" His mind burns with an anger I'm desperate to escape, but he just tightens his hold.

"But you know what, Chloe? Today I did. Today, if I had not had an iron grip on my emotions, if I hadn't walled off your emotions from my own, I would have attacked my father, and ensured the death of everything that matters to me." He clutches me desperately to him and I know I'm included in those things that matter. Maybe one of the only things that matter.

I wrap both my arms and mind around him, pushing comfort and forgiveness towards him, and maybe a little bit of something I'm not ready to name. His hands smooth up my back and into my hair as I nestle into his chest, soaking up the comfort.

"I would do anything for you, Chloe," he says into my hair. "But I won't be the cause of your death."

"Why'd you keep his plans secret from me?" I whisper, not wanting to restart the fight, but needing closure.

"It's part of the oath, Chloe. We can't go against his wishes, because he believes that is to harm him. It would invoke Hera's wrath."

"How are you still able to be with me then?"

He winces. "A technicality. He doesn't believe I would be interested so, he hasn't ordered me not to touch you." He sighs. "Ares is self-centred. And arrogant. With a short temper."

"That doesn't sound like someone you should be supporting," I say.

He frowns. "But despite all that he acts for what he sees as the greater good. If he didn't, we would have taken our only exit route long before now." Death. His only exit route's something I don't want to contemplate. Thank the gods Ares held his shit together long enough for Boss to find me.

I breathe in his earthy scent, relaxing as I haven't all day. "Well, he'd better see that the greater good is you by my side, or I'll make him see it."

He smiles into my hair. The rosy glow of his mind seems to caress mine, almost like his hands are doing to my skin. I'm so relaxed, I almost forget. But . . .

"And his big baby making plans?"

Boss stiffens. "I suppose we are going to have to figure out how to shake him off without breaking the oath."

I roll my eyes. "Do you really think it's going to be that easy?"

He nibbles along my neck and all thoughts fly from my head.

"I think that's something we shouldn't be worried about right now," he says and my breath catches.

"And what should I be worried about?" The anticipation is killing me.

He moves lower, kisses trailing down my collarbone and into the vee of my shirt.

"Well, Princess, you should be worried about the fact that there are far too many clothes on in this room right now."

His fingers trail up my ribs, taking my shirt with them. Every nerve ending fires, sending me into an inferno of lust. Reaching up, I place my lips to his ear. "Take me to bed," I whisper. Boss throws me over his shoulder as I open the link between us wide.

Emotions and sensation overwhelm me as I sink into bliss.

CHAPTER ELEVEN

Chloe

A SCRATCHING AT THE door and persistent whining wakes me the next morning. I groan, rolling over and attempting to bury my face into the hard chest next to me. Boss chuckles as I yell, "Come back in an hour, Bailey!" The whines turn into howls, enough to wake the whole complex, and Boss rolls out of bed. I hear the latch unlock and an over-exuberant hellhound greets me.

"Jesus, Bailey." The idiot still thinks he's a puppy, wriggling all over the bed and licking my face as he settles his considerable weight on my chest. At least he smells better now. "Get off, you dumb mutt!" He whines, but eventually gets the point and jumps off me after I elbow him in the ribs. Boss's deep baritone laugh sends warmth all through my body, and I find myself grinning stupidly. The man has a wonderful laugh. His weight settles onto the mattress again and all thoughts fly from my head as his lips take mine in a gentle caress.

My fingers trace his brows, sharp cheek-bones, even as my tongue skims his full lips. There is nothing about this face I don't love, even the scratchy rasp of stubble that reddened my cheeks after our frantic love-making. He groans his disappointment as he pulls away from me and his weight is gone once more from the bed.

I link with Bailey and prompt him to look at Boss. I'm not above using any means at my disposal to ogle that tight behind. Someone has brought our bags here during the night, and Boss is currently unpacking his suitcase into the wardrobe. "What if we have to make a quick get-away?" I ask, slightly confused by his actions.

"I'm hoping not," he says. "But even if we do, clothes are replaceable." He pads back over to the bed. He plunders my mouth again with an intensity that leaves me breathless as he moves back to the suitcases. "I'm hoping that when all this is over, we can come back here and spend some time together, just you and me."

"I want that too." The man knows just what to say to turn me into a puddle of goo.

"Would you like me to unpack yours as well?" I hesitate. "It's okay. You can tell me what you need and I'll make sure it is perfect. Colour coded, correct?"

I try to swallow past the lump in my throat. Such a simple thing to have me on the verge of tears. Sensing my turmoil, Boss wraps his mind comfortingly around mine, while continuing to unpack my clothing.

It's then I remember the second half of Hephaistos' gift. Thankfully, Caleb had packed it.

"There's something for you in the front of my suitcase." Boss pauses as his fingers touch the wooden box, then he pulls out the matching band to my bracelet.

Without hesitation, he puts it on. The click of the latch closing seems to echo around the room and Boss gasps in a little breath. A wash of warmth seems to flow between us. It's comforting and makes me smile.

"Hephaistos said we would be able to find each other instantly with this, no matter how far away from each other we are." Boss's elation writhes through our link like a happy puppy, sending me into a fit of laughter. "I take it that's good news?"

"Of course it is!" He sweeps me into a hot kiss, leaving me reeling when he moves back to the clothing. "Now I can find you instantly when you try to run from me."

"Not going to happen." My determination's clear in my voice.

"You say that now," his tone's turned so serious I instantly pay attention. "But what happens the next time something shakes our foundations? What happens when my father puts his foot down?"

I send all my new feelings flying down our bond, letting him bask in it for a little while before pulling back.

"We'll cross that bridge when we come to it," I say firmly.

"Yes. I will cross bridges, mountains, oceans to get back to you." Though there's a teasing thread in his voice, the seriousness of his tone leaves no doubt that he's telling the absolute truth. "Nothing will keep me from you."

I clear my throat nervously. I'm tempted to tell him how I'm feeling but the enormity of it makes me uneasy.

Silence stretches.

The moment's lost.

"Deimos contacted me earlier to say he was meeting his men shortly." He puts the final T-shirt away and comes back to lay with me on the bed. "We will need to move out with Caleb as soon as possible if we are to find Ligeia. Her night of rest should almost have healed her. She will be on the move shortly if we don't find her first."

I sigh. "Okay. I'll have a quick shower and we can join them in the common area." Slipping off the bed, I use Bailey's eyes to make my way towards the bathroom.

"Can I join you?"

"Can you be quick?" I tease.

His thoughts turn hot and predatory, making me smile as I duck into the bathroom. "The question is, Chloe, how fast can I get you to explode?"

Extremely quickly, it turns out.

THE COMMUNAL HALL IS a domed, sunlit room that's so big our voices seem to echo. Deimos is long gone with another of Caleb's cousins. "Couldn't we have found a less . . . spacious . . . location for planning?" I ask.

Bailey's exploring outside and the emptiness is making me nervous, despite the comfort of Boss at my side.

Aeden jumps in, eager to be involved in our plans. "I suppose we could have, but we thought that more space might make it easier for you to do your thing." He waves at my eyes, then winces as he realises it might not be PC to point them out.

"I don't think it makes a difference, mate, but thanks for the thought," I reply with a raised eyebrow.

He throws me a wry grin in response. His enthusiasm's contagious. Boss draws me closer to him, his thoughts turning a lurid green.

Closing my eyes, my breathing evens as I send my thoughts out wide, searching for Ligeia's thought signature. It's closer than I expected, still over the water, but not nearly as washed out as it was yesterday.

"What are the closest islands to this one?" I ask.

"Ang Thong Marine Park is not far away. It has many islands, most of which are small and uninhabited, perfect for hiding." Aeden's full of information. My gut tells me we're on the right track.

"Let's move in that direction then. Boat or plane?" I ask the boys.

"Boat," Caleb immediately replies. "It's much easier to scope everything out on the water than in the air."

"Plus, all three of us can captain a yacht, and we'd have to hire a plane otherwise."

"Do we have a yacht here?" I ask.

Phobos laughs. "*I* have a yacht here." His thoughts turn wispy with longing. "I like to sail when I can, and this is the perfect area for it."

"Done then! Captain Boss, take us to your ship!" I say as I salute, earning another chuckle. I may make this my mission in life.

"How about I take us to the docks? Avoid the drive in the *thing* you guys are calling a 4WD?" Caleb's still unimpressed with our Fortuner. I snicker behind my hand, earning a half-hearted growl from Caleb. He needs more practice. Both twins manage that threat much better than he does.

As we move off to gather the few things each of us think are indispensable for our mission, it strikes me that the last few days has been a massive learning curve. I'm almost grateful to the Council. I'd been tiptoeing around, trying to figure out how I was going to live my life, but had become so fearful I wasn't even trying. My morning jogs were about the most adventurous things I'd done in months. I'd felt crippled by my eyes, when in reality, my mind was the problem.

Now I've taken my fate into my own hands, learning to use my skills, taking risks for the good of others. It feels good. Powerful.

I'm so close to finding the truth about that night, I can almost taste it.

Then there's Boss. Our future shines bright before me, a full moon over an endless highway. There's no way I can convince myself that the man in the vision isn't Phobos. It stuns me that there's such beauty in the future, such contentment.

I know there'll be difficulties, but knowing what's in store . . . Well, it makes me more determined to see things through.

The trip to the yacht is short and uneventful. Caleb opens a gateway into another out-of-the-way storeroom, this time at the marina, and Boss, Aeden and I step through behind him. When we reach Phobos' yacht, my jaw just about hits the ground.

Bailey sticks closely to my side, providing me with ample opportunity to share his vision. There're magnificent yachts scattered right across a small, sheltered bay, but we're heading towards the largest of them all.

"What the hell do you need to be compensating for, Boss? Guaranteed no woman ever complained," I say incredulously, and he blushes.

Blushes.

My big, strong warrior blushes like a little girl at some innuendo. I try to keep a straight face, but my silent laughter floods our link, earning a grumble from the recipient. Caleb and Aeden are chuckling out loud, not even bothering to try and spare Phobos a little embarrassment.

"It's ocean-worthy, and can sleep at least ten members of my family, which is handy for covert missions." His attempt at defending himself just makes us laugh, Caleb the loudest and me in a teasing guffaw. Highly attractive.

"There's nothing *covert* about that, mate," Caleb adds his two bob's worth to the argument. If anything, Boss goes redder as he leads us up onto his floating palace.

Bailey trembles against my hip as we cross the gangplank, terrified of the water. I keep my hand on his back in reassurance. It's moments like these I realise he's far braver than he acts. The mutt's still moving past something that terrifies him senseless. Now that's courage.

The yacht's even more beautiful on board. The gleaming mahogany decking stands out sharply against the white of the fibreglass, every fitting polished to a golden shine. It screams money and though I've grown up in a pretty wealthy family, we've nothing compared to this.

"Big boys and their toys," I mutter as Bailey and I look around.

I find my way over to a long white lounge as the others get the ship (is that the right word?) ready to cast off. The motor rumbles to life so I disconnect from Bailey, giving my mind a rest. I'd thought a yacht would rely entirely on the wind, but the motor's a good contingency plan for emergencies and would also be good for navigating out of difficult docks.

"I'll distract the hound, shall I?" asks Aeden. Bailey's doggy mind is full of terror. Water is definitely not his thing.

"I think he'd appreciate that," I say, nudging Bailey towards Boss's cousin.

A moment later the coppery scent of raw meat tickles my nostrils and Bailey instantly perks up.

"Good move, warrior." I laugh as Bailey immediately follows him below deck.

The gentle breeze caresses my face as I relax, closing my eyes. This feels like the right course of action, it chimes deep in my body. Sending tendrils out to find Ligeia's easy this time and I lock onto her almost instantly. I solidify the connection in my mind, building it into a thick rope, then add Boss into it. He's standing at the helm, directing us out, so he makes some minor adjustments to our course as he gets new information from me.

I smile. This isn't difficult at all.

Heaven help the Council if they decide to move against me when I'm at full strength. Boss's savage agreement with my thoughts holds a satisfaction that echoes my own. They won't be able to find me unawares.

We clear the bay and Caleb lets out a whoop as he unfurls the sails, obviously familiar with the vessel. Bailey whines, once more on deck with Aeden. The big lug's seasick. I won't be going below deck the rest of the journey.

I feel a grin tug the corners of my mouth wide. The yacht's lurched forward in a rush, pushing us ever closer to Ligeia.

I spread my awareness out further, touching all the individuals in the area, then further again. I coil my awareness through both land and sea, the islands giving me a sense of peace I can't find in the city. They thrum with energy and a heavy awareness that touches mine, offering both love and comfort. It's so beautiful, I'm thankful again for the gifts of my forefather.

Bailey's still shaking underneath the table, eyes screwed shut, but I don't need eyes when my awareness spreads this far. The yacht rises and falls with the waves, lulling me into a pleasant lethargy. Unfortunately, it's over too soon.

Caleb furls the sails and the noise of the engine is abruptly cut. The reverberation of the anchor hitting the seabed thrums through me.

I frown at Bailey.

"He'll be all right here with me, Chloe," says Aeden. The man's staying with the yacht in case we need a quick get-away. I send a grateful smile his way.

"Thanks, Aeden," I say.

Boss grabs my left hand and Caleb the right as he traces us to shore, leaving the other two behind. The Siren's so close my body's humming with our connection, urging me towards her.

Boss still has hold of my hand and he uses our shared link with Ligeia to make his way through the dense vegetation, Caleb bringing up the rear. I'm so focussed on my connection with her and the world around me that the forest becomes a pulsing blur and Boss sweeps me into his arms. I've become a liability.

The connection between us leads our group to a cave. Metallic and heavy, the scent of blood both repels and excites me.

She's here.

I build on our connection, sending reassurance through the bond I've formed with her. Ligeia isn't having it—her shriek breaks the link between us, sending an icy spike through my brain. I slam hands over my ears but it doesn't help dispel the ringing.

"Ligeia!" I call, desperate to disrupt her agonising shriek. "My name is Chloe Santos. I'm the only Seer in existence and I'm here with Phobos, Son of Ares and Caleb Swift to ensure you live long enough to seek your revenge."

We wait. None of us are stupid enough to enter the den of a wounded Siren, so I use the time to slip behind Boss's eyes. There are brief hints of movement at the entrance, making my warrior shift uneasily. I tap his shoulder then slip downwards to stand by myself.

"We know you are hurt, Siren, and we also know what you were seeking, and where." Phobos' voice is muffled by dense foliage, but still manages to boom across the clearing.

"I recognise your voice, Son of Ares. Forgive me for saying that I'm a little doubtful of your intentions, considering your past exploits." Her voice is a sinister whisper on the wind. We all hear the threat in it.

"You don't know me, Ligeia, so you have no reason to trust me." Caleb's voice startles me. I thought he'd been taking a backseat in these proceedings. "But we're all here to help you—you and the others."

"Others?" She's playing dumb and it pisses me off.

I've touched her mind and I know she's no idiot.

"Yes, Siren, you aren't the only one with missing family members, just the one who found their captor first." My temper snaps. "Now get your butt out here and help us track down that bitch and her minions. I want my family back, and some fucking answers!"

Sometimes, a dash of truth and a whole heap of anger can do what sweet words can't.

The woman who makes her way out of the cave is stunning, despite the fact one of her wings is still healing before my eyes. Her luscious red locks twirl around a sweetly rounded body that might as well have been naked, for all the good the rags scattered over her did. She throws her head back, letting out a harsh laugh.

"You, Chloe Santos, I like." I feel like I've just managed to shart a rainbow, the words are that momentous. She turns to look at the guys, eyes raking in scorn over Phobos, but settling with interest on Caleb. The man's blushing—what is it with these guys and blood flow?—a deep red and he can't seem to figure out where to rest his eyes. I could tell him the face is the best option, but like most heterosexual males, his eyes are drawn inexorably to the lady lumps. Her lips curve upwards in derision.

Dude, you seriously just blew any chance you ever had of tapping that. My voice in his mind seems to shake Caleb from his stupor, but not before Ligeia dismisses him with a sneer.

"And who might you be missing, Chloe? If you are the last Seer, your line is ended." I ignore the little tug of sadness at those words.

"There are two halves to every whole, Ligeia. The rest of my family are Muses." I sigh. "It's a long story, but my family are victims of this as much as you and yours. I had a vision that led me to you." She strides forwards, experimentally flexing her almost healed wing, and Boss shifts so he's in front of me. She stills, one hunter assessing another, then nods in begrudging respect at my man.

"And what do you hope to achieve, little Seer?" There's that name again. I wonder if I can erase it from everyone's memories. "Persephone has the denizens of the Underworld at her command, and Hades isn't lifting a finger to stop her."

"You saw, Hades?" Boss asks quickly.

She hesitates. She wants to throw him under the bus but is too honest.

"No. I don't think he supports her, but neither is he acting against her, and that is worse." Her mouth lifts into that now-familiar sneer. "The man is spineless, unable to act even when faced with proof his 'love' is a duplicitous snake." I can't help but agree with her.

Boss cuts in quickly, trying to rush us out of here. "You have about ten seconds to make your decision, Ligeia, before we are attacked where we stand." A furious shriek echoes through the undergrowth. Suddenly I feel what he does, that malicious darkness creeping closer to us, gaining speed and momentum. It's not the same as the darkness that attacked me in my bedroom, but it does have echoes of its power.

Ligeia's head snaps towards the sound, eyes flaming with her anger. I drop from behind Boss's eyes and fling my awareness in a net around us, sacrificing vision for strength. Each filament of my net wraps itself around an attacker and I take the time to worm my way into their minds. I don't know if what I'm going to attempt will work, but it's worth a shot. There are at least fifty mind signatures out there. I suppose we should be grateful there aren't more.

They emerge from the trees, both flapping and crawling, creatures of nightmare who had been bound in Tartarus. The air seems to vibrate with electricity, and it's then I realise we're seated within the calm before a storm. I can smell it, the ironically earthy scent of rain, and realise we'll not have the advantage of the sun.

"Is anyone else disturbed that Persephone has released monsters from Tartarus?" I ask, before continuing, "And can someone tell me how smart they are?"

"They may look like beasts, but they think like humans. Careful." Ligeia's explanation is brief but all I need in the moment.

"I give you fair warning creatures of the dark, you have no idea what you are walking into. Turn back now and I will spare you the fate your mistress will suffer." Boss is too chivalrous.

Ligeia launches herself at them without warning, singing a darkly dangerous melody that crashes around us.

The creatures shriek again, this time in agony.

My awareness of the men follows them forward, but I only leave a tendril of my thoughts with them. And Ligeia. Enough to protect them from what I'm about to attempt. I throw my strength out through the web I've made, burrowing into the minds of the creatures. This time they're aware of me, their attention turning in my direction, sensing the danger.

Too late.

Sweat pours down my forehead as I jerk on the web, and in mid-flight, the creatures turn. Low growls and shrieks rumble from twisted throats as they start to stalk their own brethren. Their minds are mine and now so are their bodies. If I stop to think about it, I know this new skill will terrify me, so grimly I continue.

Boss draws back to me, wrapping me in his arms as I begin to sag. The effort to hold the compulsion is immense. Instinctively, I know that if I lose focus for one second, I won't have the strength to regain what I've so painstakingly won.

Unlike a Siren's song, this influence won't last beyond the strength I have in my body. The creatures are tearing at each other, thoughts riddled with bloodlust, but also fear. They're aware they're being influenced but powerless to stop it. It makes my stomach heave, almost as much as Boss's display of his power outside my apartment.

When there's only a handful left, I drop my web. It doesn't take long for Ligeia and Caleb to deal with those remaining. Exhaustion has sapped me, but the corners of my mouth lift with pride.

Well done, Princess. Boss's thoughts echo my own. I relax into his arms as the others join us.

"Well," Caleb's cockiness comes out to play. "That worked. Anyone up for round two?" Groans all round.

Ligeia's thoughts are in turmoil, but a thread of determination's winning out over her distrust. "I will come with you."

Her words and thoughts are stilted, slightly archaic. I wonder how long she's been on her own, but I'm too sensitive of her fragile trust to try to find out.

Then she adds, "We will find our families and we will make that bitch pay for everything she has done."

Maybe not so archaic.

Did they say bitch back in who-knows-when? Or is she translating from Greek? Either way, I'm impressed.

Without fuss, we make our way back to the yacht, leaving the bodies for the sunlight to destroy. Bailey greets me enthusiastically as we board, then runs away to hide below deck. I don't know whether he's smart or a chicken shit. It's time to point out the elephant in the room. "So . . . we know there's a possibility the Titans are free if these Tartarian clowns have been released." Tartarian. I like that. Think I'll keep using it.

"Some, maybe. But not all." Ligeia has settled beside me while the boys do their thing, getting us out into the blue.

The one good thing about the coming storm's that the winds are favourable. Still, it took us an hour to get here, so we'd better get a move on.

The spicy scent of Ligeia's anxiety wafts around her and I begin to understand the depth of her fear and also her courage, that she would face Persephone on her own because she was ill-informed and didn't know who to trust.

"The Titans are bound deeper than their minions. However" —her voice drops, becoming a mesmerising murmur— "I am sure they haven't breached the walls of HIS prison yet. The tiny hints of his darkness I have sensed around us are fractions of his power." Her inner walls tighten around her thoughts, locking down her emotions with: "Either that or he is still weakened from when Zeus struck him down."

"Are we talking about who I think we are talking about, Ligeia?" I ask.

"Kronos," Boss answers for her, moving over to join the conversation as Caleb takes the wheel. "The only one whose power could become an issue is Kronos." Ligeia shivers, her arm feathering against mine before she firms her resolve.

"Yes, Son of Ares. Kronos' destructive power could destroy us all."

I frown, not liking where this is heading.

"So, some idiot is releasing nightmares from Tartarus." I'm totally confused. "But why? Surely Persephone isn't stupid enough to think she can control them? Granted, the woman *is* an egomaniac, but surely she hasn't gone that far?" We're all silent as we contemplate the lunacy of this move. There has to be a bigger plan, but none of us can figure it out.

"Would Persephone have the guts to pull something like this on her own?" Caleb's voice floats back to us, making us question her actions further.

Ligeia laughs bitterly. "No, she wouldn't. Take my word for it, the woman would not have the spine to take any action by herself. She must have an accomplice." There's a world of hurt in her voice, and I make up my mind to find out what makes this woman tick. She's a mystery—and I desperately need a friend I can trust.

"Right, so the plan of the moment is to take out Persephone, free the Sirens and Muses, then track down the puppet master, yes?" I try to sound more confident than I feel.

This is a massive undertaking I'm not sure we're equipped for. I sense the agreement of the others without them voicing it. The puppeteer's freaking me out.

Boss's thoughts are a soothing blanket around mine, lending me his calm. I sigh. As soon as we dock, things will be different between us. Most likely other Immortals will be there, maybe even Councillors. I hate having to play nice with arseholes, and nothing Boss can say will convince me that Ares and his siblings are nice people. Well, maybe Hephaistos, but he's different.

I'm not wrong. Whatever Boss sees as Aeden manoeuvres into the bay has him distancing himself from me.

One guess as to who's waiting at the dock.

Exhaustion threatens to swamp me, but I square my shoulders as we glide closer to doom. Perhaps exhaustion has me wallowing in melodrama as well. Ligeia stands firm beside me and just as we nudge the dock, I remember the state of her.

"Oh my god! I forgot to offer you new clothes! Surely there's something on this boat that will fit you?" I'm rambling, mortified I forgot something that could be so important. Ligeia's laughing affectionately.

"You truly are wonderful, little Seer." She reaches up to gently cup my face, but at the first touch of her hand, I automatically flinch and hang my head, hiding the scars. That's all it takes for confidence to flee.

She doesn't back off but places one sharp talon underneath my chin applying pressure. It's look up or be impaled. I tilt my head upwards, linking my mind with hers though I'm terrified of what I'll find. She lets me rifle through her surface thoughts as she speaks. "Never hang your head, Chloe. You are not weak, you carry battle scars—wear them as a badge of honour."

I open my mouth, about to spew forth some bullshit. I don't really believe in self-preservation, but she shushes me. "You just showed more strength on that island than the majority of the Council can muster together, and still you are ashamed of your appearance." Her words make me hesitate, think about why I hide my face, my eyes.

"You need to learn to love yourself." She backs off, laughing to herself. "Although maybe I should not throw stones. It took me a good thousand years to learn that lesson and you are . . . maybe one hundred years old?"

I smile ruefully. "Thirty."

She laughs again. "I take it back! You're doing well, just try to refrain from hanging your head in my presence again."

The woman's mercurial. One moment anger rushes off her, the next she's advice and laughter. I wonder if age has affected her, but I don't think so. I think she moves to her own beat, a force of nature.

Bailey finally makes an appearance, pressing into my leg in apology as we disembark. I grin, gently ruffling his fur to tell him all's forgiven and slide behind his eyes.

Strong waves of lust are flowing over the yacht. Caleb's got it bad for our Siren. She's refused my offer of clothing, and I know from a quick ruffle through her thoughts it's to impress upon those present the seriousness of the situation. It shouldn't be necessary, but standing next to Ares on the dock is Hermes.

Ligeia's anger rises above all else as she eyes the former god. Hermes looks ready to bolt. Ares himself shifts uncomfortably and I grin, ready for a showdown.

CHAPTER TWELVE

Chloe

THERE WAS NEVER GOING to be an easy time for Ligeia to come face to face with her attacker again, but standing half-naked while about to embark on a rescue mission was probably the worst possible scenario.

"I take it back, Chloe. I will not work with this sadistic, despotic, son of a bitch. No," she continues, "That's an insult to dogs. Hermes is worse than a maggot crawling beneath our feet." Ares at least looks confused by this statement, but Hermes's gone a sickly shade of green that doesn't match his colourful Hawaiian shirt. Can someone please tell the man we're on Koh Samui, not Honolulu?

Caleb grabs her hand tugging her urgently to the side. I don't know what he says to her, but by the time he's done, Ligeia's back at my side glaring daggers at Hermes. The man in question's currently having his own whispered conversation with Ares, who looks ready to shoot flames. Hermes is backing away but Ares looms menacingly above him, which seems to intimidate him enough to stay still. It makes me like Ares a little bit more.

Behind the two are a group of lesser immortals, descendants of Hermes and Ares, but also with them is Hephaistos. Bailey gives a cheerful yip at the sight of him. The hulking man, dressed in modern combat gear, carries an impressive array of weaponry. I don't know why it surprises me, but I suppose I'd half expected him to come to battle in leather and armour.

I hold firm to Bailey's eyes as Hephaistos wraps Ligeia in a big bear hug. For the first time since I've met her, she fully relaxes, allowing his warmth to wash over her. Caleb's disappointment is so strong, I don't even need to touch his mind to feel his emotions. If I were a nice person, I'd probably let him know that the affection coming from Hephaistos is brotherly.

But I'm not that nice.

"Little Ligeia," the depth of emotion in his voice is almost overwhelming. "We'd thought you lost to us. Where have you been?" Unfortunately, this brings Ligeia's attention back to Hermes.

"Oh, I don't know, Uncle. I may have been minding my business, recovering from my losses in the water around my island." Hermes tries to inch away but Ares has his wrists in an iron grip. "I may have been there for over 500 years, content in my own company before *someone* found me."

All eyes move to Hermes who quails under the scrutiny.

"I may also have been abducted, tortured and raped repeatedly over what feels like a lifetime until some idiot forgot he was holding a Siren and freed my mouth."

Her smile turns cruel. "How are you feeling, Hermes? Everything working well? Fighting fit, as they say?" He moves to lunge at her, but the shackles of Ares' hands are unbreakable.

"You fucking bitch!" Froth forms at the corners of his mouth. "When this is over, you are dead! Dead, you hear me?" I sense Ligeia's satisfaction too late to intervene, even if I'd wanted to. Nonetheless, worry churns in my stomach as her intentions become clear.

"Then you won't mind me challenging you, here and now?"

Hermes' mouth opens and closes like a fish. A challenge in our world is to the death and only invoked under extreme circumstances. Hermes is one of the ancients and should easily be able to defeat Ligeia, but the curse of her song still sits and I doubt victory would be that easy. Instead of speaking, Hermes nods resolutely.

"I think we should take this back to base." Phobos' words cut through the tension like a knife. "We are attracting attention."

Indeed, local fisherman peer at us, curiosity shining in their eyes. Can't say I blame them. Hawaiian shirts, combat gear and tattered clothing are probably not a combination you see here regularly.

We hastily make our way towards a convoy of SUVs that have Caleb's head shaking in subdued sadness. Bailey sticks close to my side, Boss immediately behind me as we pile into the vehicles. Ares tries to manoeuvre himself into my vehicle, but between Caleb, Ligeia, Hephaistos and Boss, there's no room and he retreats in graceful disgust. I breathe a sigh of relief, letting go of Bailey's eyes and just relaxing into my man.

"I see you both wear the bracelets." Hephaistos' voice is warm and soothing but it still jolts me out of my comfort zone.

"Chloe gave it to me this morning. Will you fill me in on how it works?" Boss asks respectfully.

"It contains a tracking beacon that is keyed to your energy signatures. Because of your bond, it was easy enough to tune it to your linked energy fields, and much like Chloe does naturally, you should be able to sense her location." Concern flows in waves from him. "I've been filled in on your vision."

For a minute I wonder which one, and then I remember there's only one that could imply Boss had 'lost' me.

"I don't like the fact you were alone. Hopefully, this should allow help to find you quickly," he says quietly, tapping my bracelet. It hums a little in response.

Boss sends a wave of warmth and comfort my way. The bracelet flares further to life like a tiny electric current, reminding me it's there. I stroke it gently and the sensation subsides. There's more life in Hephaistos' creations than in some of our oldest Immortals.

"We have to make it through this afternoon and the night first," I say.

Weaving a tendril of my mind through Ligeia's is easier than I thought. Her rage still burns like a bonfire leaving her vulnerable to my invasion. I tie off the thread and leave it there, needing it to understand her motives.

"What were you thinking?" I blurt, horrified by Ligeia's actions. "We need all the help we can get, and killing Hermes may very well send all of his line scurrying back into their rabbit holes."

"Hey, I resent that!" Caleb's attempt to lighten the mood falls flat. The silence stretches as Ligeia refuses to answer. "In all seriousness though, I think you'll find with Hermes gone, the others will be only too eager to help." His assessment lets me relax a little.

"That's good, but what about your sisters, Ligeia?" I press. "How'll you find them or revenge if Hermes manages to kill you in a couple of hours? Did you think of that?"

Her rage fills the vehicle and it's not only me who can feel it now. The others shift uncomfortably in their seats, waiting for the explosion. They don't wait long.

"I will accept no help from that man." She screeches, causing all of us to clutch our ears. "He will die and so will his friends when I find them. I will sing to them so they shred their own skin from their bodies. Slowly. Nothing will stand in the way of my revenge, no one will kill that monster but—"

"Enough, little one!" Hephaistos' rumble cracks like a whip across his niece, Ligeia's, tirade. She stops abruptly and it's then I feel the trickle from my nose, smell the copper. I don't think I'm the only one left bleeding from her outburst. My ears are ringing painfully, too.

"Okay," I say gently. "Have your revenge. Just make sure you live to save your sisters and my family." Her resolve firms like a rock in her head, a deadly calm settling. We wait in silence as Caleb drives the SUV up the mountain again, each lost in thoughts of what we have to lose.

Boss doesn't touch me again as we exit the vehicle and though I'm disappointed, I understand. Ares' eyes burn into my back as I follow Bailey out the back door, though I'm too tired to link with the hound again. Hopefully, it won't always be this way.

I stumble as I attempt to take a step, and Hephaistos quickly grabs my arm, the chivalrous move covering my weakness. Boss's jealousy is like a wave, expected at the contact, but it's Ares' reaction that's unusual. There's a slight hint of disgust, then pity, which he quickly tries to mask as he orders everyone around. The disgust I get, but why the hell does he pity me?

Maybe I'll be able to get through to him after all, convince him it's for the best if he forgets his interest in me.

Unfortunately, I think it'll all depend on whether his emotions outweigh his ambition.

Hephaistos leads me in the direction of the communal hall, and I understand that we're going to the clearing outside it, with enough room for the combatants to manoeuvre. Nerves jangle in my chest as I think about the possible outcomes. My terror for my new friend is so real, I can almost taste it. It's then I stop stock still as my eyes burn with the intensity of a solar flare.

Ligeia's pressing an attack, her sword swinging effortlessly as Hermes struggles to parry. Though he's lauded as fleet of foot, he stumbles, coming to his knees on the ground. Ligeia raises her sword for the killing blow, blood fever in her eyes. Only she can't see his triumphant smile. One second he's on the ground, the next behind Ligeia, his own sword moving in a forceful arc towards her head . . .

Hephaistos's waited patiently through this, having turned me towards the jungle on the pretext of showing me the local flora and fauna. I'm beyond grateful.

"Do you want to tell me, or should I get Phobos?" he asks.

I smile. It's not every day you find a friend so understanding.

"He knows already, the man's just about living in my head at the moment." He chuckles and I get a mental nudge from Phobos letting me know he heard that. *Serves you right,* I send to him, earning a mental chuckle. *Can you make sure she knows his plans?*

Already there. His conversation with Ligeia's short and to the point. I fill Hephaistos in on my vision.

"She will beat him, Chloe. You have just seen to that." He squeezes my hand in encouragement as he embraces his savage glee. I blink in surprise.

"So, you aren't a Hermes fan, huh?"

His excitement only ratchets higher. "Whatever gave you that idea?" Hephaistos' dry sarcasm matches mine.

"I wonder . . . could it be the satisfaction at Hermes' predicament that just about wafts off you like a perfume cloud?" I ask flippantly.

He stops me.

"Hermes has done many questionable things in his life, and hasn't been taken to task for them because of his unique position." I nod my understanding. "This is the first time in millennia that there has been a descendant of Hermes strong enough to hold the veil of Olympus themselves. The time is ripe to get rid of that madman."

"There's no one who deserves the honour more than Ligeia." Somehow my bottom lip has made its way between my teeth. "I just don't want her hurt. She's been through so much." He squeezes my hand again and a warning flare of jealousy fires from Boss.

"Your kindness is a credit to your line, Chloe." His thoughts drift to Boss. "I hope he knows what a treasure he has found." I blush from the roots of my dark hair to the tip of my nose. There've been more compliments flung my way in the last three days than in my entire existence.

We walk together towards the others. Ares's distracted by the battle to come and doesn't notice Boss move to stand behind me. This in itself isn't unusual for a bodyguard, but the fingers moving in soothing circles on my back probably look a bit suss. I don't want Ares to notice but it feels too good to tell him to stop, particularly when the hand strays lower.

"Enough, Phobos, or you'll ruin any chance you have at a future with the girl through your own jealous actions."

Boss stiffens beside me at Hephaistos' whispered whip of words and surreptitiously moves a half step further behind me. I sigh, both remorseful and frustrated. I hate sneaking around, but I understand why. Ares will require dealing with very shortly.

"Do you want to use my eyes?" My breath leaves in a grateful rush at Boss's offer. Bailey sits patiently by my side but it's so much easier to share with Boss and I'm exhausted.

I slip behind his eyes, revelling in the comfort of him there with me. Ares helps Ligeia into leathers. Hermes by one of his sons. Traditionally, they must fight with the double-edged short sword *xiphos* and wear the armour of our homeland, though I can see the swords are made of steel, not the traditional bronze. This will make the leather jerkins nearly useless, though perhaps it's all for show.

When the old ones fight, it's more about their gifts than their skill with a sword. These two will be relatively evenly matched. It'll be difficult for Ligeia to use her voice as a weapon when she's exerting herself physically, and Hermes is still crippled by her curse, so I think they'll rely more on weaponry than is usually the case.

Hermes swings his sword experimentally in wide circles around himself as Ligeia stretches her limbs. His posturing goes unnoticed by Ligeia who takes her time to make sure everything's fastened comfortably and the sword's well-weighted. Finally, Ares calls them into the centre of the clearing while everyone gathers around him. A blue wall springs up around them, flickering with flashes of lightning. Caleb's sweating so much, I know it's his doing.

"By the laws of the Council, a challenge has been made and accepted. Will the combatants step forward?" Both move surely towards the God of War. "Any skills you possess may be used in this battle. There are no rules, only that you may not leave this circle until one of you is dead." Both nod, one determined, one craftily. Ares moves backwards. "You may begin on three. One. Two. Thr—"

Hermes lunges forwards, swinging forcefully at Ligeia's head, fully intending to end it immediately. She laughs, darting effortlessly to the side and slicing at his ribs in the same motion. There's a deep groove cut into his jerkin, though no blood can be seen, it's a reminder for him to be careful.

My nails dig into Hephaistos' arms, but he maintains a stoic expression. Boss's thoughts are clinical, examining every angle of attack with me as Ligeia and Hermes attack and counter-attack. They're testing each other, neither gaining any advantage from the constant to and froing. It's then Hermes attempts another overhand swing. Ligeia easily slides away, but not before she lets out a piercing shriek, all she can manage under the conditions. Wincing, I raise my hands to my ears to check for blood, but find there's nothing of the pain from the car. She's in control, her attack is directed at one person, and one person only.

Hermes staggers, blood seeping from his ears, but as Ligeia moves in for the kill he lashes out, sword raking across her calf. Her wings erupt from her back as she shrieks in pain, helping her regain her balance as Hermes skitters away. Blood seeps from the wound but the woman ignores it, the force of her fury carrying her forward.

Though he raises his sword to parry, with each thrust Hermes is steadily pushed back towards the boundary circle. Finally, his back brushes against the blue lightning and an enormous bellow escapes his throat before he can contain it. He launches himself to the side, narrowly avoiding Ligeia's next swing, but as he passes she lands a roundhouse kick with her uninjured leg into his already raw back.

Though he's lauded as fleet of foot, he stumbles, coming to his knees on the ground. Ligeia raises her sword for the killing blow, blood fever in her eyes. Only she can't see his triumphant smile. One second he's on the ground, the next behind Ligeia, his own sword moving in a forceful arc towards her head.

Hermes has finally decided to use his gift.

Caleb lets out a warning cry and the circle shivers, then miraculously holds. Only, Ligeia has not been idle. Forewarned is forearmed. Her mouth opens, one triumphant note fills in the clearing, stopping Hermes in his tracks. She bends and slides from under his sword, continuing her heart-breaking song directly into his ear. Tears leak from his eyes, face a horrified rictus of pain as his muscles seize.

Ligeia doesn't pause, a manic grin appearing as blood starts to pour from his eyes. His ears. His mouth. Hermes collapses in a fleshy heap at her feet as Ligeia croons a lullaby to him. All resistance has faded. He's a vacant shell staring at his killer with sightless eyes.

Finally, she stops singing. His chest's no longer moving, but it isn't finished. She pulls her sword from the ground, stands statuesque above him, and with one swing severs his head from his body. The sword flies again and again until all that is left is pulpy flesh.

She looks around the circle as Caleb drops the barrier. All are silent, waiting.

"It is done. The terms of the challenge have been fulfilled," Ares intones.

Blood drips casually as she strides towards the edge of the circle, wings flared behind her back. There is no hitch in her stride, which would betray her wound. But it gapes open, dripping blood behind her. There's no way I'd be walking if it were me, and yet I feel the pain radiate across our bond. Even though she's shielding, it's strong, so I send a little comfort back to her. She doesn't stop as she makes her way towards the communal hall but I feel her gratitude all the same.

I reluctantly pull away from Boss's mind, giving up the use of his eyes with a sigh. Though it's easier, I still need the rest being alone in my mind affords. The people around us are hushed, and I can't tell what the repercussions of this event will be, only that it needed to happen.

"Andrew, Martin, salvage what you can. We'll bury him as befits his station but that'll be the last we speak of our forefather." Caleb's voice is hard as ice as he talks to two of his cousins. It's then I realise he'll have to assume Hermes' rank.

I don't see whether they follow his commands, but I feel the *whoosh* and *pop* that accompanies a Hermes tracing, so they must be doing something right. Hephaistos places his right hand on the small of my back, Boss just restraining a growl. He leads me inside as I let out a sigh. Males and their possessive egos. Caleb stays behind, though I am sure this isn't where he wants to be right now. And definitely not who he wants to be with.

"I cannot tell you how happy I am that we will not have to deal with Hermes anymore." Hephaistos' satisfaction seeps through both his tone and his thoughts. "She did a marvellous job. I was particularly impressed with her lullaby. Masterful." I stop, turning incredulously towards him, disturbed by the tone of the conversation. Though I can't see him, I sense his confusion.

"You act like this was just a walk in the park, afternoon tea with your dearest Mumsy! How can you be so removed from the savagery that just took place?"

Hephaistos's quiet for a minute, and I think he isn't going to answer me, but then his words reach to the pit of my soul. "Because over millennia you switch off or go mad." His acceptance and sorrow are clear. "You either find ways to cope with the soul crushing weight of loss, or you lose yourself. Like Hermes." He gathers his thoughts. "He was not always like this, this depraved monster. Once, he was brave and honest and the first to stand up for what is right."

His thoughts are heavy, crushing. Images flicker—a young Hermes, standing up to both Ares and Zeus when the occasion called for it. The past is the past, but this helps. It makes me see the possibilities, what good can become if the positive isn't fostered.

"Hold on to love, Chloe." The sadness in his voice tears at my heartstrings. "Hold on to love, because that is the only thing that will save you from the darkness of millennia."

"But you're still strong, and look at how much you have lost."

"Love," he says. "Memories of love enough to last a lifetime. Make sure you have the chance to experience those or there is no telling what you might become, with your power."

His words carry the weight of the world. I must speak to Ares. But not before I've slept.

CHAPTER THIRTEEN

Chloe

THE TROUBLE WITH THE best-laid plans of mice and men is that nothing ever goes as intended. Bailey and I make our way towards the cabin, bypassing the communal hall for some much-needed rest. Boss has put Ligeia in the hut closest to ours. I'm assuming that it's normal for a bodyguard to sleep close to their charge, but I'm too tired to check whether that'll cause problems with Ares. And to be honest, I don't care. I crawl into bed, push my lump of a hound off it, and instantly fall asleep.

I'm woken by kisses gently feathering their way down my spine. A contented smile spreads as I register Boss's warmth, our connection flaring strong and true. I'm torn between whether to roll over and kiss him senseless or pretend to still be asleep and let him continue.

"I know you are awake, Princess." The kisses don't stop, so I relax into the mattress. "But you are going to have to choose. Do you want me to continue like this?" The kisses inch along my arse, moving towards my inner thighs. "Or move on to sweeter pastures?" A long, slow lick grazes my inner thighs and the outside of my vaginal lips, a tantalising glimpse of what's to come.

I squirm closer, silently begging him to continue what he's started, but he just moves away, stopping mid-stroke. "Boss!" I groan. "Please!"

"I asked you to choose, Chloe." The calm tone's irritating, but not enough that I'll forfeit what I want.

"Just do it. You know what I want, why draw it out?"

"I want to hear you say it. Want to hear the words through those gorgeous lips of yours."

"Lick me, Boss, make me come." I have no patience for games right now and fortunately, Boss caves. He flips me over, mouth closing over my clit, sucking with an intensity that has me arching over the bed as he pins my hips to the mattress. Greedily, he laps at my honey like a man dying of thirst. Alternately, his tongue circles my clit then thrusts into my channel, the rhythm making me ache in both places. Neither's quite satisfied and I'm quivering on the verge of orgasm but having it taken away again an instant later.

"Please, Boss! Please let me come." He groans but bites gently on my clit as I scream my orgasm into the pillow. He doesn't let me rest, continuing to suck and lick almost to the point of pain before he pulls away again. Having someone sharing your mind does have its benefits.

He draws me up towards him and limply, I crawl into his lap, wrapping my legs around his waist. His cock twitches, a heavy weight on my inner thigh. My lassitude's gone in an instant when his mouth pushes hungrily at mine, tongue thrusting inside. "All afternoon I have watched as you were pawed and ogled over by other men." His fingers circle my nipple then pinch, drawing a moan from me. "I have stayed silent while you ignore me and smile at others." His fingers find their way between my folds and I move as far onto his lap as I can, rubbing my slickness against him. "Tonight, now, is my time. I may have to watch you with others in the day, but at night you are mine."

With that, he grabs my hips and without ceremony, impales me on his length. I'm so slick, but the stretch almost borders on pain from this position. He gives me no time to adjust, lifting me again and slamming me back down. Groaning, I bury my head in his shoulder, biting down as he continues to thrust, deeper each time.

"You are mine. Say it!" He doesn't need me to say it. He can feel it. He's everywhere, inside my body, my mind, my soul. We're one.

He flips me over onto my stomach, pulling away and slamming in with that astounding strength of his. I'm so full, I'm about to shatter with pleasure.

"Gods, Chloe! Say it, please!"

"I'm yours," I breathe into his ear. "Always." With that, I come apart in his arms as he does in mine.

We collapse onto the mattress where I curl into his side.

"I love you Chloe," is the last thing I hear as I drift off to sleep again.

★ ★ ★

"WELL, WELL, WELL. ISN'T this interesting?" Ares' voice first thing in the morning is not what you want to wake up to, particularly in a compromising situation. Despite the menace in his tone, no physical reaction follows and Boss slides cautiously from the bed.

"Father, I know that you—"

"You know that I what, Phobos?" Anger's simmering, slowly reaching boiling point. It crawls over my skin leaving me shaking in shock. "Knew that I had plans? Knew that she was intended for me?" There's a sudden thump and a groan from Boss. *Fuck.* Has Ares attacked his own son? A *thud* sounds as a weight falls to the floor. I hastily search for Bailey, but the hound's nowhere in range. "There had better be some explanation for this treachery. It is taking all my willpower to keep from grinding you into the dust."

Frantic now, I desperately throw my mind at Ares. Surprisingly I slip easily inside, perhaps because his rage clouds his thoughts. My mind weaves tendrils effortlessly through the shifting space, then I tighten my web.

Ares immediately loosens his hold on Boss, leaving him shaking on the floor. I don't have time to check him, so I send soothing thoughts his way. The thread between Ares' mind and mine is stretched taut like the string of a bow, making it easy to navigate towards him. As I touch his face, Ares exhales some of his rage, letting the calming influence of my mind take hold.

"What're you angry about, Ares? Really?" He takes a shuddering breath, my web compelling him to tell the truth.

"My son is in bed with the woman I thought was meant for me." The words are a truth, but not the whole truth.

"That isn't it. Look deeper."

"My son is becoming stronger than me."

"Again, a truth, but not the whole truth. What is it you really fear?"

"I'm being replaced. My seed is no longer fruitful and it is now the responsibility of the next generation to continue our line." This is it. This is the fear that prompts him to hurt this son who's shown him nothing but loyalty over the years.

"You are not being replaced, Father." Boss is beside me, silently urging me to loosen the threads constricting his father's mind.

On instinct, I take a risk and draw a thread between Boss's mind and Ares'. Their gratitude's overwhelming as both men can now feel the intentions of the other, emotions flowing freely between the two. It's harder than I expected, and sweat breaks out on my forehead, trickling down my temples.

"You and your brother are both my equals in power now. I don't know whether you were born this way, or have managed to conceal it from me, but either of you could take my place in a heartbeat." Ares takes a breath, intent on getting everything out. "Tomorrow, or next week, or even in another hundred years, what happened to Hermes could happen to me."

"Hermes' fate became his because he did not love," Boss replies. "You still care, despite your anger and aggression." The exhale from Ares bleeds his anxiety away. As close as they are at the moment, he knows the sincerity of his son's words. "Neither I nor my brother want your place, your position."

"You seek freedom." Ares' voice is filled with awe and sorrow.

"That is all we have ever wanted, the chance to live our lives the way we wish to live them." I feel his attention shift to me. "To love as we choose to love."

"Is it so hard to believe that your sons aren't as power-hungry as you?" If I'm a little tart in my comments, I think Ares deserves it. He laughs.

"Actually, yes. They are possibly the only two of my entire progeny who do not desire power." His wry tone gives away his feelings. I don't need to be in his head to know how it wearies him. "Every other child would make a bid for my seat if they thought they could win. It is the nature of war—conquest and pride." His attention shifts again to Boss. "It would seem there is more of your mother in you than I thought, despite your gifts."

"Don't think love doesn't have its pride, Father." Boss's voice is stern. "It hasn't been easy the past few days dealing with my love for Chloe."

"About that," Ares states. "I may have had a change of heart." In the calm of this moment, he acknowledges his own feelings towards me.

"I didn't think that you were too interested in *me* Ares, particularly after I felt your response at the challenge."

He nods, slightly sheepish but still struggling with disgust, as my net still forces the truth from his lips. "My nature forces me to see physical weakness as repulsive." He almost shudders and I find myself trying to suppress a smile. "Unfortunately, Chloe, despite the fact you are a very attractive woman, the lack of sight is something I would have found difficult to overcome."

I laugh when I catch Boss's response.

The man wants to rip his own father's head off for what he sees as an insult to me, but his relief at his father's words trumps it. I send a soothing thread his way, loosen my hold on his father, then continue the conversation with Ares.

"So where does that leave us?" I ask. "You don't want me, yet Boss does. Is it so hard for you to accept that your line will be strengthened by your son, not you?"

Ares doesn't reply straight away.

That calculating thread's dominating his mind.

"No, we can make this work." His thoughts turn inwards, devising some strategy that won't diminish his glory. "Only the twins know that I had interpreted the prophecy as being about me." It figures Ares would see himself as the only option for having a powerful child destined to be the saviour of the race.

I roll my eyes. Typical. The only thing he cares about is saving face.

"Are you sure that Eros doesn't know about it?" Phobos' tone is doubtful. "He showed aggression towards Chloe at the Council meeting."

"Perhaps he suspects, but the details are not his." The silence stretches uncomfortably before Ares continues, "You two may remain together."

How magnanimous.

"But please try not to flaunt your relationship too much. There are others with the power to threaten you who may have come across the prophecy." The worry in his voice disturbs me. "Who knows if we will have the power to protect you? Or my grandchildren?"

All the threads I hold around his mind and between him and his son dissolve as I gasp in relief. My whole body relaxes as the strain lifts.

"How do you think we should manage the situation? It will come out eventually—if Chloe's prophecy comes to pass it won't be that long before it is obvious," Boss asks in tentative deference.

"Ah yes, *that* prophecy," Ares says, sending me a calculating smirk that gets my back up. What is it about these men that makes me itch to smack the stupid expressions from their faces? "Obviously, Phobos was the man in the vision?"

I nod in confirmation, but something tells me to keep the fact we are Soulmates a secret. Ares shouldn't have that much power over anyone.

"I'll need to think on this more. In the meantime, you should try to keep a low profile." Ares' suggestion has merit.

I crawl back into the bed and bury my head under the covers.

"What are you doing?" Ares asks.

"Now you can go away and leave me to my sleep." I'm sure I'm heard, even muffled by the doona, but Ares doesn't leave. He ignores me, speaking instead to Boss.

"The reason I came here is that we have received a communication from your brother." Boss's relieved sigh lifts a weight from my shoulders.

"And was he successful?" Boss asks.

"Yes. They have found the location of the prisoners. Unfortunately, they are heavily guarded, so he was unable to rescue them with the amount of manpower that was there."

"I take it they are on their way here?"

"Correct. They should be here within the next day or so." Ares pauses, thinking. "By that time, Ligeia should be at full strength, but your brother and his team will need another night to recuperate. It would be advisable to formulate a rough plan of attack today, and flesh it out with further details from Deimos tomorrow."

"The prisoners will be all right for another day?"

"They appear to be fine. Deimos said they overheard conversations that suggest in three days' time, an offensive may take place, but what that would be is unclear."

The door slides open again and an enthusiastic Bailey bustles into the room onto the bed. He noses at the covers until his wet nose finds my cheek and he lets out an excited yip. Sometimes I forget that he's little more than a puppy.

"We will expect you both in the communal hall in around an hour."

"We'll be there in two," Boss counters.

Ares chuckles. I'm shocked at the abrupt turnaround, but can only conclude yesterday's display of weakness was so disappointing, it made him have second thoughts before he discovered Boss and me together. "Fine. Two hours. We do need to have something in place before your brother arrives."

The sound of the door closing is a blessing, as are Boss's arms sliding around me. I reach upwards and the slight echo of his pain reaches me through our bond as I brush his cheek. Anger stirs, followed by heartache. No man should ever be forced to endure their own family turning on them. I turn and brush a gentle kiss on his slightly swollen cheek, showing him without words how much I care.

Unfortunately, Bailey makes his presence known again by crawling all over the two of us, enthusiastically slurping at our faces. Though he manages to wrestle him off, Boss isn't impressed.

"I shall be teaching your hound some manners." Underneath the stern tone is a lightness I find irresistible. "Unfortunately, his mistress hasn't taken him in hand well enough yet."

I take advantage and slip behind his eyes, laughing as he ushers Bailey outside again, much to the hound's disgust. As he shuts the door, I attempt to disengage, but he holds me firmly with him. Boss prowls around the bed, staring at me with a hunger and intensity that would be frightening if I didn't share it.

I stretch out on the bed, luxuriating in his eyes on me. His need stirs mine, pushing me beyond anything I've ever known. It scares me, this intensity, but I've no idea how I ever did without it in my life. Boss's lips meet mine in a demanding kiss. At first, I'm blindsided but . . .

"No offence, Boss, but you smell like wet dog."

"Wet dog? Thank you, Bailey. I guess I'll be needing a bath now." He pulls me closer. "Care to join me?" I'm so stunned by the lightness of the moment that I startle when he scoops me into his arms and carries me towards the bathroom. I want him to be like this all the time. In fact, I'm going to make it my mission in life.

He takes us towards the shower, intent on devouring my skin and turning the shower on in the process. I don't make it easy for him, stroking him everywhere as I slide down his body towards the tiles below.

It's incredibly erotic to see myself on my knees through his eyes, so I look upwards as I take the tip of him in my mouth. Though it's a little disconcerting, I can feel his response as if it's my own. I'm so slick between my thighs, it's all I can do not to jump him where he stands, but I want this more. His shaft hardens further as I suck strongly on the bulbous tip, earning a moan from the warrior before me.

"Gods yes, Chloe. Again!"

I swirl my tongue around the tip, trailing my fingers up and down him teasingly. While his length's pleasing, it's his girth that leaves me aching all over. I have to stretch my mouth around it when he thrusts and on the draw back he feels a tiny graze of teeth.

"Fuck, Princess. Just like that!"

I apply more pressure this time, careful to keep teeth covered until I reach the tip. It's too much for Boss, who fists his hands through my hair and thrusts unceremoniously into my throat. Though I thought my gag reflex would kick in, it isn't given a chance. He's too big, and his thrusts are well-timed. I've never taken a man like this before, this deep, and liked it. The water pounds into his back, allowing only a light mist to fall around me, and the sight of me swallowing all his cock through his eyes has me desperate to come.

"Touch yourself while I take your mouth." He doesn't need to say it twice. I thrust two fingers inside my pussy, using my thumb to stroke my clit as my fingers sink deep inside me. My moan vibrates around his cock as my orgasm approaches. His thrusts become harder and more erratic and I struggle to keep relaxed but in the next instant both of us fall over the edge.

His orgasm rushes through my mind, followed quickly by my own and I struggle to breathe in my sudden haze. He's shot his load into the back of my throat so I continue to swallow as his thrusts slow, then stop. I grin up at him in pride.

"That . . ." He doesn't need to say it. I felt it. "Let's get you cleaned up."

"Why? You're only going to get me dirty again."

He doesn't bother denying it, but turns me around, using the body wash to rub circles around my back and belly. Thoughts of my scars are far distant. I'm living entirely in this moment, water sliding down my body, following the path of his hands. When his fingers reach my puckered nipples I moan. Slow circles turn into gentle pinches. I gasp as his fingers trail down my stomach and stroke my inner thighs.

"Please," I beg, but Boss has other ideas.

He doesn't bother to reply as he towels me dry as quickly as possible. Doesn't say anything as I plant kisses down his neck when he carries me into the room. He can't remain silent when I grind my dripping pussy over his bare cock.

Dropping me unceremoniously on the bed, he pauses to growl at me. "You'll be the death of me, woman." I don't answer, just drag him down for a hot, wet kiss. He has no patience for this, immediately crawling down my body.

"I love the taste of you." I throw my head back as he parts my folds. From behind his eyes, I'm staring intently at my dripping pussy, a sight both intimate and arousing. His hunger's all-consuming as he dives in, feasting on my nectar. "I'll never get enough of this."

I don't bother replying. My orgasm arrives quickly this time but he doesn't allow me to rest, just pulls my legs over his shoulder and thrusts inside. He's in so deep, each thrust borders on pain, but my hands grip his arse and urge him on harder and faster until I come apart in his arms once again.

"That's three times, Princess. Let's see if we can make it a fourth in a new hole, shall we?" My butt clenches at the thought, but I yearn to be loved everywhere by him. I roll over, arse in the air, silently urging him to do what he wills.

He moves to the bedside table, returning with a bottle of lube. Gently he strokes his fingers between my thighs, my juices making them so slick the two that breach my back passage slide in smoothly. His cock is once again inside me, thrusting in counterpoint to his fingers in my arse. Before I know it, I'm on the verge of coming again, but he slows, breaking the rhythm and earning a growl of frustration.

"Not yet," he chuckles. He briefly pulls his fingers from me, dropping the lube over my pucker and his fingers. As his thrusting in both passages continues, he adds a third, then a fourth finger. My arse is burning, but I'm so full. I don't want this to end.

I know what's coming when he pulls his cock fully from my dripping pussy. The fingers on one hand are still buried firmly in my arse while the other drips lube onto his cock, stroking it so it is completely slick. The same hand then turns to my clit, rubbing firm circles around it.

As his fingers are pulled from my arse, the blunt head of his cock pushes insistently at my rear entrance. The burn is so intense, I almost tell him to stop, but then the head pops through and things are easier.

He leaves it there for a moment as I catch my breath, fighting through the pain to the pleasure as his fingers continue their forceful rhythm.

"Are you okay, Princess? Should I continue?"

I can feel how hard it is for him to remain still, but the reality is I'm desperate for him. For this.

"More. Please." It comes out as a croak as I'm choking on my pleasure, his fingers rubbing so forcefully my orgasm will hit long before he's fully inside me.

"Can't have that, can we?" he says, reading my thoughts, and uses my distraction from the building orgasm to thrust fully inside me. He stops, pulls back a little then thrusts again. It burns, but suddenly he hits something that turns the pain to pleasure. Honestly, this could also be because he pinches my little bud between his thumb and forefinger, sending me skyrocketing as I scream my pleasure to the world.

Boss loses control. His thighs smash against my arse as he continues to pound into me and I soak it up. His fingers have left my clit, digging into both hips as he impales me and with a groan he releases. His thrusts slow as we both ride out the effects of our own orgasm.

Gentle kisses pepper my back and I smile in contentment.

"Not leaving here. Tell them we'll talk tomorrow." I flip my hand dismissively in his direction. He chuckles and I smile. Two lovesick fools.

"You have two minutes, Princess."

"What?" I shake myself out of my stupor. "Two hours isn't up yet! I still have time for a nice nanna nap."

"You have two minutes until I get you back into that shower so we can clean up all over again." Oh. This is going to be a good day.

CHAPTER FOURTEEN

Chloe

ARES, PHOBOS, HEPHAISTOS, CALEB and Ligeia sit around an ancient map of the Underworld while I tune them out. Unfortunately, war tactics are virtually incomprehensible to me. As I sit in the midst of some very old, very knowledgeable generals, I begin to feel the first stirrings of inadequacy. Actually, that's a lie. I feel inadequate ninety per cent of the time. Probably what makes me so short-tempered.

The only other person in the room who feels even remotely as lost in the conversation as I do is Caleb.

"Are you telling me we can't transport directly into the Underworld?" Caleb's incredulous.

"No," says Ares, frustration beginning to show. "I'm telling you that even with all of your line transporting us, we wouldn't be able to take enough troops."

"So what's the point of us being here then?" His frustration's leaking through.

"Because there is still a need for tactical covert operations, Caleb." Ares sighs. "There are two larger entrances to Hades where we can amass our troops. However, they will be glaringly obvious to Persephone and she will have put precautions in place to counter an attack."

"This is where you come in, Caleb, you and the others of Hermes line you deem trustworthy." Boss's interjection has Caleb's attention.

"I'm listening."

"We will need a distraction, someone who can get in and out quickly, diverting Persephone's attention from the main entrances." Boss's idea's logical.

"We're good at moving swiftly, but I don't think my family's flamboyant enough to cause a big enough distraction. What we really need is—"

"Me!" Boss's relief washes through my mind and Bailey gives a yip of welcome. Who knew the big mutt had a soft spot for Deimos?

"Welcome back, Demon. Enjoy your tropical holiday? Weather pleasant on the flip side?" Caleb groans at my lame attempt at humour. Sometimes I frustrate even me.

"Actually, Chloe, it was a little unpleasant. And the company wasn't worth writing home about," he says with a laugh.

I link with Bailey, eager to see what's happening.

"I'd much rather be here with my taciturn *little* brother. Although he does seem remarkably cheery today." His pointed look in Boss's direction is sly.

He must have been communicating with Boss via their link while I was finishing getting ready.

"As women only seem to be in your company for a maximum of three minutes, I am assuming you need further education," Boss stirs good-naturedly. Colour me amazed. "In your case, the two minutes longer you've been in the world does not equal wisdom. Nor stamina."

"Yes, none of you oldies seemed to realise that Persephone was a serial pest until I came along," I interject, trying to steer us back on track. My sex life is something I'd rather isn't a topic of conversation.

"Persephone does need to be dealt with," says Hephaistos. I'll be eternally grateful if he can steer this conversation back into safe waters. Ones that won't leave me blushing. "What do you have to tell us, Deimos?"

"And what news do you have of Hades?" Ligeia's question's one we all want the answer to. "He is possibly the only one who can destroy our plan."

"Why's that?" I ask.

"Because Hades *is* the Underworld. His awareness is everywhere," Hephaistos fills in. "Everywhere except Tartarus and its polluted surrounds, that is."

"That's why we are sure that Hades is either imprisoned or in collusion with Persephone. He couldn't be *un*aware that something has been going on lately. Not with the release of the Titans' minions." Things are starting to make sense with this new piece of information from Ligeia.

"Okay. So what *do* we know, Demon?" I ask.

"I think I'll allow the man to talk for himself." Hades steps into the room. The show's a little melodramatic, but I've got to hand it to Demon, he does pull off a pretty daring rescue mission. Hades himself looks a little battered and worse for wear, but it's the sorrow in his eyes that haunts me.

"I'm glad you are with us, Hades," Ares says gently, a tone I didn't know he possessed. He shifts around the circle, drawing a chair next to him for his brother.

"I'm sure you will understand when I say I find no pleasure in this reunion, Ares." When he sits, Hades eyes seem to glaze over and I'm sure I see the sheen of tears. The other men shift uncomfortably, but none say anything. Who says you can't teach an old dog new tricks? Everyone recognises where Hades' pain comes from. It can't be easy to have been betrayed by someone you love.

Ligeia, sitting beside him, grasps his hand silently. He doesn't cling, but he does squeeze gently, acknowledging her support. "You are your mother's daughter, Ligeia. She would be proud of you." She smiles in understanding and I send my own brand of warmth her way. There are stories in Ligeia's depths I'm sure I'll never know.

"I don't want to talk about how I was captured. Suffice it to say that my wife is a very good actress." He looks lost. "Either that or I am foolishly blind."

"Probably a bit of both." Deimos' statement has us all glaring at him. "What? Love can make anyone blind. Look at Chloe!" I'm confused. "She must be totally blind if she's still making goo-goo eyes at my brother now that I'm back."

Ares cuffs him over the back of the head, yet his statement's worked as intended. A small smile graces Hades' face.

"Anyway," says Hades. "I hate to inform you of this, but Tartarus' walls are breached. There is definitely one, possibly more, Titans free. Persephone seems to be colluding with Iapetus at present."

"Iapetus? God of Mortality?" asks Ares, fear poisoning his voice. I never thought I'd hear that tone from him, and it chills me to my core.

Hades nods in confirmation. "Ironic, is it not? She betrays me only to fall in with my monstrous counterpart."

"Ironic is not the word I would use," Ligeia says. "Terrifying is more like it. Didn't it take you, Zeus and Poseidon together to lock that bastard in Tartarus?"

"Yes," he says. "But at that time we did not have our descendants to help. On the other hand—"

"—now half the original Olympians are dead or missing," Caleb finishes for him. He ticks off names on his fingers as he continues. "Zeus—went mad and had to be executed. Apollo—assassinated. Demeter—missing in action. Athena—missing in action. Aphrodite—also executed for crimes against mortals. Poseidon—missing."

Boss and Demon are stony-faced while the list goes on. Deep inside their anger burns. Both believe their mother's crimes have been fabricated in an effort to get rid of her. "And of course, who could forget the spectacular show Ligeia put on when demolishing my forefather."

Ligeia's glaring at him. Caleb's penchant for trivialising the terrifying must mean he and Demon get along famously.

"Realistically, do we have a strong enough force to re-imprison or destroy the Titans?" My question's met with silence.

Finally, Hades intervenes.

"At the moment, for all intents and purposes, it is just one Titan." His words are confident, but his face is ashen. "If, however, all of them are free . . ."

No-one says anything. We all know we're in big trouble if they're out.

"Okay, so . . . plan?" I hate dramatic tension.

Ares takes charge. "Right now, we have three objectives. Deimos, there are still prisoners alive in there, yes?"

"Yes, Father. They are imprisoned in the Asphodel Meadows, guarded by the Harpies." There's a sharp intake of breath. Everyone thought the Harpies, guardians of lost souls, would be loyal to the Council for eternity. "Persephone's rhetoric has swayed them against Olympus."

"So we need to rescue the prisoners, liberate the Underworld from Persephone's clutches and re-imprison Iapetus, sealing Tartarus in the process."

"Correct," Deimos agrees.

Talk about mission impossible!

"Then the prisoners are our distraction. Caleb!" Ares barks.

"I take it this is where my family comes in handy?" Caleb's too cocky. I'm worried it'll get him killed.

"You and your brethren will transport Deimos and a number of his warriors through Asphodel." Ares stern tone reflects my worry. Caleb senses it and turns the attitude down. A little.

"The objective being a rescue mission with lots of noise to split their attention?"

Ares nods the affirmative. "We will amass forces at each of the two entrances in this area, attacking simultaneously on my order."

"How will we counter Iapetus? He's the god of mortality, Ares! Who can go up against that?" My voice is stringent. I don't want Boss anywhere near that monster.

"That is where Ligeia and Hades come in, little Seer," says Hephaistos.

Ligeia's smile's feral, all trace of her wounds of yesterday gone from her body. "The Titans are just as susceptible to a Siren's voice as the rest of us. Ligeia will need to sing him into complacency while Hades drains the Titan's power."

It's Hades turn to look vicious, though he does bring up his own concerns. "But we won't know where he will surface. Or *if* he will."

"I have a plan for that too." Ares' voice is smug. He holds the silence a little longer to draw out the tension before he drops his bombshell. "Clymene is on her way." There's stunned silence. Did I mention how much I hate calculated dramatics?

"Clymene hasn't left her home for a thousand years. What makes you think she'll do so now?" Hephaistos asks the question we're all thinking.

"This would be the only reason she would leave her island, Uncle." My heart breaks as I read Ligeia's surface thoughts. There're reasons Clymene would do anything to ensure Iapetus is locked away again. Reasons that make my stomach churn.

Ares clears his throat. "Yes, she is on her way, and I'm told he has already been searching for her. Their link will ensure he will come straight to us if she's close enough for him to feel."

"So Ligeia and Hades get to hang with Clymene?" I clarify. Clymene's role in this is making me ill.

"She is the best bait we have." Ares reply's curt. I don't think he understands my lack of enthusiasm. I know it's necessary, but I hate the thought of using an abused woman to lure out one of her abusers. Even if said woman's a volunteer.

"Okay," I say reluctantly. "And the rest of us deal with Persephone?"

"Again correct. But the force with you, Chloe, will need to be stronger. I will lead it, but Phobos will be in charge of security around you. Choose your core team wisely, son. Persephone has already shown she will destroy Chloe, given half a chance."

Boss's fear and determination threaten to overwhelm me, so I sink more firmly into my mind, withdrawing a little from both Boss and Bailey.

"What do you mean, Persephone's shown she'll destroy me?" I both want to hear the answer and fear it.

Surprisingly, Hades is the one who answers. "I was imprisoned when I went to question your assassin, Chloe," he says gently. "Persephone killed the man after she locked me in a cell. I suppose someone in thrall to Phobos would be of little use to her."

My stomach drops. Then everything clicks.

"If she was behind that, and the attacks on the Muses and Sirens, then it's highly likely . . ." My voice trails off as the anger builds to white-hot rage.

"Yes. We assume she is also responsible for your current existence." Ares isn't gentle. Weakness won't be tolerated.

I sit in silence, digesting, and I'm not the only one. The silence is awkward.

Bailey whines, drawing Hades' attention. "I see you have developed a close bond with the pup I sent you, Chloe Santos," he says formally. I didn't know he'd personally sent Bailey to me, but it stands to reason that he had something to do with it. Good change of topic.

"Yes, Bailey's been a great companion so far, if a little . . . awkward at times." He chuckles at my diplomacy.

"He will get there. Cerberus was once a nervous pup too, if you can believe it." I can't. Cerberus is terrifying, and the three heads of his fighting form are the stuff of nightmares. "Your young one is his grandson." At my sharp intake of breath, he laughs again, if a little forlornly. His attention turns to Boss. "I'm sorry your prisoner is dead."

Boss sighs. "There wasn't much left of his mind to plumb in any case, Uncle. Thank you for your assistance."

"Clymene will be here later tonight. We will rest until then, and move out in the morning." Ares takes control of the situation again, and we all move off to our respective rooms.

CHAPTER FIFTEEN

Phobos

WE HAVE VERY LITTLE time before the attack to prepare, but in my estimation, by far the most important weakness to address is Chloe's fears. There are many that I can't help her fix but her aversion to fire, particularly that of her hellhound protector, are things that can no longer be ignored.

It doesn't take me long to catch Chloe, despite the fact she is using Bailey's eyes to find her way towards our cabin. I know what she wants—Apollo's journal calls to her and in truth, she will need to study it in-depth, before we leave. However, this comes first.

Chloe. I call her across our link, sending a wash of warmth to her, just because she likes it and that in turn pleases me. *There are some things I would like to help you with.* I feel her join me in my mind, rifling through my surface thoughts. Her reluctance for my plans is so great that she almost tells me to leave her. The words that flit through her head make me smile. No-one bar my brother has ever spoken to me like that. Then her begrudging agreement with my assessment filters through and I know I have won.

She stops in her tracks and waits until I catch her. Bailey fidgets by her side, his excitement clear. The hound is smarter than anyone gives him credit for. I am sure he senses his own role in the coming training and approves.

"You're going to ask me to play with fire," Chloe throws at me as soon as I touch her shoulder. I draw her to me, dropping a gentle kiss on her forehead. The webbed scars. It is impossible not to touch her. I want to reassure her, but she forges ahead. "I know you mean well and it *may* be necessary, but logic doesn't stop terror."

"No," I throw back at her. "But addressing your fears in a controlled environment with people you trust is an excellent way to break the bonds of fear." I feel her grudging agreement. Still, she pushes further, trying to make clear to me what I have already felt inside her.

"That warehouse stars in my nightmares, every night." I draw her closer, rubbing circles on her back. I don't tell her I've felt it with her, that when we lie together she draws me into her nightmares. Instead, I let her talk. It's not only Asclepius' line that understands healing. War destroys the mind, so my brother and I have an innate understanding of post-traumatic stress. Fortunately, we also inherited our mother's gift, a great healer on its own.

The light in the dark.

Love.

It breaks my heart to realise this is my first chance to use it fully. I had thought I loved Alala, had tried to use my gifts to help her but in comparison to what I feel now that flame was a fragile one, without the strength needed to battle her demons.

At least I understand truly now what most never do.

"I feel it, Boss. Every night, I feel the agony of the flames all over again. Every night!" Tears track down her face and I kiss them away. I don't hesitate, breathing my mother's gift into her mouth as I kiss her long and slow. While anyone not in love will become a virtual slave to my will, I am not worried. For Chloe, this will allow me to help her heal her mind. "I have to wake up every morning and face the fact that the fire consumed everything important to me."

"You are perfect." The words come out in an insistent, ferocious rush. "And you are strong. Your scars have helped make you who you are." I kiss her harder, allowing the fog to wind its way through her mind. It dulls the memories, covering them in a thin layer of warmth so that when they surface, they are no longer as sharp. As damaging. She breathes a sigh when the fog takes effect.

"I felt that, Boss." Her words are reproachful but her tone teases and I catch the small smile on her face. "Next time ask." *I'd never say no to something that helps me deal with the horror that quickly.* I nod my acceptance, knowing she will see my capitulation through the hound's eyes.

I take a moment to show her, let her see herself through my eyes, my emotions. She's beautiful, silvery scars criss-crossing tanned skin, high cheekbones and full lips that beg to be kissed. The taut, athletic body, shoulders no longer hunched but defiantly back. She doesn't even notice she's no-longer hiding behind the black-satin curtain of her hair anymore. But I do. And my heart rejoices in how far she's come in such a short time.

"We still have work to do." I hesitate. "We will need to test your limits. There would be nothing worse than finding out under fire that your fear is not as distant as we think." Her agreement comes loud and clear across the bonds as she grabs my hand and I lead her towards another of the outbuildings.

"Where are we going?" she asks, her natural curiosity asserting herself.

"Well," I say. "There are only two Immortals who have such a close affinity with fire. Can you guess?"

She contemplates a minute, then steals the information from my mind anyway. I laugh out loud at her playfulness. "We're visiting Hephaistos and Hades? What are they going to be able to help me with?"

"Hephaistos can make his own flames, throw it even, and it has the heat of the forge he manipulates." Her curiosity is a good thing. At least now she is not dwelling on her fear. "And Hades can help you with Bailey."

"Help me with Bailey?"

"Don't you remember your reaction when Bailey defended you in his battle form?" She winces, a little ashamed. "You were more scared of the flames on his back than you were of the assassin who had just shot you." I don't want to rub it in, but she needs to understand. "Hades can bring out a Hellhound's battle form with a single thought. Today, you will learn to fight with Bailey, or at least be comfortable enough with him to be able to control your fear."

When asked, both Immortals agree with my plan, following us to a clearing by the pool usually used for weapons training. Chloe's emotions dance over her face, her apprehension incredibly clear. I realise she has lost the ability with her sight to mask the emotions on her face. A fiercely protective wave rises in me and it's all I can do not to grab her and lock her away from anything and anyone who would use those emotions to hurt her.

Unfortunately, that means everyone.

Well, almost everyone.

Hades comes to a stop in front of Chloe and it makes my heart swell when he looks directly into her sightless eyes without flinching. There is a reason Hades is my favourite uncle, despite the fact he has been so blind when it comes to his wife. He doesn't sugar coat anything or waste time either, which both Chloe and I appreciate.

"Hellhounds are formidable protectors, Chloe, but unless you can master this fear of yours this pup will only be a hindrance to you. To be quite honest, I can't believe you haven't addressed this already." *Was* my favourite uncle. I move forward with a growl but Chloe laughs, stopping me in my tracks.

"And when was I supposed to practice this, Hades? In my apartment? The middle of Sydney Harbour? The Botanical Gardens? Circular Quay?" She snorts with her laughter, then quickly covers her face, mortified. Everyone else chuckles at her mortification and the tension eases.

"Fine. There wasn't an opportunity for you to do this earlier," he concedes. "We had best make the most of the one you have now."

"I thought that we could kill two birds with one stone this session." I move to take control of the situation, knowing either of my uncles will assert their authority at the first opportunity and their agenda could be very different to our own. "Once Hades can get Chloe comfortable with Bailey, I want Hephaistos to use his flames as he would in battle on the two of them." Chloe starts and a panicked look darts across her face before she masters it.

"Are you sure you want me to do that?" Hephaistos asks, picking up on Chloe's concern. "Are you not pushing for too much, too fast?" I hesitate before I share everything with them.

"I have used my mother's gift on her." Their silence speaks. The fact that Chloe is here and not a drooling mess like the assassin, speaks louder than words. My heart swells and I know I'll do anything to keep her safe. They know it too, both looking between us with intense satisfaction. "Love heals. You two should know that better than most." Both swallow, having had occasion to need Aphrodite's help in the past. My brother and I are not the only ones who miss her. Our gifts may not be as strong or as wide as hers, but this is the first time in my life that I am thankful for the double-edged sword she left me with.

"Well . . ." Hades coughs, breaking the tension. "I suppose that's my cue to get Bailey in defensive mode." He strides confidently across to Chloe and her hound. Bailey doesn't know which way to look so it is only moments before Hades locks him in place with his gaze. "Are you ready, Chloe?" he asks, eyes never leaving Bailey's, the latter having dropped to the ground of the practice yard, whining in submission.

She nods in determination, settling her feet in a firm stance. I notice her muscles lock up but decide not to say anything. She is not one of my warrior brethren and doesn't need a lecture about fighting form when she is struggling with her own nightmares.

Bailey is a few paces in front of Chloe when something alerts him that Hades is not playing anymore. Immediately the hellhound triples in size, green flames rippling down his back as he snarls menacingly at his former master.

"Okay, Chloe, Hades is going to back him towards you slowly. I want you to feel the heat coming off him, focussing on the fact that it is impossible for it to hurt you." She nods, but already sweat breaks out on her forehead as she fights her instinctive need to flee. "He's your hound, Chloe," I continue as Bailey slowly backs towards her, keeping himself between his mistress and a circling Hades. "He would never hurt you. Reach out to him, feel his heat for yourself."

Chloe's hands tremble as she makes contact with Bailey's head. She flinches, but I sense the moment she registers both logically and instinctively that while the hound is hot, her hands where she touches him are not burned, nor the heat more than she can handle.

The moment her mind relaxes fully I nod to Hades who backs away. Bailey remains vigilant as Chloe strokes him with more confidence. The green flames twirl happily around her hands and forearms yet all she feels is heat and comfort. I exhale, preparing for part two of my plan.

"Do you think you are ready for Hephaistos, Chloe?" I can feel her readiness but the other two can't, so she'll have to say something to reassure them. She's so pleased with her progress with Bailey, I have to give her a mental nudge to speak.

"I trust you." She sends a wave of affection my way. "All of you." Her sightless gaze turns unerringly towards the other two men and I know she has overcome her fear so well that she is even able to focus on using Bailey's eyes. I'm so proud of her, all I want to do is take her back to our cabin so I can show her exactly how wonderful she is but if we don't do this now, we won't have another chance before the battle. I take a breath.

"Bailey can run interference between you and fire. His skin is flame retardant, even brimstone will not harm him," I say before I gesture Hades to continue.

"He is also one of Cerberus' pups," he picks up. "Something others are not aware of with those particular beasts is that they can extend a flame retardant shield metres from their skin, but only if they are extremely alert." He moves closer to Bailey again who reacts with a warning growl and even stronger flames. Chloe doesn't flinch. "Theoretically, his shield should be able to extend to include you as well."

At this Hephaistos steps forward. This is the part I am most nervous about, though I try and wall my fears away from Chloe. She frowns a little in confusion buts shakes out of it quickly, focusing on what is happening in front of her.

"Hephaistos, I want you to throw flames towards Chloe." She blanches so I hurry on with my explanation. "Just in front of Bailey to begin with, then as he starts to implement a shield, throw them closer to Chloe." She is clutching the ruff of Bailey's neck in a death grip and his attention shifts in my direction, a snarl quickly following.

I turn to Hephaistos and look him in the eye, willing him to understand the seriousness of what I'm saying. I'm not sure how much precision work he has done with his flames in the last few years but I'm hoping he hasn't let the skill fall by the wayside. He smiles confidently then turns to reassure Chloe.

"Don't worry, little Seer." His voice is a deep baritone that soothes even me. A small spike of jealousy runs through me when I think about its possible effects on Chloe, but I shake myself out of it. I should be beyond this now. "This is something I do every day. If at any time it looks like your hound will not be able to form or maintain the shield, I have more than enough control to swallow the flame before it hits you." She breathes an audible sigh of relief but her grip on Bailey's neck doesn't loosen. At least we know she is over her fear of *him*.

Hephaistos gives no warning as tightly controlled flames sizzle from his hands to land directly in front of Bailey's enormous paws. The mutt snarls but immediately a shimmering green shield of fire licks around both him and Chloe.

Hades' eyebrow quirks upwards in surprise. "I haven't seen any of the hellhounds since Cerberus move automatically to protect their master like that, first time." His tone is speculative. "I may need to send some females to visit you in a decade or so, Chloe. His is a bloodline I don't think I want to lose." She grins through the flames, the sickly green giving her features an impish cast.

"I don't think Bailey will mind that too much." She laughs.

Hephaistos takes advantage of her distraction to hurl larger balls of flames directly at Bailey. They fizz out with a tiny sizzle as they come into contact with the shield. Bailey is in his element, tongue lolling as if laughing at the Immortal's efforts. Narrowing his eyes Hephaistos launches a deadly barrage directly at Chloe. The hound stiffens then, as the last of the balls shimmer to green, stalks menacingly towards the former God. The threat to his mistress was this time too great to ignore.

"What's the hold up?" Chloe pipes up, her casual tone causing Bailey's ears to twitch in her direction. "Have you tested his shield on me yet?" The hound sits still, confusion growing as the three men laugh. Chloe's anger starts to build as it always does when she thinks someone is laughing at her.

"Well? Hurry up I haven't got all day!" she snarls at us. Swallowing more laughter—which neither Hephaistos nor Hades even try to do—I move towards her and wrap her protectively in my arms.

"Your hound is amazing, Princess," I say as I squeeze her in reassurance. "Hephaistos just did his level best to burn you to a cinder and all he got for his troubles was a supremely annoyed hellhound stalking him." Her own mood lightens, a chuckle escaping at the visual I send her. "And if you hadn't disconnected from Bailey so early you would have seen it yourself." She blushes a little so I know I've guessed correctly that she disengaged so she wouldn't have to see the flames coming.

"All right," she says, grumpy again. Luckily her grumpy is adorable. "I suppose I deserve that little dig. Shall we practice some more?" There's my girl. My chest swells near to bursting with pride for her, but I hold myself in check. We have work to do.

"All right," I nod at Hephaistos.

"Let's do this again shall we, hound?" And with that Hephaistos lets loose with a stream of fire that would melt a hole in a boulder.

Together Chloe and Bailey stand firm, unwavering in the face of danger.

My heart lightens a little in relief.

One worry down, one hundred more to deal with before we leave. Hopefully, our best will be enough.

CHAPTER SIXTEEN

Chloe

CLYMENE ARRIVES AS THE sun sets. Boss and the other tacticians are discussing details. I need time to get my head straight. One moment I'm alone on my veranda, Bailey snoring at my feet after his big day, the next a silent presence fills my space.

She's not what I expect of a Titaness, particularly one whose husband was the God of Mortality. The term Titan's misleading—they look just like us, only their base powers are cataclysmic. Clymene hides her power well, but it's still easy to sense it roiling under her skin. Her nerves have her defences fluctuating.

Nervous myself, I attempt to send a calming thread towards her. At first, she flinches away, both mind and body, but when I hover expectantly just before her barriers, she parts them gently to let me in. Her mind's a mess, a writhing pit of dark snakes that bite at unwary thoughts. I shudder, eager to pull away but knowing she needs both my calm and an understanding of my perspective. I open myself to her in turn.

"I know why you've hidden away from life, Clymene," I say as gently as possible. Bailey's whispery huffs are the only sound filling the void. "I don't blame you. Are you sure you're ready for this?" She doesn't answer.

We sit in silence for an eternity, my mind stroking hers, calming the beasts. There's a tranquillity in our space that defies boundaries, knowledge of time or place. There's only us, and the healing of a friendship freely offered.

At first, her past comes to me in snapshots, picture windows that I can't make sense of. Her existence spans an eternity, too great for a child like me to comprehend. But then she settles on the one thing that can show me his weakness.

The moon is full in the sky as Iapetus stalks within touching distance. He reaches for her, but she flinches. As does he.

"You should go, Iapetus. There is nothing here for you anymore."

"You cannot say that, Clymene. We are wed. You always have and always will be mine."

She wrenches her gaze from the sea, turning to face him directly.

"No-one can belong to another. I may be weaker than you and our brothers, but I will no longer suffer for your ambition. Or fear."

"Ambition?!" he scoffs. "It is not ambition, but might, which sees us dominate the known world. We are Gods!"

"And yet you, who are Death, cannot father children. Our brother, strongest of us, is so terrified of his own children that he imprisons them at birth. You all want to continue our line, but your overwhelming ambition leads you to farm out your wives to Kronos in the hope that children of that union will increase your power, when ours does not."

"And what is wrong with that? What is wrong with wanting to consolidate our power?"

Her heart is in her eyes as she answers him. "That you do not know the answer to that is why you are no longer the man I loved." With those words, she thrusts every image of her time with Kronos into his mind.

The day Iapetus sent her away, even though she begged to stay with him forever.

Her first night in Kronos hall, when he made his wife Rhea watch as he raped her on the banquet table.

The second night, and all subsequent nights when he passed her around their other brothers until Hyperion was forced to heal her with his light, before they could continue with their fun.

Her joy when she found she was carrying a child, not because she wanted to be a mother, but because it would finally allow her to escape.

Her despair when Kronos found out she was pregnant and because he could not determine the father, ripped the child from her womb so he could continue his fun.

Tears drip down Iapetus' face. "You were with child?" Her face was stony.

"I was." Her toneless voice was an echo of the emptiness within. "As you would have known if you cared. If you hadn't been so self-righteous that you left me with a monster."

His mouth opens and closes, fishlike, but he can't find the right words. "But why would he do that? The purpose of you being with him was to further our line?"

She laughs in his face.

"For all your years you are a child still." She starts walking towards the cliff face.

"Why are you walking away? Clymene?"

"Our lives were about trust, Iapetus. Where has that gone?"

"I do not know what you are talking about, Clymene. Of course, I still trust you."

"But you have shattered my trust in you." Still staring at him she backs toward the edge of the cliff. He takes wary steps forward, trying to anticipate her next move.

"Tell me what you want, wife. Whatever you need, I will get it, to have you back by my side."

"Too little, too late husband," she spits at him. "You have destroyed us. Wait until you see what is to come." With that, he lunges at her, but Clymene has already launched herself from the cliff, triumph in her eyes.

"How did you survive?" I don't know if I deserve the answer, but something tells me she needs to get it out.

"The fall? Or the despair?" Her voice is rusty with disuse, barely more than a whisper across my sensitive ears.

"Both? Whichever you want to tell me about?"

"I am of the water. It embraced me, cocooned me until I felt safe to rise. I rode out the Titanomachy in the depths of the sea, deaf and blind." Her thoughts are watery, relaxed.

"When I rose, they were imprisoned. Only the women remained."

"I can't say I'm sorry about that," I say, and she laughs ruefully.

"No, I was not sorry about it either, though some of the others were until they shared my memories. And Rhea's." It goes without saying that the other Titanesses needed confirmation. Could I believe someone who told me these things about Boss? No, but we are too intertwined to be objective. "In regards to my soul . . . well, I would not be exaggerating if I told you its destruction took less than a year, but a million lifetimes to put back into some semblance of order."

"We move against Iapetus tomorrow," I say quietly. "Are you going to be okay with that?" She knows what I mean. Clymene loved him once, and now we're bent on his destruction.

"If he has not learned in all these years confined, then he will never learn." There's a hardness to her that defies her fractured soul. "A rabid dog must be put out of its misery."

★ ★ ★

DINNER'S A SOBERING AFFAIR. Clymene sits rigidly on my left, Boss on my right. Bailey's wormed his way under the table, letting everyone know in no uncertain terms he's there, eager to dispose of their garbage. There are no more plans left to initiate, just a final meal in the company of friends. Calliope's directly across from me, being the one who found Clymene and brought her here, and I find I'm actually happy to have her with us.

"You look well, Chloe, despite the circumstances." Her voice is, as always, gentle and kind. "Things are looking up in your world."

"Now we just have to get through this battle." I'm terrified. If there was some way I could force my gift to see the result of this skirmish I would, yet every time I look, I draw a blank.

Though generally their own futures are hidden from a Seer, I should've been able to sense something about the other two attacks. I spent the afternoon pouring over Apollo's book, desperate to find a hidden gem to help us. To understand why everyone's future is clouded. The only answer it gave me was terrifying—uncertain futures are black. The outcome hasn't been decided yet.

I'm scared shitless.

"We will prevail, Chloe," she says. I want to believe her. "We will prevail because to do otherwise would mean the end of us all."

"Sometimes I wonder if that would be such a bad thing." Hephaistos' voice shocks me to my core. "Think about it, Chloe. Think of all the pain our kind has caused humankind." He isn't wrong. "The only reason I am not fighting for the other side," he says, "is that I know they would do worse."

"Surely you don't believe that?" I'm horrified.

He sighs heavily. "No. You are right. But it is often hard to see the good through the bad."

He's breaking my heart. I send all my joy towards him. Not surprisingly, Boss joins me sending him happiness. After Hephaistos' mind starts to glow with contentment, we move on to the others, each in turn. Deep down, I believe it's up to us to show that there *is* something worth fighting for. That *we* are worth fighting for. I link with Boss to slip behind his eyes. All I want in these last few moments together is to see the faces of those I've come to care for.

Aeden slides a seat between Calli and me. What is it with Warriors and their cockiness?

"Cheer up, Chloe," he says, spooning mounds of food onto his plate. How can he sit there cheerfully eating? My stomach turns at the thought of food, but I force myself to eat. "We've never lost a battle yet, and this time we have the big guns on our side."

"It's the big*ger* guns on theirs I'm worried about." The dry words tumble from my mouth.

Aeden grins around a mouthful of food. He's at least a hundred years older than me but he feels like a younger brother. Acts like one too.

Ares smacks him round the back of the head.

I cough.

"Tomorrow we'll go our separate ways for a time, to an uncertain future." My voice seems to be stuck in my throat. I blink back tears, forcing myself to go on. "There are so many things that could go wrong . . ." Again, I've got to stop. I never used to be an emotional mess, but tonight I'm lost.

"But what a future it will be if we prevail!" I'm so grateful to Calli for taking over, I sink back into my seat in relief. She continues, doing what she does best—inspiring. I tune out, grateful to Boss for lending me his eyes. Being unable to see your loved ones is the ultimate curse of blindness. I thank my lucky stars I have an avenue to borrow someone else's eyes for a time. Others aren't so blessed.

The hall's full. Not just our table, but the many around it. Boss takes it all in slowly, catering to my whims. There's so many of Caleb's family here I think they could open their own international 'airline'. They fill the majority of the tables and I can only be grateful that Hermes and his sons were so prolific. It's a strong possibility they'll tip the tide of battle in our favour.

There are other warriors of Ares line here, but fewer than I expected. Boss's thoughts give me the information I need on this account. Aside from Aeden and the few here, Ares didn't know who he could trust. It's heart-breaking he believes he can't trust anyone too close to his other son, Eros. The man's maliciousness didn't go unnoticed in the Council meeting.

A smattering of individuals from other lines are dotted around the room, but the absence of the Muses is achingly clear. Ligeia, too, is feeling the loss of her sisters. I turn my head in her direction and tip her a nod of understanding, despite the fact I don't know if I've judged my distances correctly and it might be a little off.

We both have a lot to fight for, and many to make suffer, though how much use I'll be in a battle's yet to be determined. I can't even see it to give forewarning.

"Stop with the sulking already, Chloe!" The Demon has risen his ugly head. "Your face will freeze that way. How will my brother cope?" Again, he's diffused the tension with his melodrama.

"Waking up to Chloe's pout would still be a thousand times better than waking up to your ugly mug on campaign has been." Everyone now laughs at Boss's good-natured rebuttal, before Demon turns serious.

"I like you like this, brother. It has been too long since I have seen you smile." He focusses with determination on the two of us. "We'll just have to make sure nothing happens to change that."

"Believe me," says Boss. "There will be no future that does not include us in it." He rubs absently at his bracelet. "I'll not allow it."

Arrogant man. So much confidence, it buoys my heart.

I rise, Bailey startling and bumping his enormous head on the table. Glasses tip, food splatters and more laughter follow. I smile. *This* is the note I want to leave on. Disengaging from Boss and slipping in behind Bailey's eyes, I make my way back to my hut. Boss makes a move to come with me but I silently urge him to stay a while longer with his family.

Me, I have a date with a book.

Surely there's something within it that will turn the tide. For the good of an entire planet, I have to try.

The consequence of failure is too grim to contemplate.

CHAPTER SEVENTEEN

Chloe

THE MORNING DAWNS CRISP and clear. Mist floats through the trees as the sun kisses its tendrils. I disengage from Bailey, allowing him to enjoy his morning run in peace as I roll out of bed to face what comes. A beautiful day to die.

Boss and I dress in silence, each lost in our own thoughts, our bond a distant throb that brings the comfort of love. Every time we cross paths, we touch. A whisper of skin, a brush of lips across a bare shoulder. The closeness necessary.

I'm terrified.

Despite the fact that Phobos has survived hundreds of battles, the fear of losing him is very real. He hasn't had to fight a Titan before. And I haven't had to fight anyone. Tartarus' monsters don't count. Then there's the possibility that I'll have to kill someone I know, someone I've broken bread with.

Finally ready, we curl together on the porch swing, letting the first rays of daylight warm the chill in soul and skin.

"I will not let them get to you, Chloe, no matter what." Boss's voice pierces the silence.

"You can't promise that." He doesn't say anything, but I sense his disagreement anyway. I sigh. "The best we can do is look out for each other. I've been looking through Apollo's book." I hesitate, unsure of whether I should share. Eventually, I continue, "I'm going to try something, similar to what happened when we rescued Ligeia." His alarm's clear. I was an exhausted wreck after that.

"You can't do that again, Chloe. You nearly crippled yourself in the middle of a battle."

"I won't be doing it in the middle of a battle," I say, quietly urging him to understand. "From what Apollo says, I should be able to incapacitate a whole army, if only for a short period of time. It will require precision, but I've become very good at weaving fine threads."

"Chloe, if you expend that much energy you'll be out almost instantly." He's worried, but I'm sure he sees the possibilities.

"If I can do this, it's over for them in an instant. Her army incapacitated, everyone else will be free to decimate them while you deal with Persephone."

"Which would require leaving you alone. Unprotected." I feel the insistent shake of his head. "I won't do it."

"You're going to have to trust in our allies. This needs to be done, Boss. I'm not sure we can win with brute force alone, particularly without Ligeia and Hades." He knows I'm right, but his own fear of losing me is getting in the way of his tactician's brain.

"I don't know if I can, Chloe." His voice is strained.

"You can and you will." I burrow further into him, soaking up his strength and comfort as he wraps his arms around me. He doesn't say anything further, but I know I've won.

Soon the sun's high in the sky and we make our way towards the Communal Hall, Bailey once again my guide and eyes, to meet for the final time with the others. Boss and Demon embrace, that stupid man-hug that's closed fisted and back thumping.

None of us know who'll survive the coming battle. I weave threads through the minds of all our friends and family, memorising their unique signatures, hoping that each will make it back to me. The reality of war's that I know some will not.

Bailey presses into my hip, sensing the atmosphere and for once serious himself. I ruffle his fur, grateful for his affection. Little licks of flame caress my skin, but they don't burn, and I find that my earlier terror has vanished. Bailey would never hurt me, and this extends to the effects of his gifts too.

Finally, our time has come.

"Deimos, wait until I signal you to commence your attack," Ares says. He's every inch the commander, supremely confident, armour shining golden. "Caleb, can you and your brethren build your gateways to our launching points?"

Caleb grins, rallying his family to open the two initial gates. By doing it together they conserve energy, leaving enough for Deimos' operation.

I follow Boss, one hand on Bailey's back as together we leap through the void into the unknown. Bailey sticks close to my side as we arrive in a lush jungle. Both of the entrances to the Underworld are located on unpopulated islands, which is convenient for us. Instinctively, Bailey and I move for shelter as Boss directs his troops to meld into the greenery. Aeden grins as he passes, sliding a hand along Bailey's back. Almost instantly there are only snatches of fabric visible behind foliage.

Ares follows with the rest of the troops and Hephaistos, a hulking black shadow with his myriad of weapons strapped along his body. It's like a wave of black foaming from the hole Caleb has opened in the fabric of the universe. Our small team blends seamlessly with the environment. Ares' men just wash over it. Then it closes, all those of Hermes line on the other side.

From my vantage point in Ares' mind, I can hear his communication with Deimos. I didn't realise they were so close, but then again, I shouldn't be surprised.

Time for you to leave, Deimos. Fight well. His words are brief and pithy, but I can feel the respect that flows between the two, noticeable now that the twins are no longer keeping secrets.

Stay safe, brother. Boss sends as well.

I'm not the one who needs to stay safe—you had better come through this unscathed or the snoop in this conversation will pull you through hell. Literally. I laugh internally as they all withdraw into their own minds, amazed again at the twins' ability to detect me in their thoughts when others can't.

My stomach's twisting as we make our way through the undergrowth towards a cave, hidden until now. The men fan out around it, weapons of all ages at the ready. The first two disappear into the blackness momentarily, before returning and signalling the others to follow. They move forward in twos as we begin our descent into hell.

Grateful for the comfort of Bailey beside me, Hephaistos behind and Boss in front, we move with stealth and speed towards the Grove of Persephone. I walk hesitantly with one hand against the cave wall, nearly blind anyway, so I disengage from Bailey and let my senses wander. Hades, Ligeia and Clymene's group have entered through the Gates of Horn and Ivory, drawing the Titan to them. Calli's with them, and I'm grateful to whoever arranged that. If she was here, it would only be one more person I loved to look out for.

Yes, I'll admit I love her, even if she is manipulative.

Persephone's Grove is on the opposite side of the Underworld, near the Ocean Gate. This means we bypass many of the defence systems of the Underworld, but need to get through the grove, where Persephone's strongest, and try to cut her off before she reaches it.

It'll be close, and it'll mean we're stationed between Persephone and Tartarus, stocked with further allies for her, but it's the best plan we could come up with. The air becomes warmer as we move forward and the smell of saltwater seems to waft gently towards us.

"We have hit Oceanus," says Boss.

"We don't need to cross it, do we? Because I'm pretty sure you left that big boat at home."

He chuckles. "No, Princess. We will exit just on the shore. Then we must move to the Grove of Persephone." He shudders.

"Why is that such a problem?" I ask. "Surely you've seen a bunch of trees before?"

"The grove is dead, Chloe."

"Dead?"

"Yes, everything in the grove is dead. The blackened trees bear dead fruit that is rotten to the touch. Nothing living survives there. It is said to be a reflection of Persephone's womb. Barren." I wince. No wonder Persephone's messed up, if this is what she's faced with every day, a reminder of what she'd see as her own inadequacies.

"Then why are we worried, if nothing lives there? Why so silent?"

"Just because nothing *lives* there, doesn't mean there aren't dangers that move."

At that moment the atmosphere changes. No longer are we trudging through sand with the sound and scent of the sea surrounding us. Instead, our feet seem to sink, with us having to pull harder to remove them with each step. The landscape itself is hungry—and oppressive. The air's damp and heavy, seemingly solid fingers of it slide down my back.

I don't know if I want to use someone's eyes, but when a shout rings out from my left, I bite the bullet and join with Bailey. The hound's growling, looking into the black forest that surrounds us to where one of Ares men has just disappeared.

"Where has Ian gone? Phobos, did you see?" Ares is flustered. That freaks me out more than anything.

"The forest swallowed him." There's real fear in Boss's voice, so I cling tighter to the scruff of Bailey's neck. The hound's staring at a spot where thick, roiling fog inches towards us. The place where I'm assuming the man named Ian disappeared. Suddenly Bailey lets out a threatening bark and the forest erupts. Figures clad in filthy rags leap at us out of the darkness.

"Is this Persephone's army?" I shout to be heard over the cacophony.

"No," Boss replies as he swings his sword casually through the neck of his assailant. "This is the army of the damned. Not dead, yet not alive, they survive in this twilight zone alone." He continues to slash his way through the horrors who look so much like men, taking heads as easily as if he was cutting wheat. Hephaistos' fireballs are unerringly accurate as the man silently dispatches enemies with ease.

"What can I do?" I feel totally useless. Everyone else is fighting, even Bailey's an enormous flaming death machine and here I stand, twiddling my thumbs while others fall around me.

"Save yourself for when we actually meet Persephone," yells Ares, currently splattered with a thick black mucous, slightly thicker in consistency than blood. "This is a skirmish, nothing more. Your talents will be needed later."

Ares' forces dispatch the undead with brutal efficiency, though between the tangible fog they have created and their own fangs and claws, the undead have managed to steal some of our number away. I don't think they'll be coming back.

The fog's receded along with the undead, leaving a clear path through what should have been a neat orchard. Instead, blackened limbs and gnarled roots litter the ground, bulging through tortured, barren earth. The trees themselves almost seem alive, actively seeking our downfall. Still we trudge on, gaining speed as we realise our attackers aren't coming back.

The abrupt end of the grove leaves us all shocked. We stand between the River Lethe, which borders the Land of Dreams, and the entrance to the Gates of Hell—Tartarus. I take a deep breath and disengage from Bailey, sending my mind flying over the landscape.

There's nothing alive behind us, which is unsurprising given the denizens of the grove. The flickers of life in the land of dreams are insubstantial, mere ghosts of what a real mind feels like. These are the sleepers, and they're no threat. But around Tartarus . . .

Minds glow like bonfires in the night, terrifying in their numbers. Though intellectually I know that our strength isn't in numbers but talent, the fear eats at me as I compare the thousands of hostile minds to our bare two hundred.

"Umm . . . I don't mean to be a doubting Delilah, but are you sure our numbers will hold up against what's waiting?" I ask after I've fed them the information they require.

Ares laughs with genuine humour. I almost relax. "Unless that is a force of Titans, Chloe, no number of lesser immortals will be able to match us."

"Don't speak so soon," I say, sensing a stronger life force than the others. "It may not all be Titans, but unless Iapetus hasn't fallen for the Clymene bait, another of the Titans is here with Persephone." *Her* mind signature's very clear. The chaos of it's indescribable. I've no idea how it didn't leak through when we first met, but perhaps I was a little distracted at the time. "And their forces are converging on our location."

Boss moves protectively to my side.

"Do you have any idea what types of troops they have, Chloe?"

I focus back down my threads, building stronger links with the individual troops, enough so I can start invading minds. Sweat breaks out on the unscarred parts of my forehead—nerves, not strain—and I brush loose hairs back behind my ears. "Give me a minute . . ." I search amongst the many for the few who'll become a problem. "Most are small denizens of Tartarus, but there are a few worrisome ones."

"Who should we be targeting?" demands Ares.

"Two of the three Furies are there."

"Tisiphone?" Boss asks, shocked.

"No, the other two, I think. Alecto and Megaera." He lets out a sigh of relief.

"Good. They don't have Tisiphone's strength. Unfortunately, they also do not have her sense of honour." Boss's words ensure my heart rate increases dramatically.

"Tisi was guarding the gate. Where is she now?" Hephaistos sounds worried so I search but come up blind.

"I can't give you an answer to that. She isn't within my range, but that doesn't mean she's been eliminated."

"What about the Hecatoncheires?" asks Ares. This is probably the most alarming. The Hecatoncheires, or Hundred Handers, are the three older brothers of the Titans. Their strength's legendary, as they're the beings who helped keep their siblings imprisoned for millennia. With impenetrable skin and unfathomable strength, they'll be virtually impossible to defeat.

"One. There's one there." I'm both relieved and devastated by this news. The Hundred Handers are nightmares told to naughty children of Immortals to keep them in line. One hundred hands and fifty heads are terrifying to anyone, let alone a child. "Gyges, I think."

"Okay, so a Fury, a Hundred Hander, Persephone and which Titan do you think is with them?" Ares asks.

"A female!" I've managed to tap into the minds of those around her but the Titaness is a blank on my radar, shining golden but as inaccessible as the sun. "Mnemosyne, is what I gather from the minds of those around her. Her walls are too strong for me to breach."

"Isn't Mnemosyne the Goddess of Memory? That could be problematic." Hephaistos' thoughts are running a hundred miles an hour but most focus on the individual weaknesses of our enemies.

"Too late to back out now." Ares' thoughts are frenetic, excited, and so complicated I'm lost in his strategies. He comes up with and discards one after another until he's finally left with me. "Chloe, we have no choice but to use you at the start. With so many strong adversaries, we will need to be rid of the weakest quickly. Do you think you can take out the foot soldiers?"

"I'm pretty sure I can put them to sleep, but I'm not sure how long for," I offer. "That is assuming Mnemosyne doesn't have something she can counter my little tricks with. Putting them to sleep will require time and concentration."

"Chloe . . ." Boss's reluctance to speak hits me hard, so I jump into his mind before he can continue. What I see there devastates me. Gasping, I pull myself away.

"I can't! Can't do that!" My breath's coming in short snatches. My stomach's about to void, but I can't lose face in front of the troops.

"I'm sorry, Princess. We know you can do it on instinct, you showed us that when we rescued Ligeia. Now we need you to do it with purpose."

"But I don't want to kill *anyone* . . . let alone that many . . ." My gut clenches and I turn to the side just as the entire contents of my stomach make a sudden reappearance.

They may only be denizens of Tartarus, but they have lives, hopes and dreams of their own. Even if they are a little dark and twisted. Granted, Persephone has obviously been feeding them so many stories that they're now totally brainwashed, but did that mean they had to die?

"It is them or us, Princess." The reluctance in Boss's tone can't be feigned and it relieves me that he doesn't take this lightly.

The same can't be said about his father. "Hurry, Chloe, we don't have time for your feminine sensibilities." Boss takes this hard, but his words only serve to anger me.

"Feminine sensibilities??" The low growl of words that escapes my mouth surprises me. It shouldn't though. Ares has pushed too far in the short time I've known him. "Caring about lives lost is a feminine luxury now, huh?" I laugh mockingly at him, even as I weave deadly threads in Persephone's force's minds. "So glad I came out with an extra X instead of a Y chromosome, otherwise I'd be a heartless bastard like you, Ares."

I ignore his answer in favour of tying the last knots in my deadly net. Shining before me in my mind, the threads reach as far as I can see, interlacing at so many different points that I've lost track of my handiwork. The speed at which I've accomplished this is astounding and more than a little frightening. One tug on any thread and thousands of lights will burn out.

Taking a deep breath, I reach gingerly to Boss. Wouldn't want to accidentally get him caught in my net. *It's done. Let me know when you want me to become a mass murderer.*

Don't, Chloe. You know this isn't what I want. Unfortunately . . .

Yes, Boss, I know. I say bitterly. *Doesn't mean I have to like you right now. Go play chess with people's lives with your dad. I'm sure there's much you need to discuss while I steel myself to do this.*

I block him out, despite his repeated hammering on my inner walls. Eventually, he gives up, leaving me alone in my misery while the two of them organise their troops. The tension's building in my head, making me feel reckless, giddy with power. It's as if the energy from all the minds I'm attached to is slowly draining into me. Sickeningly, the power I'm gaining from their minds is desperate for an outlet.

Their own energy's about to become their undoing.

No wonder people feared the Seers, though there was no mention of this power siphoning in Apollo's book. Did he leave it out deliberately or did he just not know? I suspect the latter, and that gives me little comfort. I'm even more of a freak than my forefather.

A brush of Boss's mind against mine lets me know it's time. Both Bailey and Phobos join me, standing staunchly by my side, and despite my fear and rage, I am grateful to both. I don't know if I can do this without support. Aeden joins them, light-hearted despite the situation. Probably a truer son of Ares than either of the twins.

"We will start our attack the instant the troops drop." Ares voice grates, but I force myself to listen.

"You should be aware that I won't be able to handle any of the challenging ones myself. I'm stretched thin as it is." I don't share with them that given an hour or so, the build in power would be enough to take at least one out as well. We don't have an hour. And I'm not about to share the extent of my skills with someone who'll be quite happy to use them to his own advantage.

"That's fine, Chloe, you worry about the foot soldiers. Leave the generals to us." I almost add him to my web, almost weave a thread through his condescending mind, but at the last instant, remember he's needed.

The power building inside my brain's electrifying my body. Riding me hard to do something I know I'm going to regret, but that remains a necessity. Taking a deep breath, I take hold of an imaginary thread and pull.

The thud of two thousand bodies hitting the ground heralds the unravelling of this tapestry of life. All lights in my mind wink out before the backlash of energy brings me to my knees.

I know nothing but blackness anyway, but the lack of mind light in the darkness when a moment before there was a city of them, throws my mind into an abyss.

I'm a murderer.

A murderer.

Red stains my hands and I'll never get it off my skin.

Out of my mind.

CHAPTER EIGHTEEN

Chloe

DESPAIR HAS ITS OWN shape and form. Words wash around me, but nothing seems to infiltrate the dense black cloud for more than a minute. I'm floating in eternal blackness, listening to my own silent screams, though I know there's still a battle raging around me.

"I can't leave her like this! She's—"

"You must! Persephone has drawn too many . . ."

Their words float in the blackness, but I don't acknowledge them. I can't. Right now, my sightlessness is a blessing, the panic around me muffled by the fog. I know there's something I should be doing, but the actions escape me right now.

"Hephaistos has the Furies well in hand and Ares fights the Hundred Hander, but even he struggles. You must join them! I'll guard your lady!" That voice pierces the fog . . . One of Ares ilk . . . Aeden. Slowly, the fog's receding, though I wish it wouldn't. The clash of metal on metal intrudes into my floating world.

"Mnemosyne's decimating our men one by one! Paralysing them so they can't fight back. They can't stand against her!" Aeden's urgent pleas seem to be falling on deaf ears. Boss's indecision infiltrates my mind, along with an awareness I'm returning. I take a deep breath, just as a large snout snuffles into my face.

"Bailey!" I nearly choke on a mouthful of fur, but all is forgotten as Boss draws me into the comfort of his embrace.

"I had thought you lost in your darkness for good, Chloe." His mind frantically reaches for mine and I let him in, giving him the reassurance he desperately needs. I'm not broken. Not yet.

I don't know if I'm still lost or not, but at least I'm aware of what's happening around me.

"Why aren't you fighting?" The fog's threatening to return, but I push it insistently away.

"You needed me and—" Anger suddenly surfaces.

"You're not fighting because of me?" Sometimes I think men are truly idiots. "I'll be fine right here. I'll cast my nets out and call you if you're needed." Imperiously I wave him in the direction of the battle sounds. "Off you go!"

A dry chuckle comes from Aeden. No doubt the man relishes seeing Boss get put in his place. "This overgrown child can stay with me. Surely he's strong enough to keep little old me from finding trouble." My attempt at humour's pretty lame, but Aeden chuckles anyway.

Boss doesn't.

"Trouble always seems to find you, Princess." I try to smile but my mouth doesn't want to comply. My heart hurts. I thread my mind with Boss's, giving him a mental nudge in the right direction.

"Off you go. Aeden and I'll be fine here by ourselves."

Still he lingers. Fury starts to bubble inside me.

"If you don't go now, we are done." Panic strikes through the link. "Don't make my actions be in vain."

Boss hesitates briefly, but the rising tide of my anger sends him scurrying off towards the battle. Immediately I crumble.

"You aren't nearly as well as you led him to believe." I don't dignify Aeden's statement with an answer, just flop exhausted into the grass and send out my weak little feelers towards the battle. I've no bloody clue what's happening but at least I have a finger on the pulse. Bailey moves in closer, standing vigil on my left while Aeden hovers to my right. His desire to be in the thick of it hounds him, but loyalty to Boss keeps him here.

"Mnemosyne's becoming a problem, is she?" His fear for his family floods the tenuous bond, almost pushing me out. I'm much weaker than expected.

"She'll have all of them murdered without them raising a weapon! All it takes is her attention focussing on one, then . . ." His words send my heart into my stomach. The similarities between Mnemosyne and me are uncanny. The only difference is . . .

"One at a time, you say?" I feel his agreement. "Do you trust me, Aeden?"

He focusses on me for an eternity, long enough that I fear he won't hear me out. "I do. If Phobos trusts you, then so do I."

"I need you to lend me your strength." I'd read about this in Apollo's book but haven't had the chance to try it. Attempting this in the heat of a battle could be disastrous, but if Mnemosyne gets her hands on Ares or Boss, this will all be over in a hurry.

He takes a deep breath. "What do I need to do?" His fear's clear. It's deeply ingrained among the older generations to distrust Apollo's line but he does it, for his family.

"I need you to drop all walls. That's it for the moment." He does it immediately and I weave my threads in a series of knots around his mind. The strain's almost too much. Sweat pours down my face, over my brows and into my eyes. The sting gives me the shits. Surely eyes that can't see have no right to hurt so much! Finally, the last length is tied off and Aeden's mind becomes firmly attached to mine. I take a few deep breaths, willing calm even through the screams of the dying. I don't have time for weakness.

"Okay, now I want you to close your eyes. You should be able to visualise the rope from your mind to mine. The threads are focussed on the area of your third eye." I feel it the moment he finds the thread. Rather than being overwhelmed, he instinctively firms the connection, adding his own threads to mine.

"Now, inside you there's a well, the source of your power. I'm going to draw on the well. You need to tell me if you feel lightheaded," I warn. The danger of me draining too much is a very real possibility. "I'll be too focussed on the battle to be able to monitor you properly once I engage Mnemosyne."

"Are you sure you can do this, Apollo's Daughter?" His anxiety's high, but his resolve firms when he feels my certainty. "Fine. Let's begin."

I don't question him again, drawing directly on his strength as I fling one strong net out to find Mnemosyne. It doesn't take long. Her own web's out, searching for her next victim. Unfortunately, her attention's settled on Ares, who's just dispatched the Hundred Hander. She casts her net as mine finds her.

Ares sinks to his knees, oblivious to the battle raging around him. I send another of my webs his way, but can't penetrate her hold. Her laughter echoes in my mind

"Focus on the woman?" Aeden's growl is a wake-up call. Break Mnemosyne and we break her hold on Ares.

I throw our strength into my net wrapped around her mind. Arrogantly, she has no defences up, perhaps believing none can touch her. We sink inside, expanding our web as she comes to the realisation she's been compromised.

No! Her hiss echoes, a sibilant whisper designed to beguile. *You will not control me, Apollo's dirty secret!* Immediately she attacks the fibres we've been weaving, cutting down each one we craft. I struggle to retain my hold on Aeden's power as she pushes me backwards. He's not strong enough for this and we retreat inch by inch into my mind. I become aware of Aeden panting in exhaustion and fear just as her laugh echoes in my mind.

She's followed us back. Too weak to raise my shields, I scream as she rapes my memories, inserting her own in turn.

The imprisonment of brothers by ones who should have been family.

The ignominy of hiding among the humans.

The lies of those she considered sisters.

I fling back Clymene's memories at her but she laughs scornfully. *Yes, child, I see she has been feeding you her own tales. You seem to forget however that we are Titans, built to withstand, built to rule. Clymene was weak if she could not suffer in silence for our cause.* The horror of her statement hits me, and I drop to my knees.

The woman is deluded. What happened to Clymene isn't acceptable, no one should have to suffer—

She thrusts her own memories at me, not gently like her sister, but slamming them bodily into me. I crumble under the pressure of her brothers' hands and teeth. I'm ripped apart by their brutality. And through it all, I can feel the satisfaction she has that what they're doing will bring greatness, even as she rides the pain. Her smugness undoes me even as I retch, trying to empty an already void stomach.

Clymene was weak! And so are you if you think—

Light and strength flood me. Desperate, I latch onto Aeden's offering driving the bitch back to her own body and tugging desperately on all my threads. What's left there cuts through her mind like a scythe and she shrieks, her agony silencing a battlefield.

Ares is once again upright, my link with him flaring brighter as his fury sends him staggering to where Mnemosyne writhes in the dirt.

Abruptly, all strength leaves me.

As I'm thrown back into my body, I gradually become aware of the shallow breathing beside me. Aeden.

The thread between our minds has snapped. I can't feel him at all. Just hear the rattle as he struggles to breathe.

"Aeden?" My own breath comes in short pants as I desperately reach for where he struggles for breath. Bailey whines and nudges me, but I don't even have the energy to use his eyes.

"I'm . . . fine . . . Chloe." His tone belies his words. Pain saturates them. Finally, my hands find his and I latch on, trying to feed him my strength but the bridge is shattered beyond repair. It's then I comprehend what he's done.

"I told you to tell me. Not feed me more!" I'm crying, great gulping tears that threaten to consume me.

"It's done." I can almost feel his smile, but it just makes the tears torrential.

"It might have been necessary, but now I'm a murderer. Again."

"No," he breathes. "I've made us both saviours." A last gurgling breath leaves his body before he's still.

He may have turned the tide of this battle, but my heart's shattered. I don't ever want to experience this again. Bailey howls in the distance and for a moment I wonder what he's doing so far from my side.

Abruptly, unfamiliar arms circle my body, cloth covering my mouth. Someone drags me away from the battle as my mind's silenced.

CHAPTER NINETEEN

Phobos

A **BATTLEFIELD IS THE** ultimate drug of choice for those of my father's line, yet despite being typical of my family, running away from Chloe and towards the battle feels wrong. I am uneasy, but almost all of our enemies are still on the field, Persephone cackling insanely as she ruthlessly uses the plant life to swallow our soldiers. Killing both her and Mnemosyne will win us this battle but the latter is too far away at the moment for me to do anything about, so I lope towards Persephone, hoping to take her by surprise.

Those soldiers who have managed to avoid her traps are dispatched ruthlessly after she swirls dust in the air around them. The velocity of the particles is so extreme, it's like tiny knives stabbing into unsuspecting eyes. The blinded men are easy to kill, especially since she has all but exhausted them before they even reach her.

I break into a sprint to take advantage of her current distraction with one of my cousins, but it is over so quickly for him, she has turned in my direction before I'm even halfway to her.

"Here he comes!" She squeals in delight, her smile a rictus meant to charm but instead disturbing. "Finally, a challenge. Hello, Son of Ares. Come to see what it means to be destroyed by Spring?"

I don't answer, instead using all my agility to leap and twist away from the tree roots and plants she sends flying in my direction. None touch me, but then I am in range of her dust storm. I immediately close my eyes tightly, but the sand seems to have a mind of its own, desperately seeking a way under my eyelids. I screw them up tighter but that small lapse in concentration is all it takes for one of her roots to snare my foot and have me on the ground, inching towards its mistress even as I struggle to regain my feet.

With a roar, I slash behind me with my sword, the force of my strike freeing me from the accursed greenery. I won't make the same mistake again. Persephone cackles in glee, sending out more tendrils that swipe viciously at my face. The sting of open wounds is distracting but I smile. With her petty attack, she has given me the information I need to combat her plants while closing my eyes.

I relax, freeing my mind of everything but my sensitivity to motion and sound. There are advantages to being one of Ares line, on top of the strength, speed and stamina. The wind whispers with the movement of one of her vines so I shift sideways, throwing it off course and lashing out with my sword. The severed limb immediately retreats but another swiftly follows to be dealt with the same as the first.

My grin turns nasty as I make my way towards Persephone. I can smell her fear as I get closer, then abruptly the wind dies down as she turns and runs towards the grove. She won't get far.

My strides eat up the ground as she desperately throws half-hearted attacks of greenery in my direction, which I easily dodge. Harder by far to avoid are the crumbling pits that open up in front of me, often at the last minute, and the roots that follow trying to drag me down with them.

Eventually, Persephone is within range of my knives.

I let one fly and with a solid *thwunk,* it buries itself into her shoulder. Though she staggers she keeps her feet, knowing that gaining the safety of the grove will up her chances of survival significantly.

She doesn't have that long.

Another three of my knives follow the first, one in the other shoulder and one in each calf. She drops like a stone, writhing in agony as she waits for death to catch up. I don't make her wait for long.

"You should know by now, Goddess of Spring, that I *never* miss my mark," I say with a sneer. Kneeling beside her,

I drive another knife into her chest, just below her heart. She shrieks in agony, but the knife hasn't hit any vital organs, the intention being to cause maximum pain so she can't concentrate to use her powers. I need time to question her.

She spits in my face, trying to provoke me into killing her. With some of the younger ones, this may work but she forgets my brother and I are the oldest of Ares' line. We have more control over our emotions than any Immortal living.

"That wasn't nice, Persephone." The words are calm but my soul is screaming as I reach up to the knife in her shoulder. I twist it, digging it deeper into her flesh, grinding bone. A fresh wave of screams and curses rain on my head but I ignore them to begin asking questions. "Let's start with the all-important question—why?" I'm truly baffled by her actions and the Council will need as much information as they can if they are going to fix what she has wrought.

She laughs. Pain pinches her brow and colours her tone yet still she laughs. "You deserve it, Phobos," she cackles. "You all deserve it, every last one of you power-hungry asshole males who think you can manipulate people's lives." I'm confused. It must show on my face because she laughs again. "It won't hurt if I tell you now because the damage is done, my plan set in motion and there's nothing you can do to stop it."

She takes a deep breath and for the first time since the battle started, I see a trace of sanity fly across her face. It sobers her. "For years you have manipulated us to get what you want. And now I have broken the last seal on Tartarus, all of the Titans should have escaped." Her eyes narrow in hate. "You'll all finally get what you deserve, and I'll die knowing you will be coming with me."

"But Hades loves you. You have made this place together. Your power is second only to his in the Underworld. How could you turn on him, on the Council like that?"

"What?" She scoffs. "The Council who has forced me to live with a man I hated and pretend to be his dutiful little bride for most of my life? The husband who treats me like a figurine, incapable of doing any thinking for myself? The people who whisper behind my back about my empty womb?" Tears fall down her cheeks and I have to actively work to harden my heart against her. "You are all so arrogant. The Titans will give you what you deserve." She spits at me again. "The bloodlines have grown weak in that last thousand years. No-one will be able to stand up to them."

I sigh, turning around to the battlefield. Persephone isn't going anywhere, but her next words stop me short. "No-one, particularly once your little Seer has been eliminated." Her laughter echoes in my head as I frantically search the battlefield for Chloe. She is still on the hill where I left her, closer than I thought, but she is hunched on the ground, her pain echoing along our link, and Aeden is no longer at her side. As I watch she slumps over a body and I know in my heart it is my cousin.

Suddenly Bailey's ears prick and his body burns with those intense green flames as he flies towards me. I turn, knowing in that instant I will be too late to save myself, as will Bailey, but I'm determined to try anyway. The first rule of battle: Never turn your back on a live enemy, no matter how incapacitated they may seem. I watch in horror as a living wooden spear flies straight for my heart, the last attempt of Persephone to take out one of those she considers her tormenters, even though I have had nothing to do with her slavery.

In the last instant, I am shoved out of the way, sent flying off my feet. A horrific *thud* reverberates through the insane cackle of Persephone and I twist to my feet, my heart knowing what my mistake has cost.

Ares lies on the ground, a vine thicker than his fist embedded in his chest. Blood trickles from the corner of his mouth yet still he smiles. "Couldn't let her steal our hope now, could I?" The vine twists, burrowing deeper into him and my father lets out a pained groan, the only concession he will give to the agony he must be enduring. Anger roars to life within me and I leap to my feet, intent on ending that bitch now.

Only I'm not quick enough.

Bailey has arrived on the scene and without any ceremony, rips out the throat of the woman who has endangered his pack, then proceeds to tear her limb from limb. There is a savage, brutal efficiency about it, but in my bloodlust, I wish I could bring her back, to inflict on her all the pain she deserves.

A gasp from my father has me dropping to my knees again. With Persephone's death, the vine has shrivelled back into the earth again, leaving a gaping hole in Ares' chest that oozes blood. I don't know where to put my hands, where the pressure will be most effective, and for some reason, my vision is blurred. It's only when the tears start to roll down my cheeks that it sinks in. Ares draws a last breath.

A long, mournful howl from Bailey echoes, stopping all fighting in its tracks.

Another of the Olympians has fallen. There is no coming back from this. We cannot regenerate a heart, even with the help of Asclepius, and there is no-one of even close to his skill on the battlefield. No-one can cheat death.

I look at the carnage that surrounds me and my heart grows heavier within my chest. When will it end, the incessant fighting and petty squabbling? Hephaistos is still standing, having destroyed the Furies. Twelve of my cousins remain standing out of the hundred we brought with us. Mnemosyne's gift has left our forces devastated. It's with relief that I notice both her and the Hundred Hander's body being systematically carved up by the survivors.

Better to be safe than sorry.

I turn back to my father, crossing his arms symbolically across his chest and closing his eyes, but it's then it hits me.

The ridge where I left my heart is bare.

I can no longer feel Chloe's mind linked close to mine. There is so much distance between us, terror eats at me as I frantically leap to find Hephaistos.

The man himself is already at my side.

"Where is the little Seer?" Hephaistos growls, his protective streak almost as large as mine.

"She's gone!" I gasp, waving my wrist with Hephaistos cuff on it in his face. "How do I make this work? Tell me quickly! She's obviously in the midst of her vision and—"

"You have no transport!" He roars, picking me up by my body armour. "We are stuck here, with the ability to find her, but no way to follow." He shakes me like a rag doll then slams me to the ground. I let him. Nothing he can do or say to me is worse than what I'm saying to myself. "You left her alone. What kind of a Soulmate leaves his partner when danger surrounds?"

The kind who should be executed.

A large black gateway appears and Caleb steps out, followed by at least a dozen of his family and a few Sirens, wings of various hues flaring in an unseen wind. The latter look at the empty battlefield in disappointment, their leader turning abruptly to Caleb. "Send us to the other site. We will help our sister." Caleb nods and three of his brethren create a small gate to the other side of the Lethe. Hopefully, they will find the blood they are looking for there.

I grab Caleb and haul him unceremoniously to Hephaistos. "Okay. I have transport. Now, how does it work?"

Hephaistos doesn't waste any time. "Focus on Chloe through the band, not your link. See her in your third eye." I close my eyes, following his instructions as Hephaistos briefly fills a grim Caleb in.

"Got it. Now what?"

"Focus on connection and location. Firm that in your mind, then link with Caleb and share the information." She is a long way in the distance. I don't know if Caleb can manage on his own. He looks exhausted.

The man confirms it, calling over his cousins. Together they make a gateway.

"I will stay and secure the battlefield," Hephaistos says as I nod, leaping into the blackness with no idea who follows me.

I just hope I am not too late.

CHAPTER TWENTY

Chloe

THERE'S A POINT IN everyone's life where the past comes back to haunt them. Unfortunately for me, the opposite's true. The future's arrived.

Awareness comes slowly, making me fight through the fog to find it. My eyes want to stay shut and since they aren't necessary, I conserve my energy by leaving them as they are. Too exhausted to move, I take stock of my surroundings. The earthy scent of the forest surrounds me as I press my fingers into the dry leaves. Heart beating erratically in my chest, I recognise my situation for what it is—my vision has found me.

Breathing deeply, I try and harness enough energy to send out tendrils of my thoughts. It takes a number of goes, but eventually I manage it. Two minds, much closer than I expected. Hesitantly I weave my way through the trees, trying to find a safe place to hide. I've no energy left, so a fight's out of the question. Abruptly I find myself almost falling into a large bush.

The minds are getting closer so I duck down, scurrying as far under the shrub as I can then raking leaf litter over me. My heart pounds with the force of my terror, the rush of blood making my ears ring. I force myself to control my breathing and succeed. A voice rises from the left.

"She is close, brother. I can smell her fear." It's no one I recognise.

"Quiet. I can't hear anything with you chattering in my ears. You know she will end us if we fail." They're both silent for a little longer, but the first man can't maintain it.

"Do you think she was telling the truth, that we would be part of a new Council?"

"I think that she would tell us anything to get us to do this job. Fortunately, even without that reward, there is much in it for us." He lets out a short laugh that sends chills down my spine. "Can you imagine it? The opportunity to break a Seer after all this time? Without that bastard Apollo's help, they never would have beaten us."

I shudder. Titans are stalking me. Either them or their progeny born in Tartarus.

"Come out little Seer. Why delay the inevitable? You know we will find you eventually. You never know, you may like what we have in store for you . . ."

Terror floods my veins, bringing with it a short burst of energy. I use it wisely, flinging a desperate suggestion into their minds that they can hear their quarry further to their left. Furtive footsteps move away and I breathe out my relief. It won't fool them for long, but it may give me enough time to harvest some of the forest's life force. Surely plants are no different to Persephone's troops?

I lie still, knowing that if they hear even the slightest hint of movement they'll be back instantly. My mind reaches out to the life in the forest, as it did on the boat when we rescued Ligeia. The tendrils connect with each tree, each living thing around me, so I attempt to draw on their energy a little at a time. I don't want a repeat of what happened to Aeden to happen to an entire forest.

The energy slides into me, dripping into my depleted well agonisingly slowly. I'm only just starting to feel human when I hear them return.

"She must be back here somewhere. The trail is cold for miles the opposite way. Just like her thrice-cursed ancestor this one. He always had some trick up his sleeve."

More silence as they search methodically. It won't be long until they reach my hiding place. I attempt to draw energy faster but the forest moves at its own pace and I'm terrified of giving myself away.

"I still can't believe that she thinks to buy us with what is rightfully ours," the first speaker chuckles.

"She is nearly as mad as Persephone, though I think she has her own agenda that does not align with our own." The two are lost in their thoughts. "Kronos will deal with her when the time comes." I don't know who they're talking about, but it leaves a bitter taste in my mouth that there's another plotting with the Titans beside Persephone, even if they don't share the same goals.

They draw ever closer to my hiding place and it's at this point I know I'm going to die. The life I've managed to harvest from the forest isn't enough to be useful, only enough to give me the energy to run. Silent tears roll from my useless eyes as I wait for the inevitable.

The footsteps stop.

"Quiet. Do you hear that?" The jangle of armour seems to echo through the forest, lifting my heart.

"Fight or flight, brother?" They are silent with indecision until I see them realise what they are up against. There are more than one or two in this force, the vibrations of their footsteps reverberating through my cheek pressed desperately to the ground. I smile.

"Come," says the more dominant one. "She will not live long once Kronos is at full strength." They run, feet pounding in an unhurried rhythm until they are drowned out by the echo of the approaching army.

I hold still, just in case it's not the rescue I'm hoping for. A snuffling and an excited bark penetrate the bushes. Bailey snuffles around my face, my hair, slurping his enthusiasm along the way. I don't even have the heart to tell him off, I'm so happy he's here.

Abruptly I'm hauled from the ground and gathered into a bone-crushing embrace.

"Enough, Boss! I'm well, but any tighter and I won't be breathing much longer." He does let go, but only to run his hands over every inch of my body, checking for injuries he somehow thinks he can heal. Eventually, he relaxes, gathering me to him gently this time, burying his face in my hair.

"I thought I'd lost you!" His words are muffled, but no less emphatic. He brushes kisses along my brow, cheek, and finally lips. It's a gentle claiming, an affirmation that I'm alive and well. Unfortunately, it's also a claiming that's now been witnessed by a host of immortal warriors. Uneasy, I push Boss away from me, trying to gauge the reactions of those around us.

Many are his family, and I can feel the smug satisfaction ringing through them as if it's Ares own. They're pleased at this chance to further the power of their line. Others aren't so happy, particularly those who'd fought in the other battles but came to rescue me anyway.

I mark in my mind those who're very negative about this, resolving to keep them under close watch. The more ambivalent, I'll woo away from their fears and into an alliance with us. It'll be necessary that we all work together to secure the defeat of the Titans once again, only this time imprisonment's too gentle.

Turning back to Boss I ask, "How are you here? Hold on, where *is* here? And" —I know I'm babbling but I can't stop— "what happened on the battlefield? Did you get Persephone? What about the other missions? Did—"

He stops me once again with his lips. I melt, oblivious to the stares of those around us. Curling up into a contented ball in his arms, I relax finally.

"I suppose I can wait until we get back to have my questions answered." He laughs, but beneath his humour's a well of sadness so deep, I'm not sure I want to know the cause.

At that moment Caleb comes to my side and one of my questions is answered. Their mission must have been successful for him to be able to get all of these troops here . . . wherever here is.

"Thank the gods for Hephaistos, hey?" says Caleb, with a forced chuckle. "Without that little gift of yours, we would've had no hope of finding you." I'm stuck for words, my jaw flapping open like a fish.

Boss continues, "I think we're in America, somewhere. At least, I know we aren't in the tropics or Australia, judging by the vegetation." Boss's voice is low and soothing.

"I brought enough of my family with us that we can transport directly back to Koh Samui." Caleb's exhaustion rolls off him in waves. I'm almost surprised that I'm able to feel it, but the forest has fed me enough energy that my links with others seem to be firmly in place. I send out a wave of gratitude, to the forest and those in front who came to rescue me.

The forest sends back a wave of love so strong I'm surprised, but then again, I shouldn't be. The Titans themselves were destructive, and the earth has a long memory. The warriors in front relax after my sending, more inclined towards goodwill, and I thank my lucky stars they arrived in time.

"I guess I owe Hephaistos a bloody big present when we get back." I frown, puzzling over what I can do for him. "It may take me a while to find something suitably amazing though."

Caleb chuckles. "You know what makes everything better, Chloe?" His mind's on mischief and I know I don't want to hear what else he has to say.

"Enough, Caleb." I put my hands over my ears, much to everyone's amusement. "Take us home."

Caleb's cousins join together to make a gateway and one by one the warriors file through leaving Phobos, Caleb and me alone.

Just as the gate's about to close, a blackness closes in around us, terrifying in its malice. We've felt it before, in my apartment in Sydney. There doesn't seem to be any substance to it, but the echo of laughter threads through our minds.

It won't be long until I find you again, Apollo's daughter. And when I am at full strength you will beg me for mercy, as your forefather did those who stole his life. Boss slides me to the ground, the hiss of metal telling me he's drawn his sword. The voice laughs again. *My Olympian children have not come very far in all these millennia but you, little Seer.* His voice hardens. *You are too much like my prophetic son. I will be keeping an eye on you.*

The darkness and the voice fade leaving me with an anxious knot in my belly.

"Come, Chloe. Though the gate." Caleb's voice is falsely cheery.

"You heard Kronos, Chloe. He cannot touch you now." Boss's attempt at reassuring me falls flat.

"But what about in the future?"

"The future isn't written yet," he replies. "If it were, you would know it."

I breathe out a sigh of relief as Boss grabs my hand, leading me through the gateway.

At least we have some time to plan before the Father of the Gods moves to action.

The gates of Tartarus are open.

Kronos has been unleashed.

CHAPTER TWENTY-ONE

Chloe

IT'S A VERY SUBDUED group who reconnoitre at the villa in Koh Samui. Bailey's been glued to my side since we stepped through the gateway, terrified to lose me again, and Boss isn't much better. We've gathered in the communal hall to share our experiences and the information gleaned in this ordeal.

"Fortunately, Iapetus was so distracted by Clymene's presence that Ligeia had him hooked before he was even aware of what was happening." Calli's voice is sad and I realise it must be for Clymene. The two have a very solid bond. "Hades barely had to lift a finger to drain him."

"Yes, unfortunately, it wasn't very satisfying." Hades' thoughts are still black. The man can't fathom how he could have been so wrong about Persephone for so long.

"The arrival of the other two Hundred Handers was obviously challenging enough," Deimos says dryly. When Caleb and Deimos had arrived with the Sirens they'd rescued, they'd found Hades' forces nearly decimated. Ligeia was in full Siren battle mode, blood matted through her hair and wings and Calli was desperately trying to rally those troops still left. The fact that no other Titans were there reeks of a trial, a test to judge the extent of our capabilities.

One I think we failed.

"By the sound of it, I don't think we came off best in this little skirmish they organised," I say into the silence. "In fact, I think we were tested and came up wanting." There's a chorus of arguments from around the table but most tellingly, Boss and Demon are silent. They know I'm right.

"At least we managed to save the Muses and Sirens," Caleb retorts.

"And eradicated Persephone and Iapetus from the ranks of those against us," says Hephaistos. "Better that we don't have a viper in our midst, feeding information to our enemies."

Hades goes green at this, thinking about his own foolishness.

"But there's still one out there," I exclaim. It's at this point I realise I haven't shared with them the information I overheard from my would-be murderers. As I fill in the others Boss goes deathly silent. His grip on my wrist has become slightly painful, so I throw the feeling back into his mind. Startled, he immediately releases me, sending waves of regret down our bond. I squeeze his hand, letting him know all's forgiven.

"So, you are telling me that there is an unknown female Immortal helping the Titans?" Hephaistos asks, his anger poisoning his words. There's nothing he hates more than betrayal. Of any kind.

"And that it's possible they might have bred while trapped there?" Hades' disgust hits me with force. The denizens of Tartarus are more monstrous than the Titans, though not as powerful. "So rather than five to combat we could theoretically be facing an army."

"I do not think that will be the case." Clymene's quiet voice punctuates the tension. "The males of our species are notoriously almost impotent." I think back on the lore surrounding the Titans and realise she's right. For thousands of years there were so few of them they couldn't establish any real power base, even their children from 'lesser' species being few and far between.

A sigh of relief follows Clymene's assessment as everyone else puts together what I have. "What it does mean," I share, "is that we still have to be wary of everyone. Who knows which Immortal's allied with them?" I sense the agreement of everyone at the table.

"It means that we will have to find some way of measuring the truth of other's intentions, not just their words." Deimos is grim. "But I have no idea how we do that."

"There may be a way," Calli throws in hesitantly. Everyone's eyes automatically flick to her. "In the past, there were artefacts, imbued with the power of gods so long dead that none remember their names." There isn't a whisper of sound at our table, everyone eager to hear the rest of Calli's story. "Each of these artefacts had a different purpose and were bound to a bloodline to use." There's a groan at this.

"You're saying that even if we found one of these artefacts, it's very likely that none of us would be able to use it?" Hades groans.

"Did you lose your wits in the battle, Hades?" Calli asks mockingly. "Or did you forget where we all come from in your arrogance?" His mind says he had. "If we come from the Titans, then where do the Titans come from?"

"The long-dead gods," I whisper.

"I think it's time that I went back to Olympus and did some research," says Hephaistos abruptly. Ligeia and Caleb follow as he stands. He eyes the two of them, though what he sees I can't pick up from his mind, but it fills him with satisfaction. "I could use some help, if you two are offering."

"Anything that keeps me busy, mate. You probably need me, what with your old eyes." Caleb's cheeky retort lightens the mood, particularly when Ligeia slaps him over the back of the head.

"Mind your manners with your betters, pup." Her tone's fierce but I sense the lightness that lies beneath it. And the thin vein of attraction she's trying to hide. Apparently, so can Caleb.

"Haven't you heard, Ligeia? I'm a Councillor now!" He dodges another swipe. "That means no-one's my better." Hephaistos rolls his eyes and leaves, the other two following, still bickering.

"They are going to kill each other," Boss says, horrified by their actions.

I laugh. "No, they won't. Only chance of that happening is if they spontaneously combust before they do anything about the attraction between them." He still looks sceptical, so I share my experiences in their minds.

"Is no-one safe from your prying?" he asks good-naturedly, planting a kiss on my brow as we also exit the building. I blush.

"You know I can't help it." I start to build up to a really good head of steam when his mouth finds mine and all is instantly forgotten.

The man certainly knows how to kiss a woman insensible.

Chloe

I
T'S SOME DAYS BEFORE everything catches up with me but when it does, it hits me hard.

Ares is dead.

Of all the people I would've assumed could lose their life in this endeavour it wouldn't have been him. The numbers of the original Olympians, our forefathers and mothers, are dwindling fast, and there's few with the power to match them left standing. The Titans are down two of their number, but at what cost?

"What are you thinking about, Princess?" Boss rolls closer to me in our bed, drawing me into his chest and breathing me in. It'd been a close call. Too close for his comfort and I know I'm going to suffer from his coddling for a while yet. I wrap my mind around his in an attempt to soothe, but that just makes him hold me tighter. I don't feel like talking, but Boss obviously does.

"When I think about what could have happened . . . If we had been a minute longer or if they had decided your death was more important . . ." He swallows. I send my mind into his, letting him access my memories, my fear, and then my relief and happiness. He deserves to understand the whole, and I need someone to share the burden.

"It isn't my death that scares me, Boss," I whisper into his chest. "It's what I'm capable of in the darkness." Memories of a whole army decimated, of Mnemosyne's mind ripped to shreds, of Aeden dying in my arms rip through me. The tears come then, rolling over my cheeks and onto his chest. At least it's broad enough to share the burden.

"Never again!" he promises as he kisses the tears from my cheeks. "Never again will I ask that of you."

I sigh. "Don't make promises you can't keep."

The silence stretches until I feel it'll snap.

"I will promise you that it will be a last resort and that you will be the one to suggest it." I'd have to be happy with that. Unfortunately, it's a skill that'll undoubtedly be needed when Cronos unleashes his forces on us.

"Do you think Deimos will manage his new assignment?" Boss lets out a wry chuckle, sorrow following.

"I can't think of anyone better to be Councillor for our Line." He says into the darkness. Deimos has been ratified by the remaining members of the Council as Ares successor, despite his protests. "And thank the Gods his first act was to release me into your care."

"We'll have to watch out for Eros." Memories of the fury in his eyes when Demon announced our union will remain with me forever. If looks could kill, Boss and Demon would be dead a thousand times over. The twins don't realise it, but they have a life-long enemy in their brother.

And our lives are very long.

"Eros is not the one I am worried about. Do you have any idea who this woman is the Titans were speaking about?"

"Not a clue." I sigh. "I'd barely enough energy at that point to keep alert, let alone delve their minds for the identity of the mystery woman." He frowns, puzzling over the many options available. "Don't worry about it now. She'll reveal herself, and in the meantime, we'll prepare ourselves as best we can, and be *very* wary of who we trust."

"I'm not inclined to trust anyone but family at this point in time," says Boss.

"Well, I wouldn't trust my mother as far as you can throw her."

"Why would I attempt to throw your mother?" he asks as I groan. "Surely that is not a method you would consider for extracting information?" I stop his mouth with a kiss, likely what he intended with his ridiculous statements.

Our kiss deepens as he rolls me on top of him, reaching up to cup my face with his hands. He opens his mind to mine and I slip inside. It never fails to astound, the way he feels when he looks at me. The eyes are beautiful, sexy even, and every scar on my body is a mark of strength, the reason he's able to be mine. My gratitude knows no bounds, for whatever being sent this man, and it's truly precious to know he feels the same.

"I love you, my warrior," I whisper against his mouth as he lifts my arse and slides smoothly inside me. I rock against him, slowly, teasing as I lift nearly all the way off then grind back home again. His growl has me dripping as he swats my arse, urging me to go faster. I don't give in, but he doesn't have the patience for slow and abruptly rolls me onto my back as I laugh. It's cut off as he slams home, thrusting with all the power in his warrior body. I'm so full, I can think only of him as he continues to pound mercilessly into my saturated pussy. *This* is what I need, this reaffirmation of life. The orgasm is cresting, about to roll through me when abruptly he pulls out.

I swat his arm, feeling his chuckle as he stares down at my naked body hungrily. "You had better get back to that or there won't be any more action for you for the next 500 years." The laugh he lets out lightens my heart and I reach upwards, desperate for him again.

Instead, he pulls me to the edge of the bed as he stands, raises my hips and slides in again, thrusting deep and rhythmically. He lets go of my hips and leans forward, taking a nipple in his mouth and pulling strongly. I bow off the bed, mindlessly offering the other one. He doesn't refuse, the second nipple getting the same treatment as the first.

He surges upwards, kissing me frantically as his rhythm increases, short sharp thrusts meeting my cervix and causing me to explode.

I scream into his mouth as he empties into me, panting my name as the tempo slows then stops. Boss lifts me onto the bed, careful not to dislodge himself, and settles us spooning in the middle of king-sized heaven. His kisses trail along my shoulders and I sigh in contentment.

"I love you too, Chloe," he whispers into my ear as he snuggles into me. "You are my light in the dark. I'll never let you go." My hands flutter over my belly, wondering how long we'll have of just the two of us. I feel blessed that I've even had a flash of my future where other Seers haven't.

Light in the dark indeed.

Right back at you, lover. You're definitely the light in the dark for this blind Seer.

THE END

AUTHOR BIOGRAPHY

S.E. Welsh writes paranormal and historical romance after midnight—which is the only time her family and day job leave free. Even when writing in the wee hours, she manages to steam up her glasses regularly, though this could be due to the humidity of Australia's Northern Territory, rather than the heat of her words.

S.E. Welsh loves diet coke, books, travel and her family (though not necessarily in that order), considering herself blessed that all are around her in abundance. Her travels influence her work, as does her BArts in Ancient History, so all her work tends to reflect her interest in both.

She hopes her readers all enjoy the magic of heroes, history and heart.

Connect with S.E. Welsh

https://sewelsh.com/

S.E. WELSH